IRONY...

JAY HURLEY

IUNIVERSE, INC.
NEW YORK   BLOOMINGTON

Irony

This is a work of fiction. All of the characters, names, incidents, organizations, and dialogue in this novel are either the products of the author's imagination or are used fictitiously.

iUniverse books may be ordered through booksellers or by contacting:

iUniverse
1663 Liberty Drive
Bloomington, IN 47403
www.iuniverse.com
1-800-Authors (1-800-288-4677)

ISBN: 978-1-4401-3938-3 (pbk)
ISBN: 978-1-4401-3939-0 (cloth)
ISBN: 978-1-4401-3940-6 (ebk)

Printed in the United States of America

iUniverse rev. date: 6/17/2009

For Patty,

the most amazing

woman I ever met.

ACKNOWLEDGEMENTS

Where does one start? You complete a novel, and then the lessons begin. I am forever indebted to my wife Patty for encouraging me to undertake this endeavor, and for providing me with the space and the time to bring it to completion. To John, Kaitlyn, and Brian, what can I say? You have the greatest mother in the world, but what am I telling you that you don't already know? Your mother and I remain convinced that God bestowed upon us the three greatest kids in the world. God obviously endowed you with your Mom's genes! To my family members, friends, and acquaintances who took the time to read manuscripts and offer helpful suggestions and encouragement along the way, I will never forget your assistance. To Lt. Detective Tom Maloney of the Boston Police Department's Sexual Assault Unit. Thank you. I'm sure you could pick the technical aspects of IRONY... apart in seconds, but you were free with your time, a true gentleman, and I was astounded by your knowledge. You epitomize what it means to be a public servant and Boston's taxpayers are fortunate to have people of your ilk to protect them. To Rick Winterson. Thanks for your advice, your time, and your willingness to impart your knowledge. To Jim Thayer in Seattle, Washington. As I've explained, the name Thayer is deeply ingrained within my heart for many reasons. I will strive to improve as I move forward, but I would be remiss were I not to thank you for all your help. Finally, to Pat Nee. As a youth, my friends and I learned many unique lessons from people like Pat Nee, Jimmy Lydon, et al. However, Pat providing me with an introduction to New York Times bestselling author T. J. English, and Mr. English's willingness to listen to my thoughts and read my words gave me the confidence to complete this undertaking. Words cannot adequately express how proud I am to have earned Mr. English's endorsement.   jh

PROLOGUE

Disbarred and publically disgraced, attorney Tim Dunlap struggled as he approached the completion of his daily workout regimen in the Spartan prison gym. Physically spent, he dropped two seventy-five pound dumbbells to the floor. The resultant bang and subsequent rattling around of the cannonball-shaped weights, coupled with his exhaustion, distracted him from noticing fellow inmate Vincent "Pick" Piccorino sidling up beside him.

"Follow me," Piccorino said, walking down a usually guarded hallway.

Sweaty, tired, and now apprehensive, Dunlap dutifully followed him into an area known to be off-limits to inmates. His nervousness heightened when a prison guard appeared.

"Use this room, Pick," the guard said. "Just bang on the inside of the door when you're done."

Billy Turpin, the prison guard, or double agent—depending on one's perspective—had a younger brother who was a recent beneficiary of Pick's largesse. Deeply in debt to a local bookmaker, his brother's choices boiled down to a life on the run, or a run on his life. Having financially bled all acquaintances, including Billy, he made one final appeal to his older brother. Turpin lacked the money to help him, so he had jeopardized his job—and any previously held principles inherent to keeping it—by enlisting Pick's assistance.

Pick had straightened the matter out in ten minutes with one phone call and without a single cent changing hands. The intrinsic value of having a prison guard beholden to him was now paying dividends for the former Boston organized crime leader.

"Thanks, Billy, we only need about ten minutes." As soon as the guard closed the door, Pick pointed at a chair, "Sit down."

A sweat-soaked Dunlap dropped into a metal chair.

Pick got right to the point. "What's up with this fucking Bobby Barron character?"

"What do you mean?"

"Look, I've been hearing that this guy framed you since the day you got here. I guess I'm a little confused about why you've never gone after him. I mean, with your background, you've got to know a lot of people, right?" Pick surveyed their institutional surroundings, and added, "Just not the right ones, I guess."

"Yeah, no kidding. It's—"

Pick interrupted him. "I want to make a proposition."

"What do you have in mind?"

"I'm not going to lie to you. We ate your case up when it was all over TV and the newspapers. What's that old saying? Misery loves company? We chalked up your conviction to the fact that you had a dark side like the rest of us."

"Listen, Pick—"

Pick thrust his right hand up like a traffic cop. "Let me *finish!* Everybody in here thinks this guy framed you. You're a famous lawyer, yet you've never done anything about it." He paused, shrugging his shoulders for effect. "You've got to be guilty, right?"

Dunlap shook his head. "I had nothing to do with it, Pick. I *was* framed. I just don't think it was Bobby Barron who framed me."

"Are you fucking nuts? This guy is living large while you're locked up in here with all these degenerates and you don't think he did it? Let me ask you something. If *you* didn't do it, and *he* didn't frame you, then what am I missing here? Did this fucking broad rape herself and then give herself a beating for good measure?"

"Pick, you've been good to me. I'll never forget your help. I know this sounds crazy and it may be difficult to believe, but I knew Bobby Barron well. In fact, I was thinking about offering him a spot in my law firm."

Pick rubbed his prominent jaw. His squinting and disbelieving brown eyes burnt a hole through the center of Dunlap's skull as he absorbed the explanation.

Dunlap continued, "This kid was sharp. He had a ton of street smarts, but he also had a tendency to let his emotions get the best of him. Over time, his acquired experience diminished that tendency proportionately. He was almost there when all this went down. It's inarguable that my case put him over the top. It couldn't have come at a worse time for me; but I always knew he had the talent."

"What do you mean?"

"He was a county prosecutor. They don't make much money, and they work long hours for what little they do make. Most of them are waiting for that one break. My case represented his opportunity to success. It's the S equals P plus O equation."

"What are you talking about?" Confusion supplanted the disbelief in Pick's eyes.

"It's an old tenet: *Success* is simply *preparation* meeting *opportunity*. You can prepare for something all your life. Without an opportunity, you'll never succeed. I represented his opportunity."

"Whoa, whoa; you're telling me he was a good kid ... a *friend*. You're telling me you were going to take care of him, and then he turns around and sticks it up your ass? It doesn't add up." Pick squeezed his fingers together. He pointed them upward, as if to pray, and waved them at Bobby. "*Please!* What kind of a dope do you think I am?"

Dunlap passed on the chance to answer that question. He valued his existence, as meager as it might be. He continued his explanation. "Just remember the equation. He was a smart kid, so he was *prepared*. He seized the evidence and recognized the unique *opportunity*. He then took full advantage of the situation. His *success* resulted from the extraordinary job he did in convicting me."

Pick provided his own synopsis. "So, you got screwed by a friend like I did. The government put my friend in the Witness Protection Program. *Your* friend is out there in the open, and you sit in here and do nothing?"

We're going in circles, Dunlap thought. He deployed a new wrinkle to illustrate the difference.

"Your friend screwed you. That's irrefutable. In *my* case, it was like teaching your kid to hit a baseball in the backyard, and then watching him whack one over the fence in front of a crowd at a Little League game. Unfortunately, in my case, the baseball went over the fence and shattered my car's windshield. I was his opportunity. He didn't *create* the opportunity; he was simply prosecuting a case that went off the rails. He lucked out."

Pick's eyes remained glued on Dunlap. He rubbed his hands through a thick mane of salt-and-pepper hair and shook his head. He wasn't buying what Dunlap was selling.

Nevertheless, the sale's pitch continued.

"What you've got to understand is that I nurtured this kid over the years, and I know he was appreciative. He was a great kid, almost like a son to me. His performance certainly didn't help me, but—" Dunlap wanted to continue, but decided it was time to reverse the pressure and cross-examine his fellow inmate. "What's your sudden interest in this?"

"Look, let's cut the bullshit. We agree that we're both here because we got screwed by someone. You've already confided in me that you lost pretty much everything. Well, I'm in the same boat."

Dunlap stared attentively, maintaining a respectful silence. The price for Pick's protection was about to be revealed.

"At least you'll be out in a few years—I'm fucked. A RICO conviction is like a life sentence." Pick chuckled, adding, "What am I telling you, for Christ's sake? I'm preaching to the choir."

Dunlap nodded. His guarded attentiveness twisted into a wry grin. As a former prominent defense attorney, he loathed the tenets of the Racketeer Influenced and Corrupt Organizations Act, or RICO.

Pick knew of Dunlap's abhorrence of this law from previous discussions.

The subdued grin was all Pick was getting, however, as Dunlap remained silent.

"I was wiped out. RICO convictions allow the government to take anything that's not nailed down, and a lot that is. My only hope is to flip the case, but I'm broke. I've given this a lot of thought, and I know one thing. I've covered your ass since the day you got here." Pick paused. With an eye-widening and menacing glare, he added. "And you *know* that."

"Pick. I just told you, I appreciate all your help."

Pick's glare intensified as he made a pre-emptive move toward Dunlap. "Do I look like a *moron?*" he shouted. "I ain't looking for your fucking *appreciation!*" He paused again, and lowered his voice, "What I'm talking about is I can't help but think that you were set up. If I'm right, I can use my contacts on the outside to leverage this prick Barron. In return—"

"A *quid pro quo?*" Dunlap asked, finishing Pick's thought. "Is that your plan? You help me get out of here, and if you succeed, I work on getting your case tossed?"

"Exactly," Pick said with a smile. Bright white teeth dominated his leathery olive-skinned face. "So what do you think?"

"Where do you want to start? First, I don't think Bobby Barron framed me. Second, I don't have a license to practice law, but we could work around that. Let's just say this works, you know—the *first* part—and I get out. What protection do *you* have that I won't screw you, or, even if I do help, that I'll succeed?"

As Pick calculated a response, Dunlap continued.

"I know the first part of your answer is you have plenty of friends out there to remind me of my obligation, and I wouldn't screw you anyway, so that's really not a concern to me. But, what if I *can't* spring you? I have to be honest. I'd rather do my time than take the chance of getting out early and not being able to free you. I don't want to spend the rest of my life looking over my shoulder if I can't keep my end of the bargain. You've got to understand, there's no guarantee I can pull this off." Reinforcing that thought, he added, "Just getting *me* out is a long shot."

An animated Pick's voice rose several octaves, "Yeah? Well let *me* worry about that. What's the alternative? We're *both* doing time. You were framed—I think—and I got screwed by a guy who was supposed to be my best friend.

Yeah, you'll walk in a few years, but why do any more time than you have to if you're innocent, *especially* if I can piece together a plan to spring you sooner? Plus, if you *can* prove you were framed, wouldn't you be able to practice law again?"

Dunlap nodded. His blank expression belied the fact that he knew there were no alternatives. Buying time, he said, "You've brought up a lot of good questions ... So good I don't have the answers."

1

Trisha Barron relished the thought of tackling her relatively new walking route around Boston's Harbor Point housing complex. Had she known she would be arrested and incarcerated before returning home, she undoubtedly would have shut and locked her windows in response to the unseasonably cold and rainy weather forecast for later that evening.

Such was life, best summarized when British author Guy Bellamy declared, "Hindsight is an exact science."

Harbor Point was a supremely situated oceanfront neighborhood of mixed-income housing units comprising a truly diverse population. It evolved out of the ashes, mustard-yellow brick dust, sustained human pain, and rightfully earned negative public perception of the latter years of the former Columbia Point housing development. Six and seven-story red brick structures hovered over the complex's two-story, multi-colored, wood-framed row houses ringing the complex's exterior. These row houses bordered the ocean, providing the appropriate architectural and familial symmetry when viewed from the outside.

Perched on the southernmost edge of a peninsula, its footprint jutting out into Boston Harbor, the development's northern exposure stared back at Trisha's native South Boston, and Boston's downtown skyline just beyond. It was situated just northwest of the John F. Kennedy Presidential Library and Museum and the ever-expanding campus of the University of Massachusetts, a circa 1970s red brick behemoth of inexplicable design; where you never seemed to know where you were going upon entering, or how you arrived at your destination were you fortunate enough to locate it.

Harbor Point also shared a border with the former coal-fired Leavitt pumping station. This 1884 technological wonder used the ocean's tidal flow to disseminate the accumulated human waste of Boston's indoor plumbing pioneers. The castle-like granite structure and adjacent property, now inhabited by Boston's Water and Sewer Commission, stood just south of the Massachusetts Archives building.

Trisha's new daily regimen was routed in an opposite hand fashion to her former course around South Boston's Castle Island. Trisha had inexplicably walked in the opposite direction several weeks earlier, forfeiting the historic and considerable pleasures of her former route. After all, how many people's daily walk includes their passing a castle whose roots date back to the 1600s? The formidable five-sided granite fortress, known in its origin as William's Castle, after King William III of England, was a former garrison for British troops before their unceremonious evacuation from Boston in 1776. It was now a popular site for walking, jogging, rollerblading, and illegal biking.

For years, Castle Island afforded Trisha the ability to watch kite boarders on the Pleasure Bay side of the fort, and huge cargo ships and an occasional luxury cruise liner on its ocean face. Commercial jets roaring overhead seemingly scraped the trees atop the castle, or the tops of the massive blue steel container cranes in the neighboring Conley Terminal, before landing less than a half-mile away on a contiguous peninsula constituting East Boston's *General Edward Lawrence Logan International Airport*.

Trisha walked out the front door of her Hardy Street home. When she reached the foot of her street—where it intersected almost simultaneously with Marine Road and Day Boulevard—she headed west and not east as she had done for so many years.

Trisha crossed over to the ocean side of Day Boulevard. The tranquil but chilly water rolled gently up and down the beach's sand incline, threatening the grass buffer and concrete sidewalk that lay just beyond its reach. Trish was tall and raven-haired, and her trim waist belied sinewy thighs and shoulders—not to mention her age.

The fifty-three year-old's new route, while lengthier by twenty-five minutes, actually seemed to take less time to complete. She did not run into neighbors or friends looking to catch up on lost time; there were fewer encounters with lawless bikers or unleashed dogs drifting aimlessly away from their oblivious owners; and there were myriad new sights to discover.

Trisha fell into lockstep with a tall man about her age. His aggressive pace encouraged her to increase her normal gait. Trisha welcomed the extra push. She was awaiting the results of medical tests she had taken earlier that morning, and she needed a good workout.

She was confident that she could maintain his pace, as she had used the services of this pacesetter on previous occasions. She forged ahead, focusing on his fluorescent orange windbreaker with the large black "T" emblazoned on its back.

Despite the forecasted weather changes, it was a strikingly clear, sunny, and crisp autumn afternoon. Trisha wondered which direction her leader would be choosing for them as they approached the Massachusetts State Police station across from Saunders Stadium at the south end of Moakley Park.

He veered left before the police station, just as Trisha had hoped he would.

In an ironic twist, the Harbor Point area had played an integral role in a life-altering experience of Trisha's, causing her to wonder if a subliminal challenge had prompted her recent course change. She mentally revisited the incident as she pushed ahead, the memories causing powerful emotions to course through her body. Trisha changed songs on her iPod, choosing an upbeat tune in an attempt to quell these dark thoughts.

Trisha and her pacesetter had covered well over a mile and were entering the heart of the Harbor Point complex. She noticed a lone figure standing off to the ocean side of the single-family, waterfront portion of the development. She could not conjure up a logical reason why someone would be lingering there at this time of year.

Trisha's curiosity increased when the man walked toward her the moment her pacesetter had passed him.

She lengthened her stride—her previously heightened pace having suffered due to her temporary reminiscence—and she narrowed the gap between her and the pacesetter.

Dark bushy eyebrows, complemented by a week of unattended facial growth, framed the stranger's wide brown eyes. He was tall and thin, and wore a quilted beige ski coat. Its hood was up, yet the coat was unzipped.

Recalculating the space between her and her pacesetter, Trisha noticed him staring back at her, almost as if to ensure her safe passage. At one point, he seemed to be heading back in her direction, but she couldn't be sure because the hooded figure suddenly required her undivided attention.

He blocked her path and said, "Mrs. Barron? I'm here to talk to you about Bobby."

His words hit her full force. Hesitant and breathless, Trisha responded, "Excuse me? Who *are* you? Are you talking about my son?"

"I apologize, Mrs. Barron. Let me start over. My name is Mark Williams. I'm an undercover field agent with the Bureau of Alcohol, Tobacco, and Firearms. We have reason to believe that your son is involved in a series of illegal activities with several of his clients."

He flashed a leather-encased shield and identification card before tucking it away as quickly as he had produced it. "We've had you under surveillance for the past forty-eight hours. We just received a warrant to search your home for stolen material and other evidence. I've been instructed to pick you up to keep you from contacting your son, since we're also searching his apartment. I need you to come with me."

Trisha's muddled mind worked overtime. "How do I even know you're who you say you are?" she asked in an unsteady voice. Pausing, she regained a semblance of composure. "I need to make a phone call. Isn't that my right?"

"I'm sorry, but, again, my instructions were to pick you up outside your home and to deliver you back there for follow-up questioning."

"But—"

The agent seized control of the situation. "A phone call is out of the question. You'll be able to make all the calls you need once we've completed our investigation."

Trisha's options were limited. Paradoxically, as the single mother of one of Boston's most well-known legal figures, she couldn't contact her son when she most required his intervention. *Why?* she wondered. *Because he is being accused of acts more representative of the people he has successfully imprisoned in the past; or the ones he now represents. And this has been happening right under my nose ... in my own home ... and I had no idea?*

Agent Williams interrupted her thoughts. "Please come with me, Mrs. Barron." He led her away from the pedestrian path toward North Point Drive, guiding her toward one of the complex's parking lots. "I have a van parked right over there."

Technically, once agent Mark Williams detained Trisha Barron, he may have been breaking the law. Devil's advocates, or clever attorneys—like the ones her son, Bobby, used to lock horns with; or the fraternity he now proudly pledged—would argue that her ability to walk away at any time had been unfettered. With that as a jumping-off point, any characterization of this interaction as illegal would require an absurd conclusion.

Once she entered the van, however—when it was the last thing she would have ever done absent the explicit order from a law enforcement official—a definitive threshold was crossed.

Mark Williams was just one of many pseudonyms for William "Willie" Marcus, a part-time construction worker and full-time thug.

Given this skullduggery, his story was not completely fraudulent.

Several of Willie's associates *were* ransacking Trisha Barron's home at that very moment.

2

Attorney Robert Gordon "Bobby" Barron rarely sat still. He exhibited an array of personal traits that, at first blush, could easily allow someone to characterize him as an adolescent masquerading as an adult. While one could construe his frenetic behavior in a negative light, it also represented the underlying secret to his sudden and unexpected success and fame at age thirty-seven.

For Jill Thurman, it was hardly first-blush time. She observed Bobby's actions with the trained eye of her profession as she sat in his plush office in a recently constructed high-rise building adjacent to Boston's bustling South Station. The momentary chaos engulfing him presented a stark contrast to the obvious trappings of success and wealth that seemed to define a more staid existence.

"Where's that file, Marie? I need to get my act together, and I'm not getting any help here." Bobby continued to mutter under his breath as he shuffled through the paperwork and manila folders littering his desk.

Marie Phillips, a slender black woman, appeared in the doorway to his office. Bobby's secretary since he abruptly quit his position as an assistant district attorney in Suffolk County eighteen months earlier, Marie appeared unaffected by his outburst.

She brushed past Bobby and snatched his beige London Fog overcoat from a stainless steel coat rack. Her right hand disappeared into its pocket, and she removed a partially rolled-up manila folder. Staring up into her boss's cobalt-blue eyes, she said, "Bobby, you walked in, and I handed this to you. I even reminded you not to forget to pack it for court."

Marie thrust the folder in his direction, causing a wrist-full of assorted jewelry to chime in rhythm with her action. She gave him a look that a mother might cast upon a wayward child. "You looked right through me, *as usual*, and shoved it in your coat pocket as you walked away."

"What would I do without you?" a blushing Bobby said. He accepted the folder and tossed it in the general direction of the briefcase sitting atop his desk. Grinning at his guest, the redness in his face still evident, he said, "Jill, you're not going to tell people how screwed up I really am, are you?"

"Who'd ever believe me? You're Boston's Golden Boy," teased the tall and particularly well-proportioned Jill. Thick auburn ringlets framed the flawless complexion and striking facial features of the senior staff writer for *About Face* magazine, a Boston-based publication that provided juicy interviews with the latest and greatest beautiful people. Jill winked at Marie. The two had met thirty minutes earlier while waiting for the habitually tardy Bobby. "It would take someone more powerful than I am to knock you off your throne," she teased.

Jill had secured the plum assignment through subtle inner-office manipulation. Bobby and Jill were hardly strangers. She had approached her boss and successfully parlayed a ginned-up version of having briefly dated Bobby during their undergraduate days at nearby Boston College. She was now poised to generate what would amount to little more than the latest puff piece on one of Boston's hottest cult heroes. Her success subjected her to the inevitable, albeit understandable, envy of several of her female co-workers.

She was also not averse to rekindling that old romance, especially now that Bobby was famous. Being seen in his company certainly wouldn't hurt *her* career. He had been fun to hang out with in college. She assumed his sudden fame and wealth had done nothing to diminish his ability to enjoy life.

He's also quite easy on the eyes, she thought, admiring his thick black hair; the deep cleft in the center of his taut chin; and the top-notch physical condition he maintained. Bobby's stylish gray wool suit, custom-made white-on-white shirt, and flashy purple silk tie complemented his natural attraction.

Bobby was packing the recently recovered folder with the rest of his paperwork when the phone rang.

Marie turned to him as she headed to the reception area. "Do you want to take this call?"

"I don't have time. Take a message, and forward it to my BlackBerry. I'll return it on the way to the courthouse."

Thirty seconds later, Marie reappeared, wide-eyed and visibly upset. "Bobby, you need to take this call." She turned to Jill and said, "I'm sorry, but you're going to have to step outside."

Jill planned to accompany Bobby to court in an effort to get the requisite feel of him "in action" as background for her story. Marie's sudden abruptness caught her off guard.

Marie, a product of the no-nonsense system of legendary Suffolk County District Attorney Richard "Rock" Murray, had only come to work for Bobby after he begged incessantly and offered her a healthy pay raise. She was not overly cordial under normal circumstances. The vitriolic phone call she had just taken fortified her belief that this was no time for anyone to question her etiquette or to expect compassion. "You can sit in the reception area if you wish," she said, escorting Jill out the door.

Marie returned to Bobby's office, adding to his confusion.

"Who is it, Marie? I told you I had to get going," he said, picking up the phone and placing it over his right ear before she could respond.

"Bobby Barron," he said; the usual air of confidence and panache obvious in his voice.

"I know who you are, you piece of shit. I'm going to tell you this once, and you better pay attention, you got me?"

"Who is this?" Pausing, he added, "Is this some kind of joke?"

"If you think your mother being kidnapped is a joke, then *yeah*, this is a joke."

Bobby blanched. He dropped into his high-backed black leather chair and spun a quarter-turn. This subconscious effort to regain his composure failed. His knuckles whitened noticeably as he tightened his grip on the receiver.

The caller continued, "You framed Tim Dunlap, and unless you figure out a way to straighten it, out we're going to kill your mother now, then *you* when we get our hands on you. Consider her to be a little insurance for the time being, but you better start thinking about how you're going to make this good."

8

Bobby countered, "Listen, pal, I don't know who you are, or—"

The caller cut Bobby off. The conversation would be concise and unilaterally administered.

Bobby received a laundry list of commands.

"You're going to receive a phone call within the next two hours. You'll get instructions about what you're going do to straighten this shit out. Don't *make* any calls, and don't *take* any calls, until we get back to you. Send your secretary home, and do *not* say anything to her about this conversation. We're watching her. If she plays any games, she'll be joining your mother. When we call back, we'll ring the phone *once*, hang up, and then call back within ten seconds. Pick it up when it starts ringing again—*after* the single ring. You got it?"

"Yeah, but—" Bobby's feeble attempt at a response elicited a seemingly louder than usual dial tone. Bobby hung up the phone and lowered his head into his hands. He vigorously rubbed his face, then his temples, before swiveling back to face Marie.

"Who was that? What's going on, Bobby?"

"I can't get into it. You have to do me a favor. I need you to go home and wait for me to call you. I'll explain more over the phone."

"Bobby—"

"Please, Marie, you have to do this for me. I can't get into it right now. Please, just do what I'm asking." Bobby paused. Locking eyes with his secretary, he added one final "Please."

Marie headed for the door. Turning back, she said, "You're going to call me, right?"

"I'll call you."

Marie reentered the outer office and encountered Jill. "He's not coming out for quite awhile, and I have to lock up. He's dealing with an emergency. You should call me tomorrow and we'll reschedule."

"Is it okay if I sit out in the main lobby? I have to make a few calls. Then I'll go downstairs and grab a cab."

Marie's intrinsic protect-the-boss-at-all-cost mentality kicked in. "Let me drop you off. You said you lived in Marina Bay, right? That's on my way home. I'll give you a lift."

"No, that's kind of you, but, like I said, I have to make some calls, and I wouldn't feel comfortable talking in front of anyone. Thanks, anyway."

Jill had outflanked her. Marie persisted, "You sure? I don't mind—"

"I'm sure," Jill said, flashing a glistening smile.

The two women gathered their respective belongings and headed out the door.

Marie stopped to secure the main door.

Jill exited toward the common lobby adjacent to the bank of stainless-steel clad elevators. She chose a thick, upholstered chair to set up temporary shop, and then placed her cell phone to her ear. She did not want to engage in additional conversation as Marie approached her.

Marie pushed the down button and waited as Jill pretended to speak into her cell phone. An understated dual-toned chime preceded the opening of the elevator doors. Marie entered the car, laughing quietly to herself. Despite all the technological advances in noted developer Hynes Johnson's building, it was common knowledge that getting a cell phone signal in its corridors was impossible. Conspiracy theories abounded about why, but the more central issue for Marie was her innate sense that Jill wasn't going to allow this temporary setback to deter her from getting back in to see Bobby.

Jill repositioned the chair once the elevator doors closed, giving her an unobstructed view of Bobby's office door. She attempted to reach him by phone, to no avail. She waited several minutes—time enough to ensure that Marie didn't double back—before resorting to a more aggressive approach. Grabbing her belongings, she headed back to his office, where her initial knocking turned into a heavier thumping.

Neither approach produced tangible results.

"Oh, great," Jill muttered.

A heavyset security guard—in full regalia—was heading in her direction. "Can I help you, ma'am?"

"No ... yes," Jill stammered. "Actually, I came out here to make a call on my cell phone, and I seemed to have gotten myself locked out." She grinned sheepishly at the guard.

"Do you work here?"

"No, I'm a magazine reporter," Jill said, showing him the visitor's pass pasted on her coat. "I'm doing a story on Bobby ... uh, Mr. Barron," she said, pointing at the ornate gold-leafed and deeply shadowed surname on the opaque glass portion of Bobby's office door. "He's inside, but I can't get a signal on my cell phone to call him. Is it possible for you to open the door?"

"I'm sorry, but I can't do that. Company policy."

Jill nodded, tacitly acknowledging the common sense behind such a rule.

The guard knocked on the door, but his efforts went unanswered too. Turning to Jill, he shrugged. "There are payphones in the main lobby if you want to try calling from there. I'm going to have to accompany you down there anyway. I'll be glad to show you where they are."

Jill gathered her belongings for the third time in the past ten minutes. She followed him to the elevator, and they rode down in silence.

When the doors opened at the lobby level he pointed to Jill's left. "The phones are right over there if you want to make that call, or you're welcome to make yourself comfortable in the lobby. It's open to the public until six p.m."

Jill thanked him. Locating a chair, she was delighted when she detected a cell phone signal. She dialed Bobby's office.

As the phone rang, she noticed Bobby bound from an elevator toward the bank of previously pointed out pay phones.

Why would he leave an office full of phones to use a pay phone? Jill thought. She stood up and walked in his direction to find out.

Bobby rummaged through a handful of coins. He was too preoccupied to detect Jill's approach. He dialed his mother's house, and her voicemail kicked on. Bobby slammed the phone back onto its metal hooks and pondered his next move.

"Who are you calling?" Jill asked quietly.

Bobby spun around.

"What's going on, Bobby? Is there anything I can do to help you?"

"I can't talk right now," Bobby said, before noticing the cell phone in Jill's right hand. His mind kicked into overdrive. *They know I have to stay in the building, and they know about Marie, but Jill is an unknown.* "Has anybody approached you since you left my office?"

Jill hesitated. "Yeah … I was trying to get back into your office, you know, after Marie left, and a security guard threw me off your floor. I was getting ready to leave when I saw you come out of the elevator."

"Come with me," Bobby said. "Quickly, I don't want anyone to see us," as he flashed his security pass for the guard.

Fortuitously, Jill's visitor pass was still attached to her lapel.

Jill peppered Bobby with questions in the elevator. He deftly fended off her inquires with a series of esoteric responses.

As they exited onto the seventh floor, Bobby asked, "Can I use your cell phone?"

Bobby sensed Jill's confusion and ad-libbed. "I'm waiting for an important call, so I can't tie up the office phone or my cell phone. I'm not sure which one they are going to call me on."

Jill handed him the phone, but warned, "I don't think it's going to do you any good. I tried calling you from out here earlier, and I couldn't get a signal."

"That's because of the concrete walls that support the elevators in the core of the building. Everyone's always complaining about that, but it'll work fine in here." Bobby unlocked the main door and led Jill into the outer office, then his office, double locking each door behind them.

Bobby punched in a number. He thrust the phone back in Jill's direction when it went unanswered. His impatience was palpable. "How do you shut it off?"

Jill accepted the phone and turned it off. Remaining true to her professional training, however, she surreptitiously stored the number as "Bobby" for future reference. *You never know.*

"What's your cell number, Jill?"

Bobby scribbled it on a lime-green Post-it note and asked Jill for her cell phone again. He quickly dialed another number. Following a brief pause, he said, "Mickey, it's Bobby, I need to talk to you right away. The only way you can reach me is at this number, six one seven – five five five – three eight five eight. Don't call any of my other numbers, and don't go near my house or my office until we talk. Call me as soon as you get this message. It's important."

3

Tim Dunlap sat in a tiny cell in the Riverfork Institute of Correction in the otherwise bucolic central Massachusetts town of Farrell.

Often referred to by its acronym, criminal circle insiders derisively referred to the facility as Rice University.

Dunlap's fate had still not fully sunk in, despite having endured eighteen months of incarceration. He represented the exception to the conventional wisdom that time heals all wounds. The disgraced and disbarred attorney was a former college hockey star who had migrated to Boston from Albany, New York, in the late 1960s.

He proved to be as productive in the classroom as on the ice. After graduating from Boston College, he received a *juris doctorate* from Boston College Law School. His Double Eagle status—an eagle being the school's official mascot—while inconsequential in most parts of the country, carried significant weight in Boston's insular political, legal, business, and social worlds.

Dunlap had no intention or desire to return home after graduation, despite being the son of a politically wired operative in New York state politics. He remained in the Greater Boston area after passing the Massachusetts bar exam, spending his formative years learning the ropes and making his bones in the Suffolk County District Attorney's office. He made the appropriate contacts and acquired enough knowledge and experience to free him from the long hours—and the short pay—associated with public service.

His small criminal defense practice eventually flourished. This success provided him unilateral discretion over whom he dealt with and what cases he accepted.

He also never lost his insatiable appetite for Boston's nightlife. Armed with professional success and the commensurate wealth and notoriety that accompanied it, he remained a byproduct of his raucous years of college in the socially liberating 1960s. Despite his predilections, Tim managed to maintain a public reputation that was above reproach. In the ensuing years, he juggled an attractive, loving, and seemingly normal family life in one of Boston's tony bedroom communities, with an endless string of unquestionably attractive girlfriends.

As his prominence rose in proportion to his frequent successes in the courtroom, his obsessive ability to hide even the most obscure aspects of these dalliances from his wife and three children—two sons and a daughter— became as much a part of the game as the hunting or catching of his prey. His prurient behavior could easily have led to his downfall. He simply wouldn't allow that to happen.

Dunlap had become a fixture on the "talking head" legal circuit congesting cable television over the past decade. He possessed an uncanny knack for formulating unique opinions, invariably succeeding in separating himself from fellow panelists, regardless of the venue or the subject. But all that meant little now as he sat in his share of the ninety-square-foot cell; he took no solace in being one of the most learned felons in the country.

Instead, thoughts of hatred and vengeance filled his head. These thoughts were offset by one significant problem. He had no tangible target to focus on or attack.

His downfall originated out of a case that had begun with minimal media coverage, even in the face of his involvement. A subsequent and unexpected chain of events had initially exploded onto the front pages of daily newspapers across Massachusetts, then well beyond, as its ugliness continued to unfurl.

Tim had been defending a fifty-year-old Boston man with a thirty-five year history of arrests and convictions. The vicious rape and subsequent battering of a sixteen-year-old girl were the latest allegations against this jack-of-all-trades felon.

The victim had valiantly attempted to fight off her attacker, her bravery only provoking him to beat her once he had satisfied himself sexually. She mustered the courage to come forward. The resulting trial focused more on the accuser than the accused.

Dunlap had used all of the textbook tricks—and even formulated a few innovative tactics of his own—in his attempt to discredit the victim and derail the case of Suffolk County Assistant District Attorney Bobby Barron.

As his aggressive and tasteless strategy gained momentum, a corresponding law-enforcement investigation quietly unfolded. This investigation forced an unusual suspension of the rape case pending the findings of the parallel investigation.

When the rape case resumed, Dunlap's client walked away—unscathed and contemplating legal options of his own—due to a sensational turn of events.

His erstwhile attorney couldn't share in his victory, however, because he now found himself in the crosshairs of the scope formerly focused squarely on his client.

Skeptics came to understand the rationale behind Dunlap's initial involvement in such a low-profile case. DNA evidence uncovered in the separate Boston Police investigation established that the rape and subsequent assault had actually been the handiwork of defense attorney Tim Dunlap.

In retrospect, his willingness to discredit the victim and invalidate her claims was infinitely more self-serving than anyone could have imagined. His voracious sexual appetite had finally splintered the usual boundaries of his extramarital affairs.

In a subsequent high-profile jury trial, the verdict was that the prominent attorney had set up his unknowing client for the outside possibility of taking the fall for Dunlap's transgression.

Dunlap had maintained the internal controls inherent to any defense attorney. This particular layer of a much more intricate plan left him well positioned in the event he was unable to clear his client of the pending charges.

Dunlap swore he had been set up. What remained unclear and confusing to him was by whom, and why? Having lost most of his accumulated wealth—not to mention the support of his wife and two of his three children—any attempt to reconcile his precipitous downfall always began with the consideration of who benefited most by his demise.

Bobby Barron was the always-obvious first choice.

Boston's cynical media reveled in the irony of Dunlap languishing in prison while Bobby assumed his former colleagues' unoccupied seat in the ubiquitous media circus left behind. With youthful exuberance, "Black" Irish handsomeness, the testicular fortitude of an inner-city kid, and an unanticipated but deeply appreciated bonanza in the form of good luck, Bobby Barron quickly became a ringleader and a star attraction in that extravaganza.

Despite accomplishing this at his expense, it still didn't compute in Tim's mind.

Bobby was a stand-up kid from Southie, as South Boston was more commonly known.

The pair enjoyed a lengthy personal relationship that bordered on a mentorship. Dunlap often thought about how much Bobby reminded him of himself, and it was uncanny how their professional paths had paralleled each other, albeit a generation apart.

Ironically, as he had explained to Pick Piccorino earlier that day, he had been harboring thoughts of offering Bobby a spot in his law firm before this surreal turn of events.

Dunlap understood Bobby's role as a prosecutor and, admittedly, would have followed a similar course of action had their roles been reversed. Nonetheless, he consistently concluded that Bobby Barron would never backstab him.

Without exception, however, this mental reconciliation invariably preceded the same nagging thought: *Or would he?*

The berating Pick Piccorino had administered earlier that day exacerbated this recurring thought.

4

Trisha knew something was amiss. She accompanied Agent Williams to his van, where he directed her to the rear of the vehicle and handcuffed her to a metal seat stanchion, explaining that he could lose his job if he didn't do so.

They passed through the intersection of Harbor Point's North Point Drive and Westwind Road before heading down Harbor Point Boulevard. They turned right, passed through a security gate, and exited the development onto Mount Vernon Street.

Why would the security gate go up automatically? Trisha wondered. She adjusted her eyes from the sights beyond the windshield to the dashboard, and then the van's steering column. At that point, the aggregated and surreal series of events become irreconcilable. *Why would a law enforcement agent be using a bright yellow-and-black screwdriver as the vehicle's ignition key?*

"Where are we going?" she asked in an unsteady voice, adding, "and why is there a screwdriver sticking out of the ignition?"

Trisha peered through the van's side window. It would be impossible to attract anyone's attention. In stark contrast to the vehicle's transparent front windshield, a deep gray tint shrouded the remaining glass.

Agent Williams reacted to Trisha's inquiries by increasing the volume on the radio. He veered right as they passed the Doubletree Hotel near the west end of Mount Vernon Street and hugged the perimeter of the sidewalk adjacent to the Bayside Expo Center parking lot.

A defining moment was about to occur as they approached Day Boulevard. Turning right at the traffic light meant he was heading toward Trisha's home, as promised. A left turn negated all previous assurances. It would also justify the fear growing exponentially inside Trisha's mind and radiating through her body.

They climbed the short, S-curved hill, straddling the white-striped lane divider lines. Agent Williams approached the blinking red traffic light in a manner that would readily allow him to proceed in either direction.

Trisha looked on helplessly as the white goalposts, giant mint-green light stanchions, and Saunders Stadium scoreboard became visible through the rapidly defoliating trees. The setting sun merged seamlessly into the alternating shadows of Boston's skyline, creating a hypnotic display of pinkish-orange light dappled against a distant sky-blue backdrop.

When they reached the blinking red traffic light, pseudo ATF agent and career criminal, Willie Marcus, barely slowed before turning left and driving away from Trisha's home.

Trisha's heartbeat accelerated in almost direct proportion to the increasing speed of the vehicle.

◌

Mickey Carberry did not receive many phone calls from Bobby Barron. The lifelong friends' relationship had undergone significant restructuring once Bobby had joined the DA's office.

Mickey's goals and interests definitely conflicted with those of the assembled prosecutors pulling duty over at the Suffolk County courthouse.

The essence of their existence required putting people of his ilk behind bars, and their success—or lack thereof—was how social experts calculated the results. Mickey Carberry roaming the streets represented an isolated failure on their part in making Boston a safer place.

Despite philosophical differences, Mickey and Bobby maintained a bond of youthful faithfulness and friendship. In Southie's parochial world—as in many close-knit neighborhoods across the country—most cops know the robbers, and their paths crossed often.

Mickey and Bobby's relationship had enjoyed a recent resurgence.

Bobby's new role as a defense attorney required him to extricate people from legal predicaments.

Mickey, as luck would have it, possessed an endless list of acquaintances whose sole mission in life seemed to be keeping Bobby gainfully employed.

The pair grew up envying each other. Bobby was the athletically and scholastically gifted kid who never threatened the outer limits of his potential. Mickey was several inches shorter than Bobby was, but thicker and more muscular due to regular free-weight workouts designed to stave off potential replacements or the ever-present and always ambitious wannabes.

Mickey's classic Celtic mug would blend in seamlessly on any Dublin street corner. Menacing steel-gray eyes and a constant growth of thick, dark facial hair, never quite a beard, yet never clean shaven, encouraged people to provide him a wide berth. This was usually a wise choice.

He was the youngest of seven brothers. As a youth, he was a below-average student, but an animal when it came to playing sports despite being devoid of any marketable skills.

While Mickey would have given anything for Bobby's natural talent and knowledge, Bobby pined for Mickey's recklessness and never-back-down mentality. Their respective strengths complemented each other and represented the underpinnings on which their friendship was constructed and maintained.

Mickey slowly strayed down the wrong path.

While Bobby pursued his dreams in college and law school, Mickey stayed behind, majoring in mayhem, with related minors in anarchy and lawlessness.

Once Bobby realized the depths of Mickey's involvement, he could do little to help his friend. Acknowledging that professional disaster was unavoidable if they maintained their connection, he had no choice but to distance himself from his friend and his friend's equally volatile acquaintances.

Mickey kept his ear close to the ground when it came to Southie's criminal activities. Despite tonight's mysterious phone message, and the subsequent cryptic return phone call that culminated in a nervous and guarded Bobby asking to meet him at an out-of-the-way bar in Southie, Mickey had an inkling about why they were meeting. Besides, Bobby had told him to run a tab until he got there. He would get a free buzz out of this venture if nothing else materialized.

O'Bannion's Tavern sat off the beaten path of one of Southie's main thoroughfares. Mickey headed up East Broadway and turned down a side street. He located a parking spot he was confident he could maneuver his Jeep Cherokee into with a little work. It was half a block from the bar and was probably as close as he was going to get at this time of night.

Mickey heard shouting as he bounced back and forth off the bumpers of the two cars between which he was trying to park. He paused to pinpoint the source and was caught off guard by a guy screaming obscenities at him through the driver's side window.

Mickey lowered the window.

The guy stepped back; and Mickey shoved the door open forcefully, exiting the car.

The screamer, a good-sized kid—and undoubtedly an experienced bully—had an equally large sidekick.

The sidekick looked familiar to Mickey.

Mickey, a well-known figure around Southie, looked even more familiar to the sidekick, who advised his friend, "Relax, man, it's no big deal."

Mickey scanned the surrounding area as the sidekick attempted to calm his friend.

The screamer approached Mickey.

Mickey squared up, but displayed the palms of his hands—eight inches apart, around chin level—a wordless yet internationally accepted signal that he was not looking for any problems.

The screamer—ultimately identified as Scott by the sidekick—was ignoring his pal's counsel. He had just left a frustrating encounter with an attractive young woman who dumped him after he'd spent two expensive hours of plying her with alcohol. He was intent on taking that rejection out on someone. What more could he have asked for than Mickey's haphazard parking habits?

"You fucked my car up, moron."

A great line to kick off negotiations, Mickey thought.

Scott had no clue he was bartering with a legend.

Mickey resorted to a soft-sell approach. "Look, pal, you're fucked up. You don't know what you're talking about. Do yourself a favor and drop it."

The sidekick weighed in immediately. As buzzed as he was, he knew who they were dealing with and seized on the opportunity. "Come on, Scott. Forget about it. Let's get out of here."

"No fucking way. He hit my car."

Mickey offered him some wiggle room. "Look, buddy, I'm heading down to O'Bannion's. Come on down, and I'll buy you guys a drink."

The sidekick sensed a clumsy attempt at a setup. He turned to Mickey and said, "Thanks anyway, but we've got to get out of here. Go ahead. You go. We're all set."

"Fuck you, we're 'all set,'" Scott said to his friend. He turned back to Mickey, "If you walk away, I'm going to give you a slap."

Scott's highly unadvisable threat unwittingly resulted in a means to seal the deal. "I want your license and registration, or I'm calling the cops," he said, waving his cell phone in Mickey's face for added emphasis.

Scott calling the cops was simply not in Mickey's best interest. Terminating these negotiations became his top priority. *Besides, I need to get down to the bar in case Bobby shows up.*

"Hey pal, you want to pass papers? Fine, we'll pass papers," Mickey said, a discernible tone of resignation obvious in his voice. Mickey opened the driver's side door and reached into the console between the Jeep's front seats.

Scott stepped back, beaming in his pending moral victory.

Mickey emerged from the car with a large manila envelope. As he reached in for its contents, he asked, "Do we really have to go through all this?" with a heightened level of deference.

"Just give me the fucking papers and stop—"

Scott's final few words of drunken bravado never escaped his lips.

The item Mickey removed from the envelope was not an automobile registration, or a driver's license, but an admission slip—replete with the compulsory ambulance ride to Boston's closest hospital, in this case, the

Tufts-New England Medical Center—in the form of a flat, leather-clad, steel sap with a flexible-spring steel handle.

Scott's mouth was still motoring when Mickey struck him squarely, just above the left eye. The ensuing attack—about twenty seconds or so—was savage.

The sidekick's failure to intercede allowed Mickey's vicious blows to rain down unabated. The sidekick finally attempted to intervene as the tempo of the beating slowed down. His success with Mickey paralleled that of Scott.

Mickey immobilized him with a vicious blow across the bridge of his now-broken nose. He then tossed him on top of his beaten, bloodied, and unconscious pal.

Mickey reached down, snatched the dazed and bloodied sidekick by the collar, and propped him up against the door of his car. He was intent on purchasing additional insurance before he left. He bent down closer to his victim and hissed, "If I ever see you or this piece of shit again, I'll kill *both* of you. You understand me?" Endeavoring to drive one final and important point home as a river of blood flowed from the sidekick's nose onto Mickey's left hand, he added, "You open your mouth about this to *anyone* and you're fucking dead. You got me?"

The sidekick nodded feebly.

Mickey straightened out his clothing. He then wiped the bloodstained weapon, and then his hands, on several untainted portions of the sidekick's formerly fashionable blue denim shirt. He stuck the steel sap back into the manila envelope and placed it inside the center console of the Jeep. Once he locked the driver's side door, he headed to O'Bannion's as if nothing out of the ordinary had occurred.

For Mickey Carberry, this was easy. This type of behavior was commonplace in his world.

∽

Despite its inner-city setting, Trisha Barron's Hardy Street neighborhood consisted of homes that were more typical of those found in the neighboring cities and towns that made up Boston's bedroom communities. Equipped with garages or off-street parking—a rarity in South Boston—closer inspection proved they were mostly two-family homes.

Trisha's home sat perpendicular to the area's predominantly parallel traffic flow. It was adjacent to the Massachusetts Bay Transportation Authority bus line on one end and the Atlantic Ocean on the other. Despite the absence of any Do Not Enter signs, people simply didn't travel down Hardy Street unless they had business on Hardy Street.

Her parents originally owned the home, which they passed down to her when Florida's Gulf Coast beckoned them.

Trisha had lived here her entire life, save for several rarely discussed months back in her sixteenth year.

Trisha's son, Bobby, had come to occupy the larger second floor unit of his mother's home three years ago.

It had been a godsend for Bobby at the time. His assistant district attorney's salary precluded him from affording anything remotely close to this on the open market. Given his significant increase in income in the interim, he had been systematically renovating it to his liking. Consequently, a variety of trades people came and went in a steady flow each week.

One downside for Bobby was that he was still smuggling in dates like a high school student. His newfound financial independence had somehow fortified Trisha's assertion that her grandmotherly biological clock was ticking.

Bobby found his mother's peculiar diagnosis to be a bit of a stretch from all of the obvious perspectives. He was having fun. Taking a wife—never mind parental responsibilities—was unfathomable at this point.

Whenever Bobby's mother advocated marriage or children—an increasingly recurring topic in recent months—Bobby's thoughts invariably digressed to Tim Dunlap and his predicament.

He was well acquainted with Dunlap from years of post-work prowling in Downtown Boston watering holes. While the pair used to advocate from opposite sides of the aisle when it came to the distribution of justice, Dunlap treated the prosecuting fraternity with respect. Understandably, exceptions occurred whenever he faced off against any of them in court.

Outside the courthouse—and in spite of the conjectural constraints of marriage—Dunlap never seemed to have a problem hooking up with female companionship. This is what made the rape claim and related violence so difficult for Bobby to believe.

For years, Bobby had witnessed an ultra-smooth Tim Dunlap in action, never once observing a dark side that seemed so essential for what he had convicted him of doing.

℘

Willie Marcus navigated the rush hour traffic of Kosciusko Circle on his way to delivering Trisha to a Dorchester hideout. A cobbled-together trio of reprobates was tearing apart Bobby Barron's second floor apartment several miles away. While two of them dumped out anything that resembled or ostensibly concealed any legal evidence onto a glass-topped kitchen table, the third guy—and leader—reviewed the scattered contents.

He piled anything that might be helpful into a green plastic garbage bag that lay on the floor. The leader jumped to his feet when the doorbell rang. "Stay here. Don't do a thing until I get back."

"No problem," the taller one muttered. He opened the refrigerator door with a gloved hand. He needed something cold to slake his thirst.

The leader headed down the stairs toward the front door. With the lawyer confined to his office and the lawyer's mother in Willie's custody, they had entered the house under the predetermined guise of bidding a ceramic tile job, should anyone inquire.

Larry Fitzgerald stood on the other side of the red mahogany door. The Hardy Street homeowner's suspicions increased when he witnessed the trio entering his neighbor's house from the rear.

The leader opened the door about eight inches and stuck his face through the crack. "What's up?"

Fitzgerald stared into a pair of grossly mismatched eyes. He was unsure of which one to focus on. "How you doing? I'm a friend of Bobby's, you know, the *owner*. Say, are you the guys that do the wrought iron work?"

"Uh, no. We're here to measure up a tile job," the leader said, adhering to the script.

"Oh, okay, sorry to bother you. I need some grates made for my cellar windows. Bobby told me he had some people coming out to give him a bid on grates for his windows, and I thought you might be them when I saw you go around the back."

25

"Oh, yeah. No, he left the backdoor open because nobody was going to be home." The pregnant pause that followed allowed him to regain control. "Hey, I've got to get back upstairs and finish measuring."

"Yeah, right, sorry to bother you." Fitzgerald was mindful that the door was about to be shut in his face. "Hey, you got a business card, or can I get your number? I may be doing some tile work soon; maybe we can do some business?"

"No, sorry, I don't. Talk to the owner, he has our number."

"Okay, thanks for your help. Nice meeting you," Fitzgerald said, sticking out his hand.

The leader thrust a still-gloved hand through the half-open door. He gave Fitzgerald a limp handshake, pulled his arm back, and shoved the door shut. When he reached the top of the stairs he said, "Come on. We've got to get out of here."

"Hey, the man wanted us to check both apartments *and* the basement while we were here," the drink thief replied.

The short heavyset accomplice chimed in, too. "Ain't no way I'm going back and telling him we didn't finish the job. He said, 'Bring any records we could find back to the apartment.' You don't know this guy like we do. We go back there without checking everything, and he's going to lose it."

The leader relented. "Fine, I'll finish up here. You take downstairs," he said, pointing at the drink thief, "and you take the basement. Wait until I come to you to check things out, and then we're out of here. Come on, let's go!" he barked, a reminder that he was still in charge.

The drink thief went to town on Trisha's first-floor apartment. If an item wasn't nailed down, it got tossed. The only records he uncovered seemed to be personal, but he'd let Mr. Big Boss Man decide what was important and what wasn't. His job was to get everything out in the open for inspection, and he performed that job at a fevered pitch.

Larry Fitzgerald—now saddled with the additional confusion of why a guy would need gloves to measure for a tile job—questioned the veracity of this group. When he saw lights go on in the first floor of the Barron home, and then in the basement less than thirty seconds later, he had seen enough.

He went to his kitchen and opened a cabinet drawer. He dug out his personal phonebook in search of Trisha Barron's cell phone number.

એ

Marie Phillips flopped onto her creamy yellow leather couch. She revisited this evening's events and found herself wondering what had happened to Jill. Did some sort of subliminal resentment cause the jealously she felt?

Marie sipped on a bottle of seltzer water as she racked her brain over Bobby's recent cases, clients, and foes. She dialed his office on a whim, and then hung up when the phone rang. What was she possibly going to say? Bobby had clearly told her to go home and wait for *his* call.

The last thing she ever intended to do was to replicate the single-ring notification that Bobby was nervously waiting to receive.

Unfortunately, that was exactly what she had done.

5

Bobby catapulted out of his chair and nearly out of his skin. He regained a semblance of composure and sat back down when the phone rang a second and third time.

Jill asked, "Do you want me to get that?" when it became apparent that Bobby was ignoring the still ringing phone.

"Please, don't touch it."

"What's going on, Bobby? Is there anything I can do?"

Bobby remained silent.

Jill walked to a corner of the office where a satin-glossed mahogany wall housed a brushed stainless-steel Bose stereo. She hit the power button and found the unit preset to an FM station that carried the "Imus in the Morning" program, followed by a number of local and syndicated talk shows. Jill wanted to transform the somber mood. This was not what she had in mind. She pushed another button, producing Barry White's 1973 classic "Never, Never Gonna Give Ya Up."

Now we're talking, she thought, completely unaware that she had created an entirely new problem.

While the classic song still enjoyed popularity with a segment of today's generation, that popularity paled in comparison to the song's success and status from three decades earlier, when it was Trisha Barron's favorite song. While the song's sexually explicit overtones and sultry sound framed its *intended* interpretation, its potential lone dissenter was a once young, loving, and overly protective mother.

For Trisha, the song's *title*, not the intended content, captivated her. "Never, Never Gonna Give Ya Up" meant something different to her, as well as to Bobby, once he was old enough to comprehend her carefully edited explanation.

Regardless, it was the last thing Bobby needed to hear. He exploded, shouting, "Shut that off! You've got to go, Jill. I need to be alone. I've got problems here, and I need to be able to think."

Bobby's outrage startled Jill. She silently formulated an argument aimed at convincing him to allow her to stay. In an attempt to shut off the stereo, she hit another button, changing the band to an AM station. She was not helping her cause.

A news announcer droned, "... both men were taken to Tufts-New England Medical Center for treatment. We have learned the hospital expects to release one of the men later this evening. The second one is in serious condition with severe facial and head injuries and will be held overnight for additional testing."

A flustered Jill stuck her face closer to the unit, searching for the On/Off switch.

The announcer continued, "Police are currently searching the K Street area near East Broadway in South Boston...."

"Don't turn that off," Bobby yelled. He bounded in Jill's direction. "Listen," he whispered, placing his index finger to his lip to buy her silence.

"Again, in a just-breaking story, Boston Police are investigating the brutal beating of two young men. Initial evidence gathered at the scene, coupled with the extent of the injuries to at least one of the victims, leads police to believe that some sort of gang-related attack took place on two victims in the East Broadway and K Street area of South Boston. Police are currently combing the area for clues. As new information becomes available, we will be updating our listening audience...."

Bobby stared at Jill and said, "That's right around the area where I told Mickey to meet me. I hope he's okay."

જી

"Jake, Arthur wants to talk to you," Matty Shearin yelled. He handed over the hardwired headset to his friend of over twenty years.

As foreman Arthur Williams' phone man, Matty was accustomed to a variety of signals funneling through him to the other members of their steel erection crew. His primary job was to ensure the smooth transmission of signals from his gang to crane operator, Larry Geran, or, occasionally, Larry's oiler, Joe Cameron. The cab of the Manitowoc crane—which served as Larry and Joe's office for ten to twelve hours a day—sat ten stories above the work floor. This location limited the crane operator's vision at times and required their operating in the blind at others, whereby Matty became their eyes and ears to the activity below.

The primary function of the alternating operating engineers and half-dozen ironworkers was to ensure that the numerous pieces of pre-fabricated steel that make up the skeleton of a building arrived safely to their respective and final resting places. Matty, Jake, and the remainder of their gang were widely recognized as one of the best in the business.

They were hanging iron for a twenty-two story office tower adjacent to the massive Boston Convention & Exhibition Center, and the adjoining Westin Hotel. Jake's gang had erected that structure several years earlier in South Boston's burgeoning Seaport District.

This transitional area was undergoing rapid change after years of underutilization. The infrastructure was well underway for an eclectic and vibrant 24-7 neighborhood connecting the parochial and insular South Boston to Boston's staid and business-oriented downtown area. The unsightly black tar parking lots—having long serviced suburban dwellers who refused to embrace public transportation—had become a tremendous source of income for many building tradesmen and women from Boston and beyond.

For lifelong South Boston resident John "Jake" Carberry, plying his trade less than a mile from the front door of his home was about as good as it could get.

As one of the erection gang's two "hooker-onners," Jake and his partner attached the lifting eyes of the steel-cabled slings, or chokers, onto the spreader hooks of the project's giant crane. The objective was the safe delivery of the attached piece, or pieces, of structural steel to the gang's two connectors. These intrepid individuals made their living perched precariously atop the unfinished structure.

The operation came to a screeching halt when Matty removed his headset.

Jake stuck the set up to his ear. He spoke loudly so his boss could hear him over the din. "What's up, Arthur?"

"Jake, we were talking about Mickey the other day. Did you ever get a chance to ask him if he's looking for work?'"

"No, I meant to go by his place last night, but I got tied up. Why, what's up? Have you got something?"

"I was just talking to Bull, and he's looking for a guy."

"What are they doing?"

"Lintels. It's a good job, buddy. You want me to see if he'll hold off until you talk to Mickey?"

Jake paused. Installing lintels, or steel angle support shelves for the bricklayers, *was* good work. He simply hated owing Bull a favor, as the guy was a jerk.

Bull was actually a skinny little guy who had acquired his nickname due to his proclivity for shooting the bull in area taverns and pubs. Nevertheless, he took great pride in the name, and those who weren't wise to his act often perceived it in a positive light; at least until they endured a night of drinking with him.

"No, I don't want to screw him up, Arthur. Tell him thanks anyway."

Arthur had been best friends with Bull's recently deceased father. Arthur had bailed Bull out of numerous barroom scrapes since his dad's passing. Armed with his undying gratitude and mindful that Jake was not going to ask Bull for anything—the only possible exception being a fistfight—Arthur floated an alternative solution. "Look, I told Bull that this was a favor for *me*. I'm going to tell him to hold the job until you get a chance to check with Mickey and get back to me. Just let me know tomorrow. I'll take care of the rest. Besides, I haven't seen that fucking kook brother of yours lately. I could use a few laughs."

Jake laughed at his boss's unvarnished honesty. "I owe you one. I'll track him down after work and let you know tomorrow."

"Yeah, no problem. Hey, the kid's here with the coffee. Tell Matty to have Larry take a strain on that bundle and dog it off while we take a break. I'll give him a holler when we're ready."

"All right, buddy." Jake relayed Arthur's message while handing the headset back to Matty.

As Jake sat on the back of the half-full flatbed trailer truck sipping coffee with Matty and his partner, "Big Mike" McClaren, he reflected on his incorrigible brother. The youngest of John and Stella Carberry's nine children, Mickey was seventeen years his junior. Jake lamented for what seemed like the millionth time about having been too busy to recognize the signs of Mickey's alternative life path, invariably agonizing over the fact that he might have made more of a difference in Mickey's life. Mickey had idolized him when he was young, as their age gap had cast Jake into a surrogate parent role early on.

Unfortunately, with an ever-expanding young family materializing as Mickey weighed his own life's choices, Jake justified his inaction with a 'he's a big boy' mindset.

As Mickey's misguided adolescence evolved into increasingly dangerous behavior and the inevitable aftereffects, it became too much for their recently widowed mother to endure.

This forced Jake's reentry into the picture.

An unwritten rule of Stella Carberry's heritage was the obligation of a mother to place extra emphasis on her firstborn and on her youngest—in this case, Jake and Mickey—whereby each was entitled to an inordinate amount of maternal attention and affection.

Jake possessed a disproportionate maturity for his age. He had his mother wrapped around his finger to the point where she was lovingly chided about it by her other children.

Mickey had initially craved and absorbed this extra attention, only to shun it as an unacceptable sign of weakness in subsequent years.

Ten years earlier, Jake brokered his untarnished reputation to get Mickey into Iron Workers Local 7's apprentice program. While he taught Mickey the ins and outs of the trade, his underlying motive was to keep an eye on him by keeping him employed on his jobs.

Mickey proved to be an outstanding worker. It took him five years to complete the required three years of apprenticeship training, due to several lapses in judgment, but ironworking was a perfect fit for Mickey. It was a rough-and-tumble business consisting of myriad unpredictable people.

Outrageous behavior was commonplace on jobsites, where the arduous and dangerous work required individuals with courage. This courage often manifested itself in a way that was not for the faint of heart.

Over time, solid work habits, ever-increasing skills, and a growing reputation as a died-in-the-wool union member were not enough to separate Mickey from the violent but lucrative criminal world. While Mickey still worked on occasion, his purpose was more an exercise to legitimize his spending than to conform to a normal lifestyle. His plan would never pass any comprehensive scrutiny, however, as he spent significantly more than he ever legally earned.

"Let's hit it," Matty Shearin hollered, snapping Jake out of his Mickey-induced reverie. Word had just filtered down from Arthur to ship the next load.

Jake tossed his coffee cup into a nearby dumpster and went back to what was, to him, the only way to make a living—honestly and without always having to look over his shoulder.

As the load of metal decking disappeared from view, Jake helped Big Mike prepare the next load for delivery. He hoped Mickey would take his boss up on the offer.

6

Willie Marcus exited Columbia Road onto Quincy Street. He pulled over, removed his cell phone from his coat pocket, and dialed a number. "Yeah, it's me, I'm almost there." After a brief pause, he continued, an increased level of agitation obvious in his voice. "Sammy, I'm only *two* minutes away."

Willie shut his phone and stuffed it back into his pocket. He threw the van's transmission into drive, and quickly pulled away from the curb.

Trisha jerked forward, then backward, in harmony with the van's ever-increasing speed.

Willie's Sacomma Street destination ran perpendicular to Quincy Street in a nondescript section of Boston's Dorchester neighborhood.

It was about to become Trisha Barron's temporary residence.

Willie turned left and climbed a small, unevenly paved hill. He turned left again, and a figure appeared out of the cover of darkness at the bottom of the driveway.

Slowing the vehicle, Willie turned left and rolled down the chewed-up asphalt driveway. Two massive oak trees off to his right provided an added level of darkness, conveniently shrouding their arrival. He stopped at the bottom of the driveway of the rundown and unoccupied two-family home.

Willie exited the van, and then reentered it through its side door as Sammy Jackson appeared by his side. Willie said, "I'm going to undo the cuffs. I don't need any trouble. You'll be treated fine if you do the right thing. We've got a problem we need to handle. Hopefully, everything will happen quickly. We don't want to be here anymore than you do." Pausing to let his words sink in, he asked, "You understand me?"

Trisha mumbled, "Yes."

Trisha gained instant relief once Willie unshackled the handcuffs.

She immediately turned around and stared at Willie. "Can you at least tell me what's going on? I mean, you snatch me off the street, making all sorts of crazy accusations against my son and—" She paused and then continued, speaking several decibels louder and with a renewed sense of exasperation. "You *kidnapped* me, and you can't tell me *why?* Are you afraid I'll leave if I don't like your answer?"

Willie stifled a chuckle. He looked at his young accomplice—who was clad, head-to-toe in an all-black outfit— and said, "Take her inside. Make sure everything's secure, just like we discussed. I've got to make a phone call."

Sammy grabbed a handful of Trisha's white nylon windbreaker. He guided her through the front door and into a short, narrow hallway that led to the house's kitchen.

Willie moved to the corner of the garage and dialed a number on his cell phone. He glanced around while the phone rang, and then whispered, "What's up? Yeah, we're all set. She's in the house ... Yeah, okay, I'll wait to hear from you."

೧

Bobby's phone rang once before going silent. He replayed their instructions in his head: *When we call, we'll ring the phone once, hang up, and then call back within ten seconds. Pick it up when it starts ringing again after the single ring. You got it?* He was sure he understood the instructions, yet ten seconds turned into five minutes and there was still no follow up call. *Did they say ten seconds or ten minutes?* He paced around the room.

Jill thumbed through a magazine, barely absorbing its content. She survived her earlier offense of tinkering with Bobby's stereo. She was afraid anything she said or did would result in another eviction notice.

The damage caused by Marie Phillips's single ring proved to be minimal.

Bobby continued to pace. Out of nowhere, he suddenly said to Jill, "I don't know what I'm going to do."

Jill tossed the magazine onto a table. She rose from the chair and warily approached Bobby. "Please don't get upset. I don't want to say anything that's going to set you off. I just want you to know that I'll do anything I can to help you. Obviously, there's something wrong. What can I do to help?"

"I don't want to make a bad situation worse, Jill. I'm sorry I got pissed off earlier, but hearing that song, especially after receiving that call—"

He stopped talking when the phone rang. *They must have said ten minutes,* he thought as he dashed behind his desk. He motioned for Jill to be quiet and picked up the receiver.

"Bobby Barron," he said, lowering himself to his chair.

"Bobby, what the hell is wrong with you?"

Bobby became apoplectic. "What the fuck are you talking about? You said you'd ring the phone once, and then call back in ten seconds. I *know* you said ten *seconds*, and then you don't call back for ten minutes. I did everything you told me to do—"

"Bobby, what are *you* talking about? It's Jeff Lydon. I called because you had a pre-trial hearing today and you never showed up. I schmoozed Old Man Flaherty. I told him you had a car accident, and you might not be able to appear. I'm just calling so you don't make a liar out of me when you see him."

Jeff Lydon was a courthouse clerk and close friend of Bobby's. He was also tying up Bobby's phone line. Bobby cut him short. "Jeff … shit … I'm sorry. Look, I can't talk right now. I've got a serious problem, and I've got to leave my phone line open. I'll get back to you." He hung up without waiting for a response.

Jill instinctively retreated, hoping Bobby would revisit the promising conversation he initiated before the phone call. *Why had he picked up that call after letting all the other calls go to his voicemail? What was with this single ring? And what were the 'ten seconds' and 'ten minutes' all about? He got anxious when the phone rang once, and then opened up to me right after it occurred. He's waiting for a single ring signal from someone … but who, and why? What's going on?*

Bobby's eyes remained unfocussed.

Jill could not suppress her curiosity. She meandered back into their previous conversation. "Bobby, like I was saying earlier, I want to help you. I'm a professional reporter. I will never repeat anything you tell me in confidence. It would destroy my credibility. Plus, I'm your friend. I'll never—"

Bobby responded with an emptiness and distinct sense of resignation in his voice. "Jill, the problem is the people I'm dealing with don't request court orders to instruct people to divulge their media sources."

"What people? Talk to me, Bobby. Please … I want to help."

Bobby continued staring vacantly. *For as long as he could remember, his mother had always taught him to follow his first instinct.*

With that as his guide, he began recounting everything he knew. He needed a sounding board, yet couldn't help but wonder if Jill would end up regretting her entrance into the epicenter of his dilemma.

ꞔ౧

Positive customer relations were a foreign concept at O'Bannion's Tavern. Their cleaning ritual consisted of wiping the same filthy, multi-stained rag across the bar every few hours and then thoroughly at the end of each evening.

It would best be described as old school, representing a classic throwback to an era when drinking was serious sport: shots of whiskey and longneck beers in a dirty, poorly lit, smoke-filled room that was easily adapted into an *ad hoc* boxing ring whenever the need arose. In the case of O'Bannion's, the need was frequent.

Years earlier, Boston's tobacco Nazis had outlawed all forms of smoking in its bars and restaurants. O'Bannion's management teamed up with a number of other local establishments in fighting the decree, but in the end, they had no alternative but to comply. In spite of their adherence to the new law, the stench of decade upon decade of legal lighting up still clung to every corner and outdated feature of the dark and dank wood-paneled establishment.

Even Mickey Carberry felt creeped out upon entering. Mindful of the establishment's well-earned reputation for harboring a drug-addled clientele, he had not set foot here in years. He'd spoiled himself by hanging out in one of Southie's new, upscale saloons. O'Bannion's attraction escaped him until he ordered a Budweiser and discovered it was seventy-five cents cheaper than he was accustomed to paying. He remained secure that he had been spending the additional tariff wisely. He eyeballed the sour-looking bartender, who was also the owner, and asked, "Can I start a tab?"

"No tabs, no credit cards," the old man snarled, pulling the now-open bottle back as collateral until some cash appeared.

Mickey was in no mood to argue. He had just dispatched the two punks up the street, and he could hear sirens wailing in the distance. The last thing he needed was to be strolling back into the area as police conducted an investigation; especially with his car still sitting, slightly askew, as a centerpiece within ground-zero of the crime scene.

Digging out a crisp twenty-dollar bill, Mickey tossed it Frisbee style at the balding, wrinkled old man. He made a mental note to pay him a return visit some night as a payback for this lack of respect. He hoisted the longneck bottle to his lips and focused on the one luxury that O'Bannion's offered—a television, complete with rotary dials and rabbit ears covered in grimy tin foil. Several steady customers would readily swear under oath that it had once shown programs in color.

Mickey was on his third beer when Bobby laid a hand on his right shoulder, catching him off guard.

Bobby motioned toward a recently vacated and bottle-strewn table in the rear of the bar and said, "Let's sit over there."

Mickey made his way to the table.

Bobby stayed behind, ordered his friend another beer, and requested a glass of water for himself.

"You're running up my water bill, kid. I'm here to sell booze," the owner barked.

"Charge me, if you've got to," Bobby replied. He was too preoccupied with his own problem to deal with this guy's shitty attitude. After throwing the grouch a couple of dollar bills from his change, he noticed the water glass had more fingerprints on it than one would reasonably expect to find in an FBI crime lab.

The Board of Health would have a field day in here, Bobby thought as he headed toward Mickey.

7

Trisha took deep calming breaths as Sammy led her down the hall toward the safe room. She contemplated her captor's intentions during the van ride, and it dawned on her that she was carrying her cell phone. Her mind was awash in thought as she focused on how she could best put it to use.

As usual, she had placed the phone on vibrate mode before leaving the house for her walk. She usually only answered it if the caller ID indicated Bobby, or her employer, Dr. Joseph Wissard, was calling. Trisha had worked for Wissard as a dental hygienist since 1973.

She convinced herself that Sammy would search her as they neared the end of the hall. If her instincts proved correct, it wouldn't take long to discover the phone.

Sammy stopped at a padlocked door and grabbed a set of keys hanging from a large nail driven in high on the opposite wall. The first key failed to open the lock, and Sammy fumbled with the oval key ring.

Trisha jumped when she heard a phone ring.

Sammy nonchalantly pulled his cell phone from his pocket and answered it. He turned a quarter-turn from Trisha to shield his voice.

She immediately seized on what might be her only opportunity to maintain contact with the outside world by tapping a preoccupied Sammy on the shoulder. "Can I use the bathroom?" she asked.

He placed his left hand over the phone and glared at her. "Bitch, what the fuck are you doing? You see me on the phone, right?"

"Listen, I need to use the bathroom. I just figured I'd tell you now rather than after you're done taking me wherever you're taking me. I saw a bathroom back there," she said, pointing over his right shoulder.

Sammy put the phone back up to his ear and said, "Dude, I'll get back to you," before slapping the unit shut.

Trisha went on the offensive. "You can stand right outside. I'll only be a minute. I've really got to go." She walked away without his permission, half expecting him to cave in the back of her head.

Sammy followed her, but all he could offer was, "Ya gotta go, ya gotta go."

Trisha turned left and entered the bathroom.

"If you ain't out in one minute, I'm coming in," he yelled as she shut the door in his face.

Trisha actually did have to relieve herself.

Trisha conducted her business. A steady stream was discernable from Sammy's vantage point on the other side of the door. This put him at ease.

Trisha weighed whether to hide the phone in the bathroom and retrieve it later when her captors would be less suspicious; or place it on her being, where she would be susceptible to an immediate body search and possible discovery.

I've got to keep it with me. I may never get another chance.

"Let's go," Sammy said. "Minute's up."

"I'll be right out. One second," Trisha said. She shut the phone off to conserve its battery. *I hope he's not a sicko,* she thought, reasoning there was only one area he *might* avoid if he frisked her. She pulled her underwear up as tight as possible, jamming the phone securely against her genitalia.

A nauseated Trisha exited the bathroom. Her heart raced as Sammy led her back down the hall.

When they entered the room, he said, "I'm going to have to search you. Take off your coat, and turn around." Almost as an afterthought, he added, "You got a cell phone on you?"

"No." Trisha's breath shortened and her heart beat continued to accelerate. She sensed an inordinate amount of blood draining from her face.

"What about mace or pepper spray?"

"Just this iPod," she said, handing him the unit she just unstrapped from her left bicep. "That's all I carry when I walk."

Her heart was on the verge of exploding as Sammy began his search.

He came uncomfortably close to discovering her contraband on several occasions, but never did discover the phone. Once he was comfortable, he produced two pairs of handcuffs and ordered her onto a bed tucked against the far wall of the room. He shackled each of her arms to the bed's steel-pipe framed headboard.

A lot of good the phone is going to do me, Trisha thought.

Sammy shut off the light and left the room. He padlocked her in from the outside.

℘

Hi, this is Trisha. I'm unavailable right now, please leave a message, and I'll call you back.

When the beep came, he said, "Trisha, it's Larry Fitzgerald, I wanted to run something by you, and I don't see your car in the driveway. Let's see, it's about, ahh … 6:15. If you get this message before ten, could you give me a call? If not, no big deal, I'll catch up with you tomorrow."

Larry recited his phone number, hung up, and returned to his surveillance post.

℘

It all began about one week earlier for lanky attorney Carl Bionda. He had been minding his business—which in his world meant sticking his nose into everyone else's business—when his cell phone rang. He had recently relocated to Florida. Licensed in both Massachusetts and Florida, Bionda had conducted a number of Pick Piccorino's questionable business dealings in the Bay and Sunshine states over the years.

An avid, albeit unlucky, gambler, he now found himself unemployed. Piccorino had been his lucrative, but exclusive, meal ticket. Worse yet, his move south had been expedited when many of the people he had stuck it to in a variety of shady deals on Pick's behalf had begun circling his wagon after his client's incarceration.

Nicknamed "The Shadow"—a play on words in conjunction with his last name, as in Beyond a *shadow* of a doubt—the moniker fit him well.

He lost his right eye in a childhood accident. The ensuing medical procedure left him with a replacement that differed in both color and content from his good eye. The combination left him with a ghoulish and frightening look.

Shadow had fielded the phone call while walking the Hollywood, Florida boardwalk, a veritable human freak show that ran parallel to North Ocean Drive, better known as Route A1A. Hollywood's beach regulations seemingly included a provision stating, "The more you weigh, the less you are allowed to wear."

Once Shadow identified the caller, he quickly sought an empty bench.

As Jimmy Mansfield laid out Pick's wish list, Bionda's recurring thought was, *Who's going to pay for this?*

Mansfield finished up and said, "Pick says he knows that you'll come through for him on this. Once he gets the information that'll help spring him, he says he'll take care of you."

"Jimmy, nothing for nothing, but I'm hurting too. Other than a few odds-and-ends, Pick was my only client. I'm down in Florida chasing a couple of leads, you know, looking to start over. Who's going to pay for me to get back up there?"

"You want me to tell him you can't do it, Shadow?" Mansfield ratcheted up his voice a notch and continued, "You think Pick's got the money to fly you up? I'm just the messenger here. Are you going to meet with him or not? I'm going to see him tomorrow, and he's going to want an answer. What's it going to be?"

Shadow knew he had no options. "I'll figure something out. Tell Pick I'll get there as soon as I can."

"Yeah, good answer. Hey, stay away from Gulfstream in the meantime," Mansfield cracked, mindful of The Shadow's predilection for slow horses.

"Yeah, good one, Jimmy. I'll see you," before hissing, "Asshole!" *after* he was sure the phone connection had been severed.

Carl "The Shadow" Bionda showed up at Riverfork three days later. He was registered as Pick's attorney, and Pick's intermediaries had set up a special place to meet.

Pick immediately subjected Shadow to his legendary wrath the moment he entered the room. "What the fuck did you do, *walk* from Florida, you piece of shit? You've got a fucking short memory, pal. I never heard you complaining when you were stuffing my money in your pockets, but as soon as I got locked up, you think you're going to walk away? Jimmy told me you were whining about having to come up here."

"Pick, I don't know what Jimmy said. I told him I'd be here, and here I am. Come on. Let's talk business. What do you have in mind?"

"I ought to break your fucking legs as a little reminder of who you're dealing with."

Once Pick convinced Shadow of his displeasure, he explained his plan and its connection to disbarred attorney and fellow inmate, Tim Dunlap.

಄

"Bobby, this guy knows a lot of people. He defended a lot of heavy hitters, you know, guys with serious juice." Mickey took a swig from his latest bottle of beer.

"Yeah, I know all that. I prosecuted a few of them, remember? But he was also a big-time player when it came to the ladies."

"What's that got to do with anything?"

"Simple. Why *now*? I just don't get it."

"What's to get?"

"His bit is winding down. With good behavior, he should be getting a hearing within the next year. Why's he suddenly willing to jeopardize everything? It just doesn't make sense. I always figured he got too drunk and took it out on that girl, you know, an aberration, the wrong move at the wrong time. After awhile, you forget about it. Things are good. Then your phone's ringing, and someone's telling you that your mother's been taken hostage."

"Tell me what they said one more time."

"Nothing complicated. They called the first time and made all sorts of threats. It was pretty ugly. They told me to wait and they would get back to me. When they called back, they claimed I had framed Tim Dunlap and I had better make it good. You know, a lot of stuff like that. There were a whole bunch of personal threats about what was going to happen if I didn't do what they wanted."

Mickey gulped another mouthful of beer.

Bobby continued. "I never really got a word in either time. The second call was a little more specific and a little less hateful. It's confusing. What do they expect me to do? Walk into court and say I was only kidding? That there's been a mistake and that I set Dunlap up?" He shook his head at the absurdity of those conclusions.

"And that's how it was left?"

"Bottom line, they must think I planted the DNA evidence. If I don't admit to it, they're going to kill my mother." Bobby shook his head and continued, "I guess I just answered my own question. They *do* want me to walk into court and say, I was only kidding. If only it were that simple."

Mickey slid closer to Bobby. He looked around to ensure nobody could overhear him. "Bobby, all fucking kidding aside, did you set him up? If I'm going to help you, you've got to level with me. I've got to know."

8

Jill observed O'Bannion's front door from the driver's seat of her Volvo. She had been sitting there for the past forty-five minutes.

She and Bobby had exited his office building separately. She hailed a cab and picked him up in front of South Station. They then directed the cab driver to Jill's car. She relocated to her present position after dropping Bobby off a few blocks from the bar for his meeting with Mickey.

Jill removed a notebook from her oversized, two-toned leather pocketbook. She dug out a pen and scribbled a series of connecting lines and boxes, endeavoring to create some semblance of order to the events of the past several hours. Constantly checking for Bobby, she was able to fill in a number of additional blanks due to his having confided in her about his problem.

Jill weighed the personal versus professional fallout and found herself at a crossroad. *Am I getting a story or helping an old friend?*

The sight of Bobby walking out the door of the bar interrupted her thoughts.

Jill flashed her high beams, and Bobby broke into a slow jog in her direction.

"How did it go?" Jill asked as he slid into the passenger seat.

"I'm not sure. Mickey's making some calls, and he's going to meet with some people and get back to me. His brother Jake showed up toward the end of our conversation and dragged him off to talk about something else. I couldn't sit still, so I took off. He probably doesn't even know I'm gone."

Bobby was talking much faster than usual. Burying his face into his hands, he took a deep breath and said, "Man, my head is spinning."

"Where do you want to go?" Jill asked.

"No clue. Let's get out of here, though. Let me think about it while we're moving."

Jill put the car into drive and turned right at the end of the block.

"Turn right here," Bobby said.

As Jill turned right again, Bobby spun around. Pointing toward the sidewalk, he said, "Pull over for a second."

Bobby peered through the rear windshield toward the street they had just exited. He was worried that someone might be following them. Satisfied by the absence of vehicular traffic, Bobby twisted back around to Jill. "All right, let's get out of here."

Jill drove to East Broadway where she encountered a red light. "Which way do you want to go?"

"Take a left and head up over the hill. I'm going to swing by my house, but I want to look around the area first. If anyone's looking for me, they won't expect me to be coming in from that direction and they definitely won't recognize your car."

❧

Billy Turpin led Pick to an unoccupied office. "Just bang on the door when you're done, Pick." He locked him in.

An old-fashioned black phone sat atop a Formica-clad desk. Pick pushed the blinking red light and said, "Hello."

Attorney Carl "Shadow" Bionda said, "We just left there."

"What did you find?"

"We tore his place apart and didn't find anything useful. We even ripped up the mother's apartment … basement too. Nothing. A few things looked promising, but once I dug into them, there was no connection. Oh, yeah, we also had a nosy neighbor come to the door to see what was going on."

"What do we do now?"

"If there's any evidence, it must be in his office, but he's on the eighteenth floor of a new high-rise over near South Station. You know, all the latest security gadgets, full-time guard desk in the lobby where you have to sign in. There's no way we'll ever get near it."

"What if we send in a new client?" Pick asked, before quickly changing his mind. "No, wait a minute. Where are those two guys I sent you?"

"They took off once they were done. Why?"

"Take this number down. Here's what I want you to do."

❧

I've got to free up my hands. If I can just release them, I can hit nine-one-one. Maybe they can track my cell phone.

"Hello, can anyone hear me?" Trisha yelled. "Can I talk to someone?"

Her arms and shoulders ached from the numbness of inactivity.

The door burst open, and the man she still only knew as "Agent" Williams reappeared.

"What did I tell you earlier?" Willie said. "You do the right thing and everything's going to be okay. Yelling is *not* doing the right thing."

"Can I please have some water? And can you cut one of my arms loose so I can relieve some of the pain and numbness?"

"I cut one of your arms loose, and the first thing you're going do is play around with the handcuffs."

Trisha knew any type of dialogue was helpful. "No, I won't. I promise. Can you do an arm and a leg, or something that will allow me to get a little more comfortable? I'm not going to play around with the handcuffs. You have my word. Besides, even if I could free the handcuffs, you have the door locked from the outside and you have the window boarded up." Trisha pointed to the plywood screwed tightly into the window jambs. "I'm just trying to make things a little more bearable."

Willie stepped back and surveyed the situation. He turned back and walked toward the door. Stepping into the hallway, he yelled "Sammy. Get in here."

47

Willie walked back over to the bed. He dug his hand back into his pocket and removed a key. He freed Trisha's left hand as Sammy entered the room. Turning to him, Willie asked, "You shook her down, right?'

"Yeah, she's all set."

Trisha twisted her left arm in a slow circular motion to encourage blood flow. The freedom felt wonderful. Her right arm was still tethered, but the added comfort buoyed her spirits. *He's right. I am all set now. I just have to get rid of them so I can make a call.*

Willie moved to the opposite corner of the bed. He attached one end of the handcuffs to the metal footboard and the other end to her left ankle.

Trisha had to cock her left leg awkwardly to keep the steel cuff from digging into her anklebone. *But at least her hand was free.*

"Will I be getting something to eat?" Trisha asked.

"Yeah, just call room service," Sammy said with a chuckle before exiting the room.

"Let's see what happens." Willie said. "Like I told you earlier, we don't want to be here anymore than you do. If you're here long enough, we'll feed you. If I hear you yelling again, the cuffs go back on both arms. Understood?"

Trisha nodded affirmatively. She forced a smile. "No more yelling, you've got my word. Thank you for making things a little more comfortable."

Willie exited without responding, padlocking her in once again.

Willie couldn't help but admire Trisha's spunk as he walked down the hallway.

He grabbed a bottle of spring water from a small cooler in the kitchen and headed back to her room to fulfill her other request.

ભ

Trisha reached down her pants and removed the cell phone from its hiding spot as soon as she heard the padlock click. She pressed the power button and waited for the phone to activate.

Sudden commotion outside the padlocked door caused her to panic. Trisha stashed the phone under her left thigh just before the door opened.

Willie walked over to the bed and extended a bottle of spring water in her direction.

Trisha accepted it.

"Thank you" she said, just as her cell phone's voice mail messaging system rang out.

She would never hear Larry Fitzgerald's well-intentioned message.

9

Jill pulled her car adjacent to the sidewalk across from the Admiral Farragut Statue, a local landmark to the Civil War hero that stood sentry over Southie's Pleasure Bay for the past 115 years.

A mild drizzle had begun to fall.

Bobby hit "M" on his BlackBerry activating the default for his secretary's home phone number. "Marie, has anyone contacted you?"

"No, no, you're the first person who has called. What's going on, Bobby?"

"I still can't get into it. I need you to go in to work tomorrow and wait for me to call. I don't know what time I'll get there. Christ, I don't know if I'll be in at all."

Bobby paused when Jill turned on the windshield wipers.

He regained his thought process and said, "Just go to the office and we'll play it by ear, okay? I need you to reschedule all my appointments. Tell everyone I had to go to the hospital. Now, we've got to be on the same page here. What did I go to the hospital for?"

"Abdominal pains?" Marie replied. "Kidney stones, maybe?"

"Yeah, yeah, that's plausible. What hospital did I go to?"

"If I tell anyone what hospital you're in, aren't they apt to call there to check up on you, or maybe even pay you a visit?"

"Yeah, you're right. That's why you make the big money," Bobby kidded.

"I'm just going to be vague. The less said the better."

Bobby silently nodded his head in agreement and said, "As soon as I hear something, or if I need something, I'll call you."

"Where are you now? Are you alone?"

Bobby looked at Jill. A smirk crossed his lips. "Yeah, I'm alone."

"Well, be careful. I'm going in early tomorrow. Make sure you call me, okay?"

"Yes, boss. I'll call you." *No sense in raising her anxiety level,* he thought. He shut off the phone and placed it on the car's center console.

"She hates me."

"*What?* Why would she hate you?"

"What do you think she meant when she asked if you were alone?"

"She's very protective, that's all."

"Come on, Bobby. She was upset earlier when I wouldn't leave after you told her to go home. Her asking you if you're alone is nothing more than a euphemism for, 'Is that bitch Jill with you?'"

"You're nuts."

"I'm nuts, huh?

"Yeah, you're nuts," Bobby said, mimicking her voice.

"Well, if I'm nuts, then why didn't you tell her I was with you?"

Bobby's smile disappeared. "You're good. What can I say? You got me."

"I'm not trying to *get* you, Bobby. I want to help you every bit as much as Marie does. I feel it's important that you understand that." Jill took a deep breath. "What do you want to do now?"

"We're going to drive by my house while I look around to see if anything looks out of the ordinary. There are only so many places to hide in that neighborhood. Head up that way," he said, pointing toward a deserted stretch of beach road that ran parallel to Marine Park.

As Jill maneuvered through the Hardy Street neighborhood, Bobby purposely avoided driving down his street.

Once he was confident that nothing was amiss on the adjacent streets, he directed her down Hardy for one final look before entering his home.

They exited onto Marine Road. Jill circled the block one final time.

As they headed down M Street, Bobby said, "Pull over here," pointing to his left.

Jill double-parked and put on her emergency blinkers.

Bobby laughed. Double-parking—sans emergency lights—was a virtual birthright for any born-and-bred South Bostonian. He stared into Jill's green eyes. "Here's the plan. I'm going to walk around and go in my house through the front door. I want you to wait *ten* minutes; and then I need you to walk down that alley."

Jill looked in the direction Bobby was pointing.

"That alley leads to my backyard. You've seen the layout from the other side. I'll unlock the backdoor. Now, this is important. Before you come in, pound on the door as if it's locked, then wait a few minutes before opening it. It's really important that you wait. Okay?"

Jill looked confused.

Sensing her reticence, Bobby said, "Jill, if you're not up to this, that's no problem. I'm just setting up a little insurance. There are other ways, you know, other things we can do—"

"No, no, I'm *in*. I just need you to go over it again. You're going around the front. I wait ten minutes and walk up that alley—" She pointed, paused, and then asked, "Am I going to be able to walk into your yard?"

"Yeah, there's a huge tree between our houses, so we never needed a fence. The Kellers own this house. They know me well. If you run into a problem, just mention my name. Don't worry about it. Just scoot up the alley and you'll be at my backdoor in seconds."

Jill digested the information as Bobby continued. "Do you have an umbrella in the car?"

"Yeah, but it's not raining that hard—"

"Take the umbrella with you. Use the handle of the umbrella to bang on the door so it makes as much noise as possible. I want you to pound on that door like a bill collector. Ten minutes, okay?"

"I'm all set."

"One more thing. I don't think you have my *home* phone number. You should put it in your cell phone, just in case."

"What's the number," Jill asked. She entered it as he recited it, and then stored it as Bobby 2.

"You better put my mother's number in there, too. If you get to the backdoor and it's locked, I probably ran into an unforeseen problem. If it's locked, I want you to call those two numbers immediately. Okay? Mine first, then my mother's."

"Is your mother's number the one you dialed earlier, right before you called your friend Mickey?"

"Yeah, why?"

"I already stored that one. You didn't think you were going to shake me off your trail that easily, did you?" Jill teased. She flashed a green fluorescent display of his name and his mother's phone number in Bobby's face.

"Hey what can I say? Like I said earlier, you're good."

Jill shrugged and smiled.

Bobby took on a more serious tone, reminding her one final time. "*Ten* minutes. If everything goes right, I'll see you in ten minutes."

ↂ

"What the fuck is ringing?" Willie screamed, shoving Trisha aside as the offending phone rang out for the third time.

"You fucking lying bitch!" Willie yelled. He grabbed the phone and fired it against the wall, smashing it into two jagged pieces. "*Sammy!* Get the fuck in here."

53

Sammy ran into the room. "What's up?"

"Everything's a joke, right?" Willie screamed. "You think you've got all the answers, don't you?"

"What are you talking about?"

Willie grabbed the larger piece of what remained of Trisha's phone from the floor. He snatched a handful of Sammy's hair with his left hand as he shoved the serrated piece of plastic against his right ear.

The more Sammy struggled, the more infuriated Willie became, and the deeper he imbedded the makeshift weapon.

"You stupid little prick! If I hadn't come back when I did, the cops would be on their way. Ten fucking times I went over it. Check for cell phones, pepper spray, anything she could use against us. You better pull your head out of your ass, kid. This is serious business. Instead of working for Pick on the outside, you'll be his fucking in-house butler if you don't wake up."

"I did search her," Sammy mumbled, "I don't know how I missed it."

Reaching into his pocket, Willie produced the handcuff keys. He cut Trisha loose, screaming, "Stand up!" as he yanked her from the bed.

Trisha stumbled as she attempted to right herself.

Willie grabbed her under the arm. "Hold her up," he yelled at Sammy. "I'll make sure there are no more surprises."

Sammy held Trisha while Willie frisked every inch of her body. Had the phone remained in its original hiding spot, Willie undoubtedly would have discovered it this time around. Once he was satisfied, he shoved her back onto the bed and resorted to his original plan. Handcuffing both her arms to the respective bedposts, he tightened each cuff an extra notch in response to her duplicity.

A horrified Trisha didn't dare utter a word.

10

Bobby turned right and began walking down Hardy Street.

He was startled when his neighbor, Larry Fitzgerald, called out his name as he descended the front stairs of his home, which sat diagonally across the street from Bobby's house.

"Bobby, I've got to ask you about those tile guys who were here."

"What tile guys?"

Larry replayed the evening's events for Bobby.

"How long were they in there?"

"Over an hour. I was suspicious, so I went over to see what was going on. I tried to find out as much as I could from the guy who answered. When he was getting ready to shut the door, I stuck my hand out to shake his hand. When he stuck his hand out, he was wearing a rubber glove. I mean, why would he be wearing rubber gloves to measure for tile?"

"What did he look like?"

"Kind of weird looking. He had crazy looking eyes, you know, almost like a glass eye or something. He was tall—"

"But they definitely left?"

"Yeah. I called your mother on her cell phone, but they left about fifteen minutes after I called her."

"You *talked* to my mother?" Bobby inched closer to Larry, almost as if to allow him to hear the answer sooner.

"She didn't answer, so I left a message. You want me to go inside with you?"

"No, but what I would like you to do is to wait about five minutes, and then come up and ring the bell and bang on the front door. Do both floors. You know *both* bells and *both* doors. I'll come down and let you in. Then I'll explain what's going on. Can you do that for me?"

"Sure," Larry said, in spite of his obvious confusion.

Bobby headed for his house. He now had Jill scheduled to be pounding on the backdoor and Larry on the front door almost simultaneously. When he reached the top landing, he reminded Larry, "Give me five minutes, okay?"

"No problem."

Bobby entered the small downstairs hallway. When he reached the top of the stairs, he found his apartment ransacked.

Surveying the damage, Bobby muttered, "Jesus ... you've got to be kidding me."

He stumbled surreally from room to room, the depth of his depression exacerbated with each passing step. A plethora of negative thoughts funneled through his head. Bobby headed down the back stairs, stopping only to unlock the exterior door for Jill. *Larry said they had the first floor and cellar lights on too. I hope they didn't tear my mother's place apart.*

Trisha never locked the interior backdoor that led from the back hall to her kitchen.

Bobby walked into what amounted to little more than an instant replay of what he had just witnessed upstairs.

Trisha was a meticulous housekeeper.

One would never have guessed. It was as if the apartment had been placed in a giant raffle machine and then endured several rather violent revolutions.

As Bobby climbed over piles of his mother's prized possessions, he never heard the bathroom door open behind him. He bent over to pick up a table lamp—and potential fire-hazard—lying atop a pile of bed linens, leaving him unprepared for the crushing blow to his back and ribs.

The baseball bat–wielding attacker immediately pounced on the now prone Bobby. His stocking mask–covered head was inches from Bobby's face. He reeked of stale alcohol as he hissed, "You planted the evidence against Tim Dunlap. We want him out *now*. You better step up and admit what you did, or this'll be a day at the beach compared to what you and your mother got coming."

Loud banging suddenly emanated from the rear of the house. The backdoor was less than a dozen feet away.

"Who the fuck is that?" the attacker whispered, rolling Bobby over. Despite the intense pain, Bobby knew he had to respond, or Jill was moments away from becoming the attacker's next victim. Bobby tried to speak. What came out was incomprehensible.

The attacker grabbed Bobby by the collar of his coat and shook him. He repeated his question. "Who the fuck is banging on the door?"

A doorbell rang out. Heavy banging and incessant clanging continued unabated from opposite ends of the house.

The attacker propped up a disabled Bobby and said, "What the fuck is going on here?"

Bobby struggled to catch his breath. He said weakly, "My neighbor called the cops—"

"What?"

"Wait, wait … listen," Bobby ad-libbed, "I don't want the cops here anymore than you do." Pausing to capture sorely needed oxygen, he continued, "Look … go down those cellar stairs," pointing with a slight, but painful, nod of his head to the left. After another exaggerated pause, and another breath, he continued, "There's a bulkhead on the left side of the cellar. All you have to do … is pull the steel bar that keeps it locked from the inside." Another breath, "And then you're out of here."

The combination of banging and ringing continued.

Bobby prayed that Jill would not emerge through the unlocked door. He continued, "Take a left and follow the path ... It'll put you on the other side of a fence. Take it out to the street on the backside of the house."

The attacker headed toward the stairs, before pivoting around and delivering a vicious kick to Bobby's already ravaged ribcage. "You better straighten this out, pal. If we have to come back again, it's going to get ugly."

Lying face down on the floor—his head buried in his arms—Bobby was unable to move. When he heard noise coming from the back hall, his only hope was that the attacker wasn't returning for one final act of retribution. His message was already clear in Bobby's head.

While Jill's scream did little to mitigate the problem, he took solace in the fact that his ribs would not be incurring additional damage.

Jill dropped to his side. "My God! What happened?"

"There was a guy waiting for me when I came down to the first floor. He hit me from behind with a bat and then used me for karate practice on his way out the door."

"Look at this mess," Jill said, gently assisting Bobby into a sitting position.

"You should see upstairs," Bobby said, resting his head in his arms, which sat atop his upright knees.

The banging and ringing continued from the front door.

Jill immediately thought the worst. Her eyes darted toward Bobby, who was too sore to pick his head up.

"Any idea who's ringing your bell?" she asked.

"That's my neighbor, Larry. Can you go let him in?"

"How do you know who it is?"

"Just go to the door and say 'Are you Larry?' I'm sure it's him, but do that if you're worried."

Jill zigzagged around the clutter before coming to a sudden stop. She looked back at Bobby and asked, "Where did the guy who attacked you go?

If I was at the *backdoor*, and this guy Larry's at the *front* door, how did he get out of here?"

"It's a long story," Bobby muttered, rolling to his right in what was to be the first stage of an excruciatingly painful attempt to stand up.

"He's *gone*," he assured her. "Go let Larry in, and I'll explain."

♋

"Christ, Mick, I don't want to preach to you, but I'm telling you, you're going to end up dead in a dumpster if you don't break away from those scumbags you're running around with."

"You sound like Ma," Mickey said, fueled by the half-dozen beers he had consumed. "Hey, where's Bobby?" he asked, just now recognizing his absence.

"I don't know," Jake said, before taking a long gulp of beer. He stood up to go, leaving a quarter-full bottle behind. Once Mickey started comparing his advice to that of his beloved mother, he knew it was time to break camp. Mickey was so far removed from a normal life that it was hopeless for him to worry about his brother's prospective fate. Nevertheless, Jake wanted to be able to look himself in the mirror and be secure in the thought that he had done everything *he* could to show him a better way. "I've got to go, pal. Be good."

"Come on, stick around. I was only kidding about the 'Ma' crack." Mickey's relationships with several of his brothers were fractured or nonexistent. But Jake was always there for him, and he enjoyed spending time with his oldest brother.

"Hey, I've got to work tomorrow. Just because you're not going to work doesn't mean I don't have to go in. Arthur's going to be bullshit. He really wanted you to take that job. He'll probably come looking for you."

"Well, he won't find me in this shit hole." Looking around he added, "What a dump. I'm getting out of here, too."

"What are you doing in here if you don't like it?"

"This is where Bobby wanted to meet." Mickey laughed and reminded Jake, "He can't be seen with people like me unless he's defending them in court. You know, not good for his public image."

"Bobby looks good. It seems so funny seeing him on TV." Looking around, Jake echoed Mickey's earlier question. "Where *did* he go?"

"Ah, he's got problems," Mickey said, waving his hand dismissively. "You said you walked down. You need a ride?"

"No, I'm going to finish my walk," Jake said, giving his brother a handshake that evolved into a hug, reciprocating backslaps, and respective 'love ya brothers,' before they finally split up.

"You sure you don't need a ride? I've got a great parking spot right up the street." Mickey smirked; but Jake had already begun walking in the opposite direction. *I hope that those two punks aren't still stuck to the side of the car,* he thought.

Mickey dug his keys from his pocket. He would soon find out as he marched toward his Jeep.

❧

"Yeah, this is Larry," said the voice from outside Bobby's front door. Confused, Larry backed off the landing and down a step upon hearing a female voice.

Larry was unsure how to react when Jill opened the door. He backed down another step.

"Are you Larry?" Jill asked again, surveying the street for any additional activity.

"Yeah, and you are?"

"I'm a friend of Bobby's. I know this looks crazy, but he's inside. He wants you to come in."

Larry inched slowly back up the stairs. When he looked past Jill, he could see the total disarray that was evident throughout Trisha's apartment. "What happened? Where's Bobby?"

"Come on in," Jill said.

Larry stopped at the door to the living room. He wasn't sure he wanted to go any farther. "Bobby, it's Larry. You okay?" he bellowed.

Still too weak and sore to shout out a response, Bobby shuffled awkwardly toward the sound of his neighbor's voice. He entered the room from the opposite end. "You guys saved my life," he said. "If you hadn't banged on the doors and rang the bells, I'd probably be dead."

Larry walked over to Bobby. "Geez, what the hell happened? What's going on?"

Moving gingerly, Bobby slowly cleared off a chair so he could sit down.

Larry followed his lead, transferring things from the couch onto a glass-topped coffee table to create enough room for him and Jill to sit down too.

"What did you say they were? Tile guys?" Bobby asked.

Larry shrugged. "That's what *they* said."

Looking around at the mess, Bobby attempted to inject a bit of humor into the situation. "Are you sure they didn't say *pile* guys? They seemed to do a good job piling everything up around here. You should see upstairs."

Bobby reached to his left and picked up what looked like some sort of bound notebook. He thumbed through it, occasionally reading passages to himself.

Jill and Larry looked on, neither sure of what he was looking at, nor how to react.

Bobby flipped through several more pages before looking up. "It looks like an old diary of my mother's." Bobby rifled back to the beginning in search of dates. The detail of the handwritten passages impressed him. He reviewed several more excerpts before closing the book. *I'll get back to it when I have time.* Looking around, he said, "Well, at least they left a lot of valuables behind."

"If they left the valuables behind, what do you think they were looking for?" Larry asked.

Jill stood up. Privy to the information Bobby had entrusted her with, she attempted to change the subject. "Why don't I start picking up some of this stuff?"

"No, hold on," Bobby said. He reverted to Larry's question and said, "If it's me they're after, why would they ransack my mother's apartment? And vice-versa. And why would they ever be after my mother? I mean, it's got to be me, right?"

Returning his gaze to Jill, he said, "I'm just going to make some piles for now, you know, so we can get around. Make sure there are no fire hazards—"

"You're going to call the police, right?" Larry interrupted. "If so, you may not want to move things around too much until they arrive. I mean, wouldn't this be considered a crime scene?"

"No cops," Bobby said. "The last thing I need right now is to get hung up with the police all night. I just want to straighten things up enough to get around. I'm too sore to sit through all that questioning right now, anyway." He moaned and attempted to stretch his aching body before adding, "I mean, you're right ... I'll call them tomorrow. I just need to sort things out right now."

"Yeah, I hear you," Larry said. "Let me help you pick up."

Bobby grabbed the diary and placed it against the base of the wall next to the front door so he wouldn't forget it on the way out. He looked at Jill and Larry and said, "Well, there's no better place to start than right here."

The finished straightening out the first floor within twenty-minutes. Feeling a bit stronger, Bobby asked Larry to accompany him to the basement, before realizing they shouldn't leave Jill behind. They invited her to join them and, once they reached the bottom of the stairs, were heartened to see there was a lot less work required down there.

After picking up the basement, they went to work on the second floor. As the tired trio collapsed around the piles they had assembled in the living room, Bobby cracked open three bottles of ice-cold Corona beer. He apologized for not having any limes, the sliced garnish that usually complemented the Mexican lager. Bobby raised his bottle in a mock toast: "To a first-class salvage crew. I don't know how to thank you guys."

Bobby slowly stood up as Larry and Jill quaffed their beverages. He headed for the stairs. He could not shake his mother's diary from his mind.

Bobby arrived at the bottom landing and stepped outside. While the cool evening air felt invigorating, he was on a mission. Inserting his key into the first-floor door, he was surprised to find it unlocked. He opened the door and stepped inside. His stomach dropped when he approached the spot where he had left the diary only to discover that it had disappeared.

After searching the first floor, he returned upstairs to his apartment, his body aching with each successive step. When he arrived at the top landing, he re-entered the room and found Jill and Larry engaged in casual conversation.

"The diary?" Bobby's voice rose. "Did you guys move the diary? I left it on the floor near the door downstairs."

"I have it right here," Jill said, extracting it from her oversized pocketbook and waving it with her right hand. "I saw it on the floor, and I didn't want you to forget it."

Bobby wanted to believe that she had his back covered, but he was equally wary of her professional background and her knowledge of what was transpiring. Bobby accepted the diary. "I was sure it was gone. With everything that has been going on, I never locked the front door downstairs. When I opened the door and it wasn't there, I thought the worst."

Bobby did not want to put the book down again. He half-heartedly offered Jill and Larry another beer.

With a muted chuckle, Larry said, "Thanks, Bobby, but I've had enough excitement for one night. Besides, Maureen's going to think I ran away."

Larry headed for the stairs, and Bobby followed. Raising his right index finger toward Jill, Bobby mouthed, "Wait a minute," a clear indication that their adventure still had some life left in it. He followed Larry down the stairs.

At the landing, Larry turned and said quietly, "Bobby, I've got to tell you, I'm still more than a little confused. Are you sure that there's nothing else I can do?"

With a nervous laugh, Bobby said, "I already told you, you guys saved my life tonight. What can I possibly ask you to do for an encore? I'm all set. If I need anything I'll call you."

"You never did tell me. Where's your mother?"

Great. Here we go with the cover-up, Bobby thought. "Good question. I'm not sure."

"Aren't you worried? I mean, with all this mess and everything?"

"No, I know where she is. Well, I don't know *where* she is, but I have a good idea."

Larry took the diplomatic approach, sensing Bobby's unwillingness to engage in a question and answer session. "Hey, you've got lot of work to do, I'll let you go."

Bobby locked the door. He headed back upstairs, each step serving as a less-than-gentle reminder of just how tired and sore his body was.

He found Jill stretched out on the couch upon his return.

Bobby flopped down, resting his head squarely in her lap. He stared into her surprised face—albeit from an upside-down perspective—and said, "All right, you're so smart. What do we do now?"

Emboldened by her not taking offense to his advancement, Bobby continued, "You said you wanted to help. Let's hear your plan."

⁓

The tightened handcuffs were the furthest thing from Trisha's mind. Her captor, Agent Williams—or "Willie," as Sammy had called him on several occasions—had made a statement that kept resonating in her mind. "This is serious business. Instead of working for Pick, you'll be his fucking in-house butler if you don't wake up." *Does this mean what I think it means? Pick must be that gangster, Pick Piccorino. He'd been sent to prison on the testimony of his best friend and fellow gangster. What would Piccorino have to do with me? But it's not about me. They said Bobby was involved in illegal activities with his clients. Yeah, and they also said they were law enforcement agents.*

Not wanting to believe it, yet unable to focus on anything else, Trisha had little choice but to conclude that she may well have become a victim of her own misdeeds.

PART 2

MAY 10, 1970

11

1970-era Boston Bruin hockey fans may well remember Derek Sanderson, a flamboyant, subsequently self-destructive, and ultimately rehabilitated celebrity. You would be a cut above the average fan, however, if you remembered Wayne "Swoop" Carleton. Nonetheless, Sanderson and Carleton's collaboration resulted in one of the most famous moments in the history of Boston sports.

The pair performed arduously behind the net occupied by Saint Louis Blues goaltender Glenn Hall on May 10, 1970.

Their endeavors—in conjunction with one particularly fortuitous click of *Boston Record-American* photographer Ray Lussier's camera—forever immortalized a twenty-one-year-old kid from Great North Road in Parry Sound, Ontario, Canada.

Bobby Orr was already a quasi-legend in New England before flipping the puck behind Hall and into the Saint Louis net to win the Stanley Cup—professional hockey's Holy Grail.

When he was subsequently pitch forked through the air by Blues defenseman Noel Picard, with Lussier ready to memorialize the horizontal majesty of the moment, Orr's aura became unquestionable.

The resulting photograph, shot from the seat of a competing photographer who had temporarily vacated the space for a cold drink—forty seconds into overtime on an uncharacteristically sweltering ninety-three degree Mother's Day—catapulted the Boston Bruins defenseman to a level that most professional athletes can only dream of achieving. His contemporaries were now limited to a handful of icons representing the absolute elite of the Boston sports world, people like Bill Russell, Ted Williams, and the "Bobby Orr of a previous generation," Eddie Shore. Despite his relative youth, Boston fans rightfully insisted on his immediate induction into this prestigious club.

May 10, 1970 also represented a time of definitive social change in the United States.

Transitioning from the tumultuous decade of the 1960s, the public's ever-growing disenchantment with the United States government had been fueled a mere six days before Orr's dramatic achievement.

The murder of Four Kent State University students—Allison Krause, Jeffrey Miller, Sandy Scheuer, and Bill Schroeder—and the wounding of nine of their classmates resulted from National Guard troops opening fire in Kent, Ohio.

From a broader and more historically significant perspective, in addition to being the birthday of dancer Fred Astaire, his 71st; and singer Bono, his 10th; May 10, 1970 represented still another day in the continuation of the Vietnam War. Eleven days earlier, President Richard Nixon ordered an aggressive escalation into Cambodia. This order conflicted with his earlier assurance of a "Vietnamization" of the war, whereby a systematic withdrawal of United States military troops would result through the empowerment and training of additional South Vietnamese forces.

For many, this brazen detour into Cambodia represented the last straw. The Kent State violence and exponential national backlash breeched any preconceived government expectations related to societal outrage.

While the mounting campaign against our nation's involvement in this war continued to escalate, it had yet to claim Bobby Barron's father, and the love of Trisha Barron's young life.

At least, that was how the story went.

12

Bobby Barron had come to learn that his single-parent existence was the byproduct of his mother's pregnancy by a boyfriend two years her senior. The simplified version of a far more complicated story was that her boyfriend had been home on leave before shipping off to Vietnam, where he died a scant forty-one days later in the Dak Kron Bung River Valley.

A member of the Second Platoon of Bravo Company, Trisha's love, and Bobby's father, Robert "Bobby" Gordon of Quincy, Massachusetts, had been killed alongside his sergeant during a prolonged and particularly vicious battle.

During his youth, Bobby romanticized the story surrounding his father's demise. He was a hero, and Bobby was justifiably proud.

Trisha's father mitigated Bobby having to grow up without a dad. Pa, as Bobby affectionately knew him, had been a willing and able surrogate, shuffling Bobby to South Boston Little League games or CYO basketball on the second-floor hardwood of the fabled Gate of Heaven parish hall.

The questions diminished over time, before enjoying a healthy resurgence with the advent of the Internet. Sporadic searches aimed at further chronicling and memorializing his dad's experiences in Vietnam had all ended inconclusively until he inadvertently came across the expansive website of a former Vietnam veteran.

He came to learn that a number of brave young Gordons had perished in Vietnam. There were two Roberts. Robert Michael Gordon from Franklin, Ohio, had been a first lieutenant in the U.S. Army. He died at age twenty-three in a helicopter crash. Robert Charles Gordon, a Marine from Buffalo,

New York, had died as a result of small arms fire at Quang Tin, a mere fifty-three days after his eighteenth birthday. Two Robert Gordons—yet neither of them from Massachusetts—created substantial evidence in debunking Trisha's long-held claims.

Bobby wallowed deeper into the abyss of an ancestral tree gone awry when his searches indicated that both Robert Gordons had died in 1967, approximately four years prior to Bobby's birth in 1971.

Additional research revealed that only one other Gordon from Massachusetts died in Vietnam. Marine Corps PFC James Paul Gordon of Malden met his demise in 1967, thus eliminating the possibility of his inclusion in any potential paternal gene pool.

The more Bobby searched, the more confused and upset he became. His once-limited investigative skills—upgraded significantly in law school–related courses and intern experiences—became a powerful source to glean knowledge about one's opponent. What made life in the courtroom easier also provided tangible proof that his mother's story, and all the facts surrounding his alleged father's life, were untrue.

Trisha carefully sidestepped his intermittent questioning, giving evasive answers whenever he broached the subject. One thing she never foresaw was the invasive power of the World Wide Web.

While Bobby had long since categorized her closely guarded secret as untrue, he was simply too sympathetic to confront her unwillingness to discuss the issue.

She didn't want to talk about it.

Bobby analyzed her refusal to discuss it and justifiably concluded that, given her reticence, he probably didn't want to hear the true story.

∾

One final matter, unremarkable, and seemingly worthy of oversight when weighing historical considerations—yet equally noteworthy when evaluating Trisha Barron's lifeline, circa 1970—was that year's Boston College ice hockey team. The team was in the midst of finishing final exams and looking forward to summer vacation. The players had recently completed the school's thirtieth winning season in legendary coach John "Snooks" Kelley's thirty-two-year tenure.

Because Boston Bruin-mania was rampant, many of Kelley's players used their connections within the New England hockey world to gain access to the Bruins playoff run.

One of their more passionate fans was Tim Dunlap. Despite being a New York native, the Eagle's star junior forward reveled in the Orr revolution. On May 10, 1970, he and several of his teammates settled in, braving the sweltering conditions of the outdated and rodent-infested Boston Garden in the North Station area of the city.

Dunlap had limited experience playing in front of similar-sized crowds in this building. He and his Eagle teammates had previously participated in two unsuccessful trips to the legendary Beanpot Hockey Tournament, a Boston institution since 1952. Notwithstanding, Tim had never encountered anything quite like this.

Orr's overtime goal shook the forty-two-year-old brick and steel structure to its core. The roof seemed in danger of collapsing, and chaos reigned as spectators dove over the Plexiglas protectors to embrace the jubilant players. With the players' sticks and gloves shed around the ice surface, there was an instantaneous scrum, the only guiding principle being every man for himself.

Dunlap and his friends were more concerned with finding the appropriate venue to celebrate the Bruins first Stanley Cup victory since April 1941. They were not going to let this moment pass without a party.

"Tim, let's go over to Southie," bellowed one of Dunlap's friends, pointing down Canal Street. "Look, people are already waiting outside the bars around here."

"Nah, let's head back to school," said another. "The place will be going crazy."

Dunlap considered both thoughts. "You're right, it'll be nuts at school, but we're always at school. I'm game for Southie."

Proud of his Irish heritage, Dunlap loved visiting South Boston. It reminded him of his hometown neighborhood in North Albany, New York.

He never imagined his innocuous choice of celebrating a Stanley Cup victory in South Boston would have life-altering effects on him almost four decades later.

The group piled into Tim's 1966 Pontiac Grand Prix. There was alcohol to be consumed, young ladies to be charmed, and a long-overdue championship to be celebrated.

For Tim Dunlap, each minute that passed represented an unacceptable waste of valuable time.

13

"Come on, I'll give you a ride."

"No, that's okay. I'm only going a few blocks."

"It's too hot to walk. Come on, I'm not going to bite you."

"Oh, that's too bad; I was kind of hoping you would." Trisha Barron wasn't quite sure how such a provocative statement escaped her lips without funneling through her normal filtering mechanisms.

Her suitor laughed, slapping the seat next to him.

Trisha remained noncommittal.

The preceding hour of a long workday had certainly precluded Trisha from categorizing this as a standard Sunday evening. However, her suitor was far from standard fare.

He had introduced himself as Tad. He was movie-star handsome, tall and athletic-looking with piano keys—in both color and symmetry—for teeth. Thick dark eyebrows, long eyelashes, and a mop of similarly thick and curly dark hair framed his large blue eyes.

He was far from the acne-challenged fellow sixteen-year-olds she regularly warded off. He was also far from sixteen. Trisha's best guess was twenty, but she hoped he was eighteen or nineteen, so they would at least share her teenage tag.

Her overly protective parents would measure the difference between nineteen and twenty in decades not years.

It had been an otherwise uneventful evening prior to Tad's appearance. Trisha was working the counter at Adamo's Variety Store on P Street in South Boston. She was looking forward to going home and catching the highlights of the Bruins Stanley Cup victory when her shift ended at ten o'clock.

He walked through the door around nine o'clock. He alternated between teasing her and building up her self-esteem by telling her how good looking she was over the next half-hour.

She was disappointed when he told her he had to get back to his friends across the street. While she toiled away, they were obviously celebrating in the Pleasure Bay Lounge—or PBL—as it was known locally.

What a difference an hour can make, Trisha thought as she weighed her options. She wanted to get in the car, yet she knew that was wrong. Her parents were expecting her by 10:15. In the end, that fifteen-minute window of opportunity sealed her decision. Figuring her choices were walk home alone or extend the friendly banter with her movie star suitor—even if only for an additional few minutes—she jumped in the passenger seat next to him.

How was she to know that he had been throwing back shots of tequila since leaving the store?

The effect of this youthful indiscretion was just starting to kick in as he pulled away from the curb.

Trisha immediately sensed a change in his behavior. The smell of alcohol overwhelmed her when he raised the passenger window to take advantage of the car's air conditioning.

"God, you're drunk. What did you do, drink everything in the bar after you left me?"

Tad slurred, "I'm fine." Laughing, he added, "Man, what a day. Bruins win the Cup, and I meet a beautiful girl."

"Yeah, well this beautiful girl's got to get home."

"Come on. Let's take a ride," Tad said, flashing his best Boy Scout smile.

"I can't. I really have to go straight home. I have school tomorrow."

"What college do you go to?" Tad asked, before adding, "Did I already ask you that? Don't mind me, I've had a few too many."

Before Trisha had to divulge the fact that she was still in high school, he said, "Shit, I've got school, too, and I've got to take a final."

"Seriously, I have to go straight home. I'd love to stay out with you, but I really do have to go home."

Tad approached the bottom of P Street. Despite Trisha's instructions, he didn't turn right until after he passed her turn at Columbia Road, opting instead for Day Boulevard.

As they headed west, Trisha said, "You missed the turn. Slow down, you need to take your next right."

By the time the information coursed through Tad's alcohol-laced mind, he passed O Street too.

"You missed the turn. You *have* to take your next right. Slow down."

Laughing, Tad accelerated the car, quickly passing several more opportunities to turn. "Come on, you don't have to go straight home. Let's take a ride."

"What are you doing?" Trisha yelled.

"Relax. We're just taking a ride ... I'll get you home."

"You have to take a right at these lights. I'm serious. Please, I have to go home."

The give-and-take continued. As they sped along Day Boulevard, Tad repeatedly laughed off her commands to turn the car around.

Trisha contemplated jumping out as they approached G Street.

Unfortunately, the traffic light changed as they neared the intersection, and Tad roared through, bearing left without decreasing the speed of the vehicle. With Columbia Park on their right and Carson Beach on the opposite side of the road, he turned left just after the Metropolitan District Commission Police Station, presumably to head out Morrissey Boulevard.

At the bottom of the hill, Trisha grabbed the steering wheel to keep him from completing the necessary right turn under the overpass.

"What the fuck are you doing?" Tad screamed, slamming on the brakes and bringing the car to a screeching halt in the middle of Mount Vernon

Street. The acrid smell of burning rubber wafted through the air conditioning vents.

"I have to go home. Now!" Trisha screamed. "Turn the car around and take me home."

"Get out and walk."

Trisha released the steering wheel, but before she could act on his command, he spun the car into a frenzied left turn.

The vehicle fishtailed wildly as he accelerated east on Mount Vernon Street. He was unaware that he was heading into the bowels of the Columbia Point housing development. The trained and fully armed members of the Boston Police Department expressed constant uneasiness about entering this neighborhood.

Moreover, Boston's trained and experienced firefighters and emergency medical technicians refused to enter the complex without an escort from those worried police.

None of this deterred Tad.

14

The Columbia Point housing development was cynically referred to as Sin City in certain Boston enclaves. Encompassing fifty acres on a peninsula that once housed Italian prisoners-of-war during World War II, its 1502 units made it one of the largest housing projects in the United States.

Home to thousands of hard-working family members during the 1950s and 60s, its precipitous decline began when the Boston Housing Authority chose to ignore its upkeep. A blatant and systematic replacement of these working families with Boston's poorest of the poor caused the deterioration to worsen considerably in the ensuing years.

As Tad sped down Mount Vernon Street, he was quickly approaching a dead end, literally and figuratively.

"Please turn around," Trisha pleaded. "This is a *bad* area. I'm telling you, you don't want to be out here."

Ignoring her plea, Tad pulled off to the far right corner of a circular turnaround designed to assist people who ventured out here, inadvertently or otherwise. Placing the car in park, a drunken Tad turned to Trisha. "You've got to learn to relax," clumsily attempting to cup his right hand behind her head.

Trisha slapped his hand away. She backed herself as far away from him as the interior of the front seat allowed.

"What the fuck is wrong with you?"

"I want to go home! Now!" Trisha burst into tears.

Bringing her feet up, she rebuffed his second advance with a kick aimed squarely at his genital area. She ultimately settled for his midsection, when he successfully deflected her left foot with his hands.

Drunk, and now enraged, Tad screamed, "You fucking bitch!"

This elicited still another assault by an equally enraged Trisha.

She never expected—nor did she see—the quick overhand punch that landed squarely on the left side of her temple. Knocked unconscious, she crumpled limply against the passenger-side door.

Tad leaned over and pulled her head into his hands. "Are you okay?"

Trisha toppled toward him. He asked her again, "Are you okay?"

Mistaking the guttural rumblings associated with her struggle to regain consciousness—conveniently coupled with her slumping in his general direction—as acquiescence to further advances, Tad began kissing her neck. In his highly inebriated state, time ticked at an alternate speed, each subsequent action independent, unlinked, and quickly forgotten.

Minutes later, a powerful combination of nausea and confusion swathed an awakening Trisha. With her underwear and shorts barely clinging to her right ankle, and her attacker's weight pinning her awkwardly against the vehicle's seat, Trisha's head was banging off the passenger-side door's armrest in concert with each of her captor's pelvic thrusts.

His weight seemed to triple upon the completion of his egregious act.

Trisha was unable to move and unwilling to speak.

Slowly, the crushing effect of his dead weight diminished when he pulled himself off her and rolled awkwardly toward the driver's side door.

Trisha tucked herself as tightly as possible to the passenger door. Not daring to take her eyes off him, her mind was a hodgepodge of conflicting thoughts. Chief among them? *I'm probably safer in a strange car with a rapist than I would be walking the length of Mount Vernon Street on foot, especially at this time of night.*

Trisha stole a glance at the analog clock on the dashboard of the still-running car. She was now thirty-five minutes late. *My parents must be panicking!* Her head was throbbing, but she knew she had to make the best of the situation. She discreetly reached down for her underwear. Slipping them a little higher onto her right leg before slipping her left leg into the appropriate opening, she slowly wiggled her hips to pull them back on, never taking her eyes off her attacker.

Tad clumsily removed a handkerchief from the back pocket of the white tennis shorts dangling unceremoniously around his lower thighs. He began wiping his midsection and groin area.

It's as if I'm not even here. His abject disregard for Trisha fueled a resurgence of rage from deep within her.

Without another conscious thought, her previous and seemingly sound conclusion of being safer inside the car than outside of it changed. Gathering all her strength, and buttressed by the renewed and adrenaline-based courage of her rage, she twisted around and viciously kicked the unsuspecting Tad with every fiber of muscle she could marshal. She drove his head into the door buck, shattering the driver's side window.

A drunken, relaxed, sexually satisfied, and thoroughly unsuspecting Tad never expected her violent response. He flopped forward, his head and shoulders landing squarely in Trisha's lap.

Trisha screamed. She frantically searched for the door handle. Still wobbly, she grabbed Tad's sweat-soaked hair with both hands. She pulled straight up on his head with every ounce of strength she could muster and thrust him to the left.

He crashed face-first into the transmission hump on the floor of the car.

Trisha reached down to grab her shorts, unwittingly grabbing Tad's handkerchief in the process. The gleam of the car's keys hanging from the ignition caught her eye. Attempting to remove them as insurance, a shaking Trisha only succeeded in ripping a group of keys from the ring attached to the ignition key that kept the vehicle running.

When Tad began mumbling incoherently, Trisha knew she had to make her move. She exited the vehicle and finished sliding on her shorts. Only then did she notice she was holding his handkerchief. Tossing it to the ground, she adjusted her wood-soled, backless Dr. Scholl's sandals, then just as quickly removed them, recognizing that they would only slow her down. She looked down at the discarded handkerchief and noticed a fancy monogram on one of its corners. Deciding the monogram was tangible evidence—as disgustingly tainted as it was—Trisha decided it could prove to be key evidence in any subsequent accusation against her attacker.

A discarded brown paper shopping bag lay in the gutter. Trisha grabbed it and tossed the handkerchief and keys inside. Rolling it up tightly, she jammed it into the right pocket of her shorts. Knowing that the only important key was still safely ensconced in the ignition, she briefly contemplated re-entering the still-running car, but she heard voices emerging in the distance.

She had to get out of there. Every second she wasted was a second of recovery time for the animal she was intent on leaving behind.

With a sandal in each hand—Dr. Scholl's solid-wood soles actually represented a pair of potentially effective weapons—Trisha took off.

Barefoot and scared, she doubted whether she would ever see the other end of Mount Vernon Street.

15

Trisha ran for ten minutes after vacating Tad's car.

The Metropolitan District Commission Police Station was now within her sight. She weighed whether to go in, but chose to keep running to get home as soon as possible. She soon passed the white-bricked Captain's Room at the foot of G Street hill, then the K Street end of the venerable L Street Bathhouse.

Trisha's mind raced. She crossed Day Boulevard diagonally and entered the "greenie," a grass and tree-lined expanse that made up a thirty-foot separation between Day Boulevard and Columbia Road. She contemplated running up L Street before deciding to stick to the safety provided by the wide-open space of the beachside park.

A car entering L Street from the west arrived at the intersection just as she exited the darkness and leaped from the sidewalk onto the street. Trisha never saw it coming. A prolonged blast of the car's horn resonated in her ears.

Goosebumps covered every inch of her body.

She veered sharply to her right to avoid colliding with the vehicle. She ran away from the car's front end, but was so close she could not see into the driver's side window. She had nothing to focus on but the top of the car's white roof as she moved toward its tail end. What she could see heightened her fear.

We were in a white car. Is that him?

Trisha reached the rear of the car, turned left, and crossed the street. She entered the next expanse of the greenie but stopped running. She turned to face the car. A combination of fear and physical exhaustion paralyzed her.

The car came to an abrupt stop, and the driver blew the horn again. It was forced to continue moving when another car pulled up behind it.

Trisha watched the white car drive up L Street, and then turn right onto Marine Road and travel in the general direction of her house. She felt hopelessly alone and burst into tears for the second time that evening. Strangely, this sudden release of emotions had a decidedly calming effect. Determined to make it home, she began a slow jog toward M Street, gradually increasing her stride to match her earlier pace.

Turning left on M Street, she was in the final stretch. When Trisha reached Marine Road, she turned right and ran headlong into her attacker. They collided violently. She bounced off him and smashed her head on the corner of a steel, rivet-reinforced, olive green U.S. Postal Service relay box.

She was less than two hundred feet from the safety of her home.

❧

Twenty-two-year-old Tommy Carr, a third-generation South Bostonian, stood over the prone figure. A probationary Boston firefighter, he knelt down to ascertain if she was breathing. He rolled the victim's head gently to the right, his left hand supporting her neck and head. With the professional training he was currently undergoing bottlenecked in his brain, he brushed aside, her sweat-soaked dark hair. He was shocked to discover that the injured woman was his long-time neighbor.

"Trisha. Are you okay?"

Two crushing blows to the same side of her head in less than forty-five minutes had taken their toll. As a semi-conscious and completely bewildered Trisha attempted to clear the cobwebs and silence the bells and whistles echoing inside her skull, the soothing voice continued.

"… okay? Trisha, it's Tommy Carr. Are you all right?"

"No," was all Trisha could muster.

Carr slowly righted her to a sitting position, gently cradling her head. "Where were you going in such a hurry?"

Trisha tried to stand up. This slightest bit of movement triggered intense nausea followed by a sudden twisting of her body and a lengthy session of vomiting into the adjacent gutter.

The next few minutes proved to be unpleasant ones for Trisha—not to mention for Tommy Carr—who had little choice but to stand by and assist his young neighbor.

☞

The two brothers visiting Columbia Point at the invitation of their cousin were facing the equivalent of life's daily double. Facing a long walk back to Dorchester's Fields Corner neighborhood, they were encouraged by the sight of a wobbly Tad alighting from his vehicle.

Tad's car was about to become their transportation home.

The older brother figured it was time to instill some street etiquette. Tad had made the unpardonable mistake of disrespecting their cousin's neighborhood when he began urinating on the trunk of a nearby tree.

"Hey, my man. What the fuck you think you're doing?"

The younger one joined in. "You must want that fucking white owl cut off? If not, you best put that bad boy away." He produced a six-inch knife to fortify the seriousness of his advice.

The older brother noticed the fancy watch adorning Tad's left wrist. Producing his preferred brand of cutlery, he said, "Give me that watch."

"Hey, I ain't looking for trouble—"

"Shut the fuck up and give me the watch!"

Tad tugged on the leather strap, but wasn't moving fast enough for his attacker's liking.

"Are you fucking deaf? Empty your pockets, too." It was almost an afterthought. The ideas were coming to him randomly, and his task was to convey the assignments once they passed through his marijuana and alcohol-laced brain.

The older brother picked up a jagged baseball-sized rock. He waved it in Tad's face. "I'm going to cave your fucking head in if you don't start listening."

Tad's hands were shaking. He continued fumbling with his watchstrap.

"You heard what the man said. Hurry up, and then empty them pockets," the younger brother piped in.

"Never mind the bullshit, just take the fucking shorts off," said the older one, smashing the rock off the back of Tad's head. He dropped the rock and switched the knife back to his right hand. He grabbed a handful of Tad's hair and placed the knife against Tad's throat. Blood from the jagged gash streamed steadily down Tad's neck, dripping onto the blade of the long silver weapon. He then coaxed Tad out of his shorts, shirt, and underwear. He knew Tad wouldn't be going anywhere too quickly without any clothes. He turned to his younger brother and said, "Go get the car."

He tightened his grip on Tad's hair, keeping the knife positioned for additional damage. "You move from this spot in the next fifteen minutes, and I'm going to run your fucking ass over. You got that?"

Tad nodded.

Fortunately, not all was lost. Tad's expensive watch remained securely affixed to his left wrist.

16

"You mean to tell me it was *you* I ran into?" Trisha asked.

Turning to face her, Tommy Carr said, "It was really hot in the house, and I had been down the beach getting some air. When I reached the corner on my way home, you flew around from the other direction, bounced off me, and hit your head on the mailbox."

Trisha was still piecing things together.

Tall and wiry, the dark-haired Carr continued rubbing his soaped-up hands and forearms under the faucet of the kitchen sink, cleaning off the final remnants of the unpleasant aftermath. He turned toward Trisha again and said, "I didn't know it was you at first."

"Did the note say what time they'd be home?"

"No."

Carr accompanied Trisha back to her house, expecting her parents to take over from there.

Instead, they found a note telling Trisha that they had gone to Maude's house and would be back shortly.

Trisha attempted to convince Carr that she was okay. "Really, I'm all set Tommy. My parents will be right along. I can't thank you enough—"

"I don't mind waiting," Tommy interrupted. His professional training had taught him that head injuries required close observation. He changed the subject, asking her again, "Why were you running so fast?"

"It's a long story. Trust me; you don't want to hear it."

Uncomfortable with him remaining, but appreciative of his support and understanding his logic, Trisha said, "I'll be right back."

She headed to her bedroom. She removed the rolled up brown paper bag from her pocket and stashed it in a long-held secret hiding spot behind a built-in set of drawers in her closet. She then grabbed some clean clothes and headed for the bathroom, intent on scrubbing Tad away, at least physically.

Just before closing the bathroom door, she shouted, "Tommy, I'm going to jump in the shower. You *really* don't have to hang around."

"I'll wait for you to get out. I just want to make sure you're okay."

The physical cleansing worked wonders. When she stepped from the tub, she heard the animated voices of her parents returning from their impromptu Stanley Cup celebration. She revisited her excuse one more time as she walked down the hallway to greet them.

While showering, she had reached an irrevocable decision that there was no reason her explanation should include any mention of the rape.

୧୭

"Tommy, stop the car, what did I just see?"

Johnny Boylan and Tommy Dailey were partners assigned to District 11 of the Boston Police Department.

As Dailey drove down Mount Vernon Street, Boylan detected some sort of movement on the south side of the road.

"Back up, Tommy," a suddenly animated Boylan said, twisting his head sharply to the right. "I swear I just saw someone walking along the fence."

Dailey slammed on the brakes of the paddy wagon. Instead of backing up, he swung the vehicle around. "You've got to be shitting me!" he laughed, "The guy's naked!" Slapping the gearshift into park, he yanked the keys from the ignition and leaped from the truck, followed closely by his partner.

Over time, what little Tad could recollect about that evening's sexual encounter, which was minimal, fell well within his recently loosened parameters of consensual sex. In fact, a review of the official Boston Police Incident Report regarding the placement of a drunken, beaten, and naked

86

detainee into protective custody failed to address any possible sexual angle, consensual or otherwise.

Read in retrospect, it would be more indicative of another misguided youth being the latest in a long line of victims who inadvertently ventured into a dangerous environment. His plight was totally representative of the criminal behavior pervading Columbia Point, circa 1970.

For Tad, the strange and twisted odyssey that would forever represent May 10, 1970 had come to an ignoble conclusion.

The good news? Trisha Barron's ill-conceived and hastily reached decision to maintain absolute silence regarding the incident was all the cover he would ever require.

17

A significantly enhanced sense of smell, coupled with an endless craving for Kelly's Landing fried food, caused a noticeable tightening of Trisha's clothes. She began to sense that the source of her growth was something more than the battered onion rings and fried clams—*with* the bellies—that were indigenous to the popular South Boston waterfront fast-food emporium.

Her previous concealment of the ordeal from her parents rendered her new story significantly more difficult to sell.

They had always chalked up the physical injuries she had sustained that evening a result of running into the mailbox. The question they always wrestled with was *why* she had been running as wildly as recounted by Tommy Carr at the time of the incident.

She retraced the entire sordid evening for her shocked parents once it became obvious that she had no choice but to come clean.

Rage, tears, hugs, more tears, an elevated level of rage, and finally, the common sense to rally around their only child supplanted their initial incredulity.

Privately, they remained unconvinced of Tommy Carr's lack of involvement. His—or perhaps *their*—story always bothered them. Trisha's father talked about pursuing the matter criminally, partially in an effort to ferret out the truth.

Trisha ultimately convinced her mother that she couldn't deal with the ramifications of living through it again.

"Besides," she argued, "what are the chances of ever finding the rapist?"

From her parent's perspective, Trisha's unyielding requirement of maintaining the status quo simply amounted to more evidence in the "Tommy Carr involvement" column.

In the end, however, Trisha's parents capitulated to her wishes.

જી

Trisha eventually ended up back home before giving birth.

She had spent three months in a wing for unwed mothers at St. Margaret's Hospital in Dorchester in an effort to avoid the gossip and scrutiny of her classmates at South Boston High School.

Her parents decided that the extensive tutoring she had received between September and Christmas left open the possibility that she could take on a heavy load in the summer to get back up to speed.

This was, of course, before recognizing the prospective responsibility of her having to care for a new baby.

This fourth-wheel represented an extended learning curve for the Barrons, leading to a series of protracted conversations on alternatives. For the devoutly Roman Catholic family, it always winnowed down to two choices: the adoption of—or the acceptance of—their first grandchild.

Bill and Ellen Barron decided, once again, to broach the subject with their very pregnant and increasingly anxious and irritable daughter during the particularly lazy week between Christmas and New Years.

"How are you feeling?" Ellen asked.

"Fat, tired, and scared," Trisha replied.

"Yeah, I remember the feeling. These last five weeks are going to seem like five years."

"Geez, Ma, are you trying to cheer me up? Because if you are, you're doing a horrible job."

Bill Barron jumped in. "Trish, your mom and I have been talking. You're a bright and talented kid. This baby is going to put a tremendous burden on your ability to lead a normal life."

"Oh, Dad, not *again*," Trisha whined. "I'm *not* going through all this and then giving up the baby."

"It's going to be tough," her father argued. "We're not getting any younger, and it takes a lot of help to raise a child."

"Your father's right, honey," Trisha's mother interjected. "The decision you make will have a lasting effect on the rest of your life."

What was always left unsaid was Trisha's parents could not shake the filthy feeling surrounding the rape of their daughter. Her child would forever represent this unpleasant and unavoidable fact.

The absolute best-case scenario Trisha could seemingly offer—in lieu of the rape claim—was her involvement with their neighbor Tommy Carr.

Trisha was having none of it. "There is no decision. I'm *keeping* the baby, and I don't appreciate this constant second-guessing or lack of support, because you're right. It *is* going to be difficult."

☙

Trisha awoke, awash in amniotic fluid, at five o'clock in the morning on Tuesday, February 9, 1971. This precipitated a frantic few moments, an expedited trip to St. Margaret's Hospital with her parents, and the birth of her son, Robert Gordon Barron.

Despite all her preparation, Trisha felt completely unprepared for such a monumental experience. Once she laid eyes on Bobby's angelic face, however, a sense of comfort overwhelmed her, legitimizing her earlier refusal to consider the alternative of adoption.

The only happier people on earth were Bobby's maternal grandparents. They kicked into full grandparent mode—partly as a matter of recompense, to counterbalance their previous adoption requests—and bestowed doting love and countless gifts on Bobby and Trisha.

It also provided a potent injection of youth into her parents. Ellen Barron became a super-surrogate force, eventually allowing Trisha to go back to school and earn academic honors while becoming a quality parent in steps, always knowing that help was only a holler away.

Trisha eventually went back to school and trained to become a dental hygienist. She graduated with honors, qualifying her for a job at the office of Dr. Joseph Wissard, a young upstart who was quickly making a name for himself in parochial South Boston.

She now had a career to support her single-parent existence and a beautiful son to rush home to each evening.

In the interim, she also inadvertently discovered the true identity of Tad.

18

The early days and weeks of parenthood ran relatively smoothly for Trisha. Nevertheless, she became bored by the mundane tasks of feeding, cleaning, and tending to Bobby. She also tired of the sedentary and lonely lifestyle that accompanied her single-parent existence.

One positive side effect of her pregnancy and Bobby's birth was her elevated thirst for reading. She had become a devotee of Boston's two main daily newspapers: The *Boston Globe* and the *Boston Herald Traveler*.

With so much time on her hands, she had even started reading the sports pages. One Monday morning in February, she became intrigued with a *Boston Globe* story about the upcoming 1971 Beanpot hockey championship game.

An annual Boston staple, the Beanpot was two nights of rock'em, sock'em hockey between three Boston and one Cambridge/Boston institutions of higher learning—Boston College, Boston University, Northeastern University, and Harvard University.

If a team won games on successive Monday evenings, the Beanpot was theirs for the ensuing twelve months.

Winning the Beanpot could legitimize even the worst of seasons. It allowed bragging rights to the schools—all located within a four-mile radius of each other. These rights extended through the remainder of the season and all the way through the various summer hockey leagues, where the paths of the respective teams' players regularly intersected.

The *Boston Globe* story highlighted the final two team's chances. It featured Boston University—the perennial favorite, having won four of the past five tournaments—on the front-page of a supplemental section of the paper's nationally renowned sports page.

After some quick research, it seemed unfair to Trisha that Boston University had won so many tournaments. The appeal of an underdog dethroning them suddenly seemed attractive. *We have to beat BU,* she thought, as she opened the newspaper to handicap the chances of their foe, the Boston College Eagles.

Trisha nearly collapsed when she found herself staring straight into the face of the animal who had viciously raped her less than one-year earlier. She didn't require a color photo to identify those blue eyes; nor would she ever forget that impish smile. She launched herself out of the dining room chair and shoved the newspaper toward the center of the table, knocking a half-full cup of Lipton tea onto her mother's cream-colored area rug.

Her involuntary scream woke Bobby from a sound slumber.

He wailed for her attention.

A conflicted Trisha needed to clean up the spilled tea and tend to Bobby. Instead, she grabbed the section and stared at the picture again, removing any residual doubt from her mind. *There's no mistaking that face.* She could not stop staring at the photo.

Given her knowledge of what he had done, she could never again consider him handsome, but hers would be the distinct minority in any impartial assessment of his physical appearance. Absent her intimate knowledge of his vulgar predilections—and the resulting taint that behavior cast upon him—one would be hard-pressed to describe him in any other way than handsome.

The caption under the picture read: *Eagle captain and star senior Tim Dunlap hopes to take home the Beanpot at least once before his career ends.* The sub-title above read: *BC intent on revenge after last year's 5-4 loss to BU.*

Where had he come up with the name Tad? *Had he been planning the rape the entire time and purposely used a phony name?* Trisha couldn't put the story down, and she eventually endured the following passage:

> Dunlap, a pre-law student, counts his mom and dad as his personal heroes. The Albany, New York, native's parents try to make as many games as possible and have the ride down the New York Thruway and into Chestnut Hill via the Mass Turnpike down pat.

"My dad's always complaining that I owe him three sets of tires," laughs Dunlap, "but he hardly ever misses a game. It would mean a lot to win the Beanpot this year, for him and my mom as much as for me." Win, lose, or draw, this is one young man with a good head on his shoulders. Tim's parents, Steven and Cynthia Dunlap, have obviously done a great job in raising such a fine young man and they have a lot to be proud of.

Trisha wasn't sure how to react. *Instead of following him around for his hockey games, they should be following him around when he's not playing hockey.* She read the story again, staring intermittently at his picture. A mishmash of contradicting thoughts created a logjam in her brain.

Bobby continued crying and the spillage went unattended while Trisha weighed the alternatives of suddenly being able to identify her attacker. With a monogrammed handkerchief, the evidence seemed incontrovertible.

Monogrammed! Trisha bounded from the chair and dashed to her bedroom.

Bobby's feeding and the sopping up of the spilled tea would have to wait.

She needed to revisit the evidence related to the sexual predator who also happened to be her beloved baby's father.

⁊

As a youngster, Trisha had a secret hiding spot for items she didn't want her parents to see.

Many years earlier, her father had constructed an elaborate drawer system inside her bedroom closet.

In a frantic search for a particularly flattering two-piece bathing suit, a young and frustrated Trisha yanked too hard on one of the drawers. She pulled it completely out of its slot, exposing a four-square-foot void of empty space behind it.

What a great hiding spot, she thought, despite being a kid with little, if anything, that required hiding.

That innocence of youth had changed on the evening of May 10, 1970, when she had placed the brown paper bag with the monogrammed handkerchief into the space. She had never retrieved it. In fact, the thought of retrieving it had never crossed her mind—at least not until now. She had to see the monogram in the light of day and determine whether it lent credence to her claim that Timothy Dunlap was not a fine young man, as trumpeted by the *Boston Globe*, but a brutal rapist.

She removed the brown paper bag from its secret location. She peered in slowly, half expecting something to jump out in her face. The evidence was still there, rolled in a loose ball, and accompanied by an assortment of keys.

Wow, I grabbed his keys. I had forgotten about that.

With much hesitance, Trisha reached into the bottom of the bag. She removed the handkerchief and unfolded it. She was surprised at how well preserved it was as she opened up the fine-linen fabric. The clearly visible yellowish stained proof of the isolated incident was obvious. The narrow, hemstitched "Script Initials," were there, but the fancy font and the positioning of the letters caught Trisha off guard.

𝓙 𝓓 𝓐

Trisha stared intently at it. It looked like "JDA." Upon further inspection, she realized the "D" was a bit larger and slightly bolder than the adjacent letters.

"Dunlap!" Trisha said aloud, thinking, *They put the last name in the middle, like the towels in my parent's bathroom.*

Trisha easily recognized the now discernable anagram, rearranged it, and began mumbling to herself, "TA ... D. Timothy A. Dunlap!" *That's where he got "Tad." It was his initials.*

Trisha summarized her findings in her mind: She had a picture of him that allowed ready identification and his initials were on the handkerchief. She grabbed the bag, and she placed the handkerchief and keys—she even had his keys—back inside. What more would be required?

Trisha rolled the brown paper bag up tightly and stashed it back into the secret cubbyhole. She then slid the drawer back into place.

Armed with this plethora of evidence, Trisha was remarkably comfortable and confident with her decision to put the evidence away and drop the subject.

You're a lucky man, Tim Dunlap, she thought. As she headed to the kitchen for a thorough hand cleansing, she had second thoughts. *No, you're a terribly unlucky man.*

She had a beautiful son that he would never know, never mind *enjoy*, and he presently required her immediate and undivided attention.

PART 3

PRESENT DAY

19

Bobby clutched Trisha's diary as he dropped into an upholstered chair.

Jill was lying on a couch; her eyes closed and her body fully relaxed.

As Bobby leafed through the diary, he was simultaneously fascinated by its content and guilt-ridden by feelings of apprehension over this unauthorized access to his mother's deepest feelings. His apprehensiveness eventually won out.

He closed the diary and stared at Jill. *How can she be sleeping?* he thought, wondering whether he would ever be able to sleep again. Acting on that thought, he stretched out his long legs and crossed them before closing his eyes.

"What are you going to do, take a nap?" Jill snapped. "I don't believe you. How can you possibly sleep?"

Bobby bolted upright. "I was just thinking the same thing about you, but I wasn't going to wake you up to ask."

"I wasn't sleeping?"

"What were you doing, checking your eyelids for holes?" Bobby joked. "You were snoring, for crying out loud."

"You're a liar." Jill leaped from the couch and grabbed Bobby in a headlock.

Their underlying mutual attraction for each other continued to smolder in spite of the severity of his problem.

∽

Mickey unlocked his Jeep and jumped behind the wheel. The two punks he'd beaten were long gone, giving him a perverse sense of satisfaction.

After firing up the vehicle, he reached into the storage compartment on the bottom of the door. He grabbed a blue metal, breath mint container and popped open the lid. Pulling out a joint, he pushed in the car's cigarette lighter and banged his head against the driver's seat headrest several times while he waited for the lighter to eject.

He fired up the joint and sucked in a lung-full of marijuana. Mickey held his breath, simultaneously filtering the events of his meeting with Bobby through his head and the marijuana through his system. *It was amazing how naïve people could be. Finding Bobby's mother wasn't going to be a problem. Nor would getting her back, for that matter. The problem would be getting Bobby to admit to any role he might have played in the railroading of this Dunlap guy. That's what this was all about. Success in deals of this nature required leverage.*

Mickey needed the calming effect of the joint. Exhaling a plume of bluish-gray smoke, he was pissed off and hurt to think his friend might be lying to him about Dunlap. Bobby coming clean was essential to their ultimate success with these people, just not for the reasons he might think.

Sucking another enormous cloud of marijuana into his expanded lungs, Mickey imagined how relieved Bobby would be to find out that his mother's safe return was a virtual guarantee.

Notwithstanding that bit of good news, he knew that he would be equally unhappy—in fact, he would be downright distraught—should he ever discover that Mickey had orchestrated Trisha's kidnapping.

∽

Trisha was now convinced she had been one-upped. Her captor's haranguing of his young protégé for failing to detect her cell phone resonated in her mind. "This is serious business, kid. Instead of working for Pick, you'll be his fucking in-house butler if you don't wake up...."

What did this mean for Bobby? I've got to get out of here. Trisha's needs presented a monumental problem. Her captors were now monitoring her more closely than ever.

With her two arms tightly shackled and her resolve rapidly evaporating, Trisha took a deep breath. Holding it for several seconds, she exhaled slowly, mentally revisiting the actions she had undertaken two years earlier.

How did I ever expect to pull this off?

20

Trisha unlocked the glass door to Dr. Joseph Wissard's office, an act she had performed thousands of times in the past three decades. She deftly juggled two newspapers and a jumbo Snickerdoodle coffee from the Java House.

It was 7:58 in the morning. Trisha arrived early to set up the operatories, turn on all the equipment, and brew a pot of coffee for the doctor and his staff. She would then pull the records for that day's patients before sitting down and leafing through the newspapers until her boss arrived.

Trisha settled into the back office after completing the rudimentary tasks. She sipped the artificially sweetened brew. She allowed herself only one cup per day, so she had learned to savor it. Then she began reading the *Boston Globe*.

A story on page 24 of the LOCAL/REGION section piqued her interest. It was above the fold, a quarter of a page, and two columns. Police arrested a fifty-year-old Boston man with a laundry list of legal woes and a history of abhorrent behavior for the vicious rape and subsequent beating of a sixteen-year-old Brighton girl.

The victim's only so-called crime had been trying to fend him off, and she had put up a courageous effort. While rape stories automatically raised Trisha's anxiety level, this one hit particularly close to home.

Trisha was sixteen when similarly assaulted.

The Brighton victim tore open the front pocket of her attacker's fashionable jeans during the attack. She managed to extract his handkerchief, amidst the bouncing around of coins and the blowing around of a small amount of paper currency, and had turned it over to police as evidence. This eerie similarity heightened Trisha's attention, but the infuriating part was contained in the story's final paragraph: "Attorney Timothy Dunlap, of the Boston-based firm Dunlap & Associates, LLP, spoke on his client's behalf. 'These accusations are baseless. I am confident that after we've had our day in court, my client will be exonerated of all charges.'"

Trisha gained a subliminal, albeit perverse, delight in chronicling Tim Dunlap's admittedly prolific career. She had little choice. He appeared regularly in newspapers or as an expert talking head in a variety of legal arguments on television. The irony of her well-guarded secret—especially in light of Bobby turning out to be such a well-adjusted person who unknowingly followed in his father's footsteps—was the satisfaction derived from the fact that Dunlap would never know about his son.

Dunlap's usual involvement in the defense of high-level criminals—or his explaining away assorted organized crime activities gone awry—cast his presence in such a low-profile case as odd. The back-story was that a local gangster had requested Dunlap's *pro bono* representation, and this guy's infrequent but unmistakable "requests" could just as easily be categorized as instructions.

Dunlap's new client was a degenerate gambler. In addition to his fondness for beating and raping young girls, he was deeply in debt to the gentleman who sought Dunlap's legal advocacy.

One unmistakable precept of the underworld is that dead men don't pay. The stark reality was that the ones who go to prison aren't too far behind when it comes to their fiduciary responsibilities.

Trisha was having none of it. While she would have understood the wise guy's untenable business position, nothing could justify a former rapist and woman-beater accepting the opportunity to defend a similarly situated sicko.

Trisha was simultaneously enraged and fearful. Naturally, she feared for the victim's long-term well being, but that was secondary. Acute rage fueled *this* fear. It was the intrinsic knowledge that—rejecting all tenets of common sense—she was about to thrust herself into a potentially dangerous situation.

After thirty-eight years of inactivity, Trisha's mind hemorrhaged egregious memories.

Suddenly, and justifiably, she deemed it appropriate for Tim Dunlap to atone for his sins, past *and* present.

✑

In 1912, Coeur D'Alene, Idaho native Leo Hannon bought out his partner of five years, and Hannon & Hillier became Hannon's Clothiers. The company flourished. In addition to their successful clothing line, a noteworthy staple of the business was their fine-linen, monogrammed handkerchiefs.

In the Dunlap family from Albany, New York, Hannon handkerchiefs were an essential and time-honored custom. Steven Dunlap harped on the importance of always having two on hand, one for personal use, and the other for unplanned but inevitable emergencies. He would jokingly describe his policy as, "One for showing, and one for blowing."

A significant consequence of this custom would not become apparent until decades later. It provided prosecutors the necessary evidence to tie attorney Tim Dunlap—a legal and social icon in Boston—to a 2006 rape and beating.

What had begun with Dunlap defending a wrongfully accused defendant, ended in his subsequent conviction and imprisonment as the actual perpetrator of the crime.

The critical piece of evidence was a semen-spattered handkerchief from an originally purchased set of three, a Hannon tradition, and stylishly initialed with a narrow, stone gray "Scripted Initials" hemstitch. While the stitched initials were admittedly those of Dunlap, he obviously shared them with untold numbers of people.

Over time, however, a forensic scientist set the stage for Dunlap's public comeuppance. She instructed the jury of the overwhelming odds of the physical evidence contained on the handkerchief being that of anyone *other* than Timothy Dunlap.

Trisha Barron reveled in her success of extracting retribution thirty-eight years after Dunlap had raped her.

For her, the end undoubtedly justified the means.

21

Bobby Barron piloted his white Dodge Durango around the corner, but was unable to pull into his driveway due to his mother's haphazard parking habits. He pulled to the curb in front of the house, shut off the car, grabbed his briefcase, and jumped out.

His mother intercepted him from the conjoined front door of her first-floor residence as he was heading up to his second-floor apartment.

"Hey, what's up?" Bobby asked, bending over to kiss her on the cheek.

"Where are you running off to? You never have time for your mother."

"Come on, Ma, I'm down here all the time."

"I need to talk to you. Do you have a minute now, or do you want me to come up after you get settled?"

Bobby engulfed her in a bear hug. Gently shoving her through the door to her apartment, he said, "What did I do wrong now?"

"Do you know anything about that rape that happened in Brighton? It was in—"

"Today's *Globe*." Bobby said, cutting her off. "I know a lot more than you think. In fact, Rock assigned me to the case. I actually spent some time working on it today."

"You're kidding. It's *your* case?"

"Yeah. Wow, what are you cooking?" Bobby asked in response to the pungent aroma emanating from her kitchen.

"I'm making a roast. You hungry?"

"What are you trying to do to me? I've got to go to the gym," Bobby whined. The garlic-laden roast was quickly trumping the thought of submitting himself to a torturous workout. He sat on his mother's couch and smothered his face in a throw pillow.

"Go to the gym. This isn't going to be ready for another hour. I'll set a plate for you, and we can finish talking then. I want to hear more about this case."

Bobby dragged himself off her couch. He walked up the stairs to his second-floor apartment, any remaining resolve for going to the gym diminishing with each step he took.

❧

Bobby leaped from his couch. He had no idea where he was as an unrelenting symphony surrounded him. He never made it past his couch after speaking with his mother. Shaking the sleep from his head, he was resolute in the fact that if the continued combination of a clanging doorbell and a ringing phone was a message, it was time to shoot the messenger.

Bobby stumbled down the stairs and ripped the door open.

His mother stood there; a broad smile on her face and a cordless phone pressed to her right ear. "I thought you were going to work out?" she asked, lowering the phone and clicking the power button.

"I was *sleeping!* Are you trying to give me a heart attack?"

"I'm sorry, honey. I knew you were hungry, and when you didn't answer the phone I walked outside to see if your car was here—"

"So what? You figured you'd ring the door bell and the phone at the same time?"

"You must be starving. Come on, everything's ready. Come eat while it's hot." She held the door open, and then followed Bobby into her kitchen.

Bobby was still shaking the sleep from his head as sat down and surveyed the feast laid out in front of him: Twice-baked potatoes with a liberal sprinkling of Asiago cheese, French-style green beans, a basket of hot croissants, and one of his mother's fabulous rib roasts, replete with Portabella mushroom–infused brown gravy.

"I knew I should have gone straight to the gym after work," Bobby lamented. The guilt-driven pang of sleeping and eating in lieu of a good workout were trumped by his physical hunger.

The mere mention of the word work provided the appropriate opportunity to catapult Trisha's curiosity to the forefront. "Speaking of work, tell me about that rape in Brighton."

"Why are you so concerned with that case?" Bobby asked as he loaded his plate.

Trisha framed her response carefully. "It just hit me hard when I read the story. She's so young. I mean, what is she, sixteen?"

"Yeah, she's sixteen. The guy's a dirt bag, a career criminal with a lengthy record ... been in and out of jail."

Trisha poured Bobby a glass of cranberry juice. "Lengthy record, huh?" she repeated, placing the glass to the right of his plate.

"Why are you so caught up in this case? I mean, don't take this the wrong way, Ma, but this stuff happens all the time."

All right, thought Trisha, *it's time to take off the gloves. I could just blurt out, "You're arguing against your father on this one." See how that sits with him.* Instead, Trisha said, "The story in the paper says this guy has some high-priced lawyer. It just seems so unfair. That poor girl is going to be dragged through the mud, and—"

"Guy's name is Tim Dunlap. He's actually a friend of mine. He's a good guy."

Trisha's heart fluttered when Dunlap's name passed through Bobby's lips. *Just not a good father.*

Bobby sliced his meat and continued, "The fact is that Tim is paid to get his client off."

"You just said that the guy has been in trouble his whole life, in and out of jail. How can he afford such a high-priced lawyer?"

"I don't get into that. I have enough things to worry about. Plus, I have other cases to deal with." Bobby began eating.

Trisha pressed forward. "I'd really like to watch this one from beginning to end," she said. "You know, see my baby in action. I'd like to see how you put a case together and, hopefully, how you'll put this guy away."

Bobby continued devouring his meal.

"Is it tougher when you have to face a guy like Dunlap?" Trisha asked, silently fighting the urge to ask, *Is it tougher when you have to face off against your father?*

"He's got a wealth of experience, which gets him a lot more latitude from the judges."

"Well, that's not fair. Why should he get special treatment from the judges?"

"I didn't say that."

"You said he got a lot more latitude from the judges. Isn't that special treatment?"

"Ma, judges are nothing more than lawyers wrapped in black robes. As many lawyers' careers progress, they end up becoming judges. Before being appointed, they're all friends, friendly adversaries, or enemies."

"I still don't understand why they deserve more latitude."

"I never said they *deserved* it. What I mean by latitude is a young guy like me might bear the wrath of a judge. Meanwhile, a guy like Dunlap escapes unscathed for performing the same indiscretion. It's not discernable to the untrained eye, but it happens. Trust me."

Escaping from his indiscretions? That seems to be his specialty, Trisha thought.

22

THE TRIAL—APRIL 2007

Defendant Tim Dunlap's head was spinning.

Despite a series of intense briefings by his high-profile legal defense team, and decades of personal experiences to fall back on in avoiding the usual pitfalls of testifying under oath, he was teetering.

Suffolk County Assistant District Attorney Bobby Barron's expert witnesses patiently explained the complex scientific evidence in a pedestrian manner, allowing the jury to grasp the necessary parameters.

The subject was deoxyribonucleic acid. More commonly known as DNA, the experts were spoon-feeding the jury its significance on living cells and the underlying information determining who we are and what we look like, both inside and out.

Using PowerPoint presentations, foam boards, and rudimentary descriptions of a complicated science encompassing nucleotides, thymine, adenine, chromosomes, uracil, guanine, chemical affinities, protein synthesis, and hydrogen bonds, the experts systematically simplified and embedded the irrevocable evidence into the jurors' minds. The totality of this evidence incontrovertibly linked Tim Dunlap to the sperm-laden handkerchief seized from the Brighton rape scene.

It was broken down for the jury in much the same manner as Dunlap's sperm had been broken down and isolated as his—and only his—in a nearby Boston Police laboratory.

The obstacle in crime-fighting circles was no longer the acceptance of this science, but the overwhelming backlog of cases dependent on its use. Unfortunately, at least for Tim Dunlap, the notoriety associated with the possibility of turning the tables on a famous Boston attorney—in a court of law, and in the absolute epicenter of where he'd practiced successfully for decades—created too salacious a story to lump it into that substantial backlog.

Subjected to the dictum that, "No good deed goes unpunished," Dunlap's reward for his *pro bono* work was an eight-to-ten year hiatus at Riverfork. He could regain his freedom sooner than the minimum eight-year sentence by maintaining good behavior, but that was of little solace.

Trisha's reward? Knowing he had nobody to blame but himself, and only her to thank.

ℜ

In the end, the means had been remarkably simple.

As Dunlap's defense team argued the merits of its client, Suffolk County Assistant District Attorney Bobby Barron pushed back at every turn.

True to her wishes, and under the guise of "seeing her baby in action," Trisha had cashed in vacation time and blended into the background as a pseudo paralegal. She took great pride in watching Bobby prepare for the case. She hoped his hard work would culminate in the incarceration of the rapist behind bars.

While Bobby shared her feelings, he had no idea they were focusing on separate targets.

Trisha's opportunity arose during an earlier explanation by Bobby of how he planned to proceed during the trial.

Bobby slid a piece of paper across his desk and systematically walked his mother through his strategy.

Unfortunately, she heard nary a word as the copy of the Boston Police Evidentiary Collection Form had taken up full occupancy in her mind after little more than a cursory glance. Initially, she took note of the victim's name. Then, listed among the items confiscated at the scene of the rape was a white handkerchief—a similar item to the one Trisha had taken from Tad over thirty-eight years earlier.

This set off a multitude of thoughts in her mind, the most notable of which was she now knew how Dunlap was going to atone for his sins.

Trisha asked Bobby how he planned to introduce the evidence.

He gave her a crash course in one of jurisprudence's most essential safeguards—chain of custody.

She encouraged an in-depth explanation of the painstaking rules required to avoid the potential tainting of evidence as a plan took root in her mind.

Bobby's effusive praise of the Boston Police Sexual Assault Unit could have rendered her idea a nonstarter. In the end, however, she concluded she had nothing to lose.

Conversely, if she *could* pull it off, the retribution would be monumentally sweet and justly deserved.

ᘒ

The Boston Police Department's Sexual Assault Unit, or SAU, was the great equalizer for citizens victimized by society's scum. Located at 91 East Concord Street and housed in what was once the maternity ward of the former Boston City Hospital, it sat on the outer fringes of Boston's eclectic South End. The aged six-story building was a dull and dirtied yellow brick and gray mortar at its base before transitioning into the more traditional red brick that dominated the surrounding streetscapes at the time of its construction.

SAU worked in conjunction with the Sexual Assault Nurse Examiners, or SANE, units of various area hospitals. These professionals descended on rape scenes with the requisite expertise necessary to sway the hardened and cynical Suffolk County juries.

In today's age of *CSI, Cold Case,* and their ilk solving complex criminal problems within forty-four minutes—leaving a full sixteen minutes for television commercials—the resulting expectations of real-life juries presented a formidable challenge. The combination of SAU and SANE, in collaboration with assistant district attorneys such as Bobby Barron, represented Suffolk County's equally formidable answer to that challenge.

Once these units completed their work, they shipped the accumulated evidence to a secured storage facility in a state-of-the-art, three-million-dollar laboratory at Boston Police Headquarters in the Roxbury Crossing section of the city. One of only eighteen such units in the nation, it was equipped with the latest forensic and serological laboratories.

Trisha had no idea what to expect when she accompanied Bobby to that facility to review the evidence.

Bobby focused on the huge cup of coffee in Trisha's hand as they approached the evidence room. "You may not be able to bring that in. Some of these people are fussier than others are. Depends who's on duty."

Bobby signed in. Several minutes passed before a member of the forensic team showed up to assist and maintain the chain of custody. After some small talk about the New England Patriots' chances against the upstart Dolphins on Sunday, the technician—who bore more than a passing resemblance to Jay Leno—asked, "What case are we looking at?"

Bobby handed him the paperwork. "Davenport. It was a rape over in Brighton."

"Yeah, yeah, gotcha," the technician said, rubbing his prominent chin several times as he stared at the paperwork. "Grab a seat. I'll be right back."

When the technician returned, he placed two items and some additional paperwork on a table for Bobby's review. The items were tagged, bar coded, and encased in sealed, heavy-duty brown paper bags.

Trisha was relieved when her coffee didn't present an issue. She was downright giddy when the technician began unsealing the bar-coded bag, which contained the items confiscated from the defendant when he was arrested.

Looking inside the bag, the technician rattled off the items from his copy of the inventory list. "There's a white Boston College T-shirt. A pair of gray boxer briefs, size large. And a pair of jeans with a ripped right front pocket."

The technician paused to read the notes. He then cross-referenced several other sheets of information. "I guess she ripped his pocket during the struggle and came away with the guy's handkerchief. She turned that into the police, too."

The technician reviewed the inventoried list again, peeked in the bag, and said, "Yeah, that's in there too."

Trisha throat was as dry as desert soil in a midday summer sun. Her body throbbed with anticipation.

Bobby broke the silence. "You're going to check the handkerchief, right?"

Nodding affirmatively, the technician rotated the bag so Bobby could see the contents. The white handkerchief was visible.

Trisha's heartbeat accelerated.

The technician then asked, "What else have you got besides this?"

"A lot of circumstantial. I can place him in the general area at the relative time through cell phone records."

"Did she ID him?"

"Partially—fifties, well built, especially for his age, nothing definitive— but it was dark. Plus, he beat her up pretty good, so there's a lot of subliminal fear. We're counting on something substantial here, something that would unequivocally tie him to her. In retrospect, we were fortunate that an arrest was even made."

"Hey, we'll see what we can find. Don't put too much stock in the initial evidence-seizing process. As you just said, it was dark. There's always a lot of confusion. The key at the scene is getting the evidence into the appropriate storage. That's when we take over."

Bobby shook his head in acknowledgement, but failed to mask his disappointment.

The technician attempted to cheer Bobby up. While it was next to impossible to satisfy eager investigators and prosecutors, he sensed Bobby's despair. He also appreciated his understated demeanor. Many prosecutors were confrontational. He attempted to cheer Bobby up. "Hey, you never know. I'll hit it hard, I promise. Don't worry."

Trisha slid her coffee cup next to Bobby's arm. *Time's running out.* She had to prolong this exercise. "Are you allowed to touch the evidence?" she asked, as she peeked inside the bag again.

"You have to wear protective gloves."

When Bobby pointed at the box of gloves, he knocked Trisha's coffee over on the table, his chair, and the surrounding floor.

"Oh no! I'm so sorry," Trisha said as she leaped out of her chair.

The technician dashed around the table to see if the spillage had tainted any of the evidence. He was relieved to discover there had been no contact as he pushed the bag toward the center of the table. "I shouldn't have allowed the coffee in here," he said sheepishly. "We dodged a bullet." He stepped past Trisha and said, "Let me grab some paper towels."

"I knew that coffee was going to be a problem," Bobby said, staring at the mess.

Trisha only had seconds to act. She pointed out a large coffee stain on the elbow of Bobby's shirtsleeve. "It's all over your shirt. Hurry up and get some water on it before it dries in. That's such a nice shirt; you don't want to ruin it."

Bobby headed in the same general direction as the technician.

Trisha removed the handkerchief from the unsealed evidence bag. Her hands were shaking. For whatever reason, it suddenly dawned on her that they might have security cameras installed to prevent such a move. *Too late,* she thought, as she replaced the handkerchief from the Brighton rape with the one from her pocketbook. *It would now lead directly to Dunlap.*

The technician returned, and Trisha accepted a generous handful of brown paper towels. She began cleaning up the mess she had purposely created.

The physical labor helped disguise the exacerbated level of anxiety coursing through her body. It did little to relieve the dryness in her throat, however.

She could have spit cotton at that point.

ↁ

In the ensuing weeks, Trisha used random payphones to call in anonymous tips about a lawyer setting up his client for a crime the lawyer had committed. Despite her repeated claims of having personal knowledge, she had no choice but to reject each opportunity to come forward and legitimize her claim.

She became apprehensive about her plan's effectiveness, as the case was heading to trial soon.

While Trisha's anonymous calls had ginned up little initial interest at the Boston Police Department, her persistence finally paid dividends.

A prominent Boston Police detective who witnessed a former Tim Dunlap client walk away unscathed from a violent crime against his cousin reached the same general conclusion as Trisha. It was time for hotshot attorney Tim Dunlap to atone for his sins.

He convinced his boss that Trisha's tip deserved review. He not only led the investigation, but also ended up working hand-in-hand with Trisha Barron's baby boy in prosecuting Dunlap.

Neither of them had the slightest clue they were prosecuting Bobby's father.

That a rapist and career criminal went free was unfortunate.

That his name was Tommy Davenport, something Trisha couldn't believe when she originally reviewed the Boston Police Evidentiary Collection Form—and that his middle name was Andrew—was more than Trisha could have asked for; but his initials conveniently matched those of Tim Dunlap.

It was this, above all else, that fortified Trisha's belief she could succeed.

In the end, it all made sense.

Especially to the jury.

PART 4

PRESENT DAY

23

Bobby fended off Jill's attacks with a series of arm and leg maneuvers. Giggling, he begged for mercy. "Come on, knock it off. I'm too sore."

"I can't believe you think I was sleeping."

"I'm telling you, you were snoring."

"You're a liar. I was wide-awake. You were immersed in your mother's diary, so I didn't want to disturb you."

Bobby changed course. "It's weird. Every time I begin reading it, I feel guilty; you know what I mean? It's so personal."

He opened the diary. Pointing to an excerpt, he handed it to Jill. "Look. It goes all the way back to when she was a kid. I'm talking before I was born."

Jill dropped back onto the couch when Bobby exited the disheveled room. She leafed through the diary, and was impressed with his mother's exquisite penmanship. She returned to the first page, intent on staying awake in spite of an ever-increasing state of fatigue.

Bobby sidestepped piles of debris on his way to the kitchen, where he pondered his next move. He peered at his watch. It was almost midnight, further limiting his options.

I've got to get some rest, he thought. *It's going to take Mickey time to get any information, and I need to be prepared if he comes up with any leads.* He worried that Jill would second-guess his weakening resolve, but he knew he was making the proper decision. When he returned to the living room, he found her sound asleep on the couch, the diary flat on her chest, yet still tightly clutched in her fingers.

He gently removed it from her hands and placed it next to a pile of clothes on an adjacent coffee table.

Jill barely moved.

Bobby reached into the pile, settling on a navy-blue fleece blanket embroidered with the logo of Salve Regina University. Compliments of an old girlfriend and alumna of the stately Newport, Rhode Island University, he covered his guest.

Bobby stopped to adjust the thermostat on his way to the bathroom. He brushed and flossed his teeth before heading into his bedroom for what he hoped would be at least a few hours of sleep before this nightmare continued.

こ

"You've got to be shitting me," Arthur Williams said. He spit out a generous mouthful of semi-transparent brown liquid from a chew of Red Man he had couched between his tobacco-stained teeth and his right cheek.

He used an already stained portion of his shirtsleeve, just above his right wrist, to wipe the residue from his mouth. He spit again and said, "That kid's fucking nuts."

Jake defended Mickey. "No, I think he wanted the job, but he'd already made a promise to help out one of his buddies. He's friends with that lawyer that's always on TV, you know, that Bobby Barron. They were meeting in a bar in Southie when I caught up with him last night. They were in deep conversation over something."

"Maybe Mickey's taking the bar exam," Arthur snickered. "I mean, he's got plenty of legal experience, right?"

Jake chuckled at the thought.

Arthur pointed to a pile of beams. "Send that load up and shake it out. I've got to go see Bull and tell him to get someone else for that job." Arthur turned back, "Shit! Hey, I've still got to talk to Mickey about something. Can you reach him and have him stop by, or give me a call?"

"Yeah, sure. Why didn't you tell me that yesterday?"

120

"Because I figured that moron would take the job. I should've known better." He muttered under his breath and fired off another projectile of liquid tobacco. "Send that load up. I'll be right back."

Jake wondered what Arthur would possibly have to talk to his brother about. He turned his attention to the pile of beams. Reminded once again of Mickey's lifestyle, Jake's 'he's a big boy' mentality kicked in.

It was automatic.

ↀ

The ringing telephone jolted Bobby awake. "Hello?"

"Robert, I don't mean to alarm you, but is everything okay? Your mother never showed up for work, and she never called or left a message. I've called her several times, and there's no answer."

Dr. Joseph Wissard was the only person on earth who regularly referred to him as Robert.

Still groggy, Bobby said, "I owe you an apology, doctor. My mom asked me to call Dorothy or Cathy and have them open up. She's not feeling well. I was supposed to call them last night and it slipped my mind. I'm awfully sorry."

"Don't worry. I just want to make sure she's all right. I also need a favor, if you don't mind?"

"Sure, what can I do for you?"

"Your mother left early yesterday to drop off some study models at the lab and to make a deposit at the bank. It was a sizable sum of money and we need to pay some bills. Could you please ask her if she made the deposit? I've contacted the lab, and she definitely dropped off the models. I just want to be sure she made it to the bank before we write any checks."

"Hold on, let me see if I can wake her. It's going to take a second. I've got to run downstairs."

Bobby placed the phone on the counter. When he turned around, he encountered a bewildered Jill. He guided her away, whispering into her ear, "It's my mother's boss. I have to explain why she didn't show up for work." Bobby led Jill into the living room and continued, "This is just going to snowball. I mean, I can cover for a day or two—"

"Well, that's what you'll have to do for now. Just make it sound bad, you know, like she won't be in tomorrow either."

"Yeah, I'll make it sound bad. Just not as bad as it really is."

⁓

"Marie, I need you to get as much information as you can from Rock's office about the Dunlap prosecution," Bobby said into the phone. "Call Mary Beth. She'll get it for us."

"Bobby, she could lose her job. You know you have to go through the proper channels to acquire that information."

Mary Beth Rosarbi was a longtime friend of Marie and Bobby. Eventually, Bobby hoped to add her to his staff. Right now, he was relying on their friendship to piece together the allegations of the people holding his mother captive.

"You've got to make it clear to Mary Beth that I would never ask her to do this if it wasn't necessary. Have her get it to you and I'll make arrangements to pick it up."

"I'll see what I can do. Anything else?"

"Just wait to hear from me. I could be calling at any hour. You've got to be prepared for anything. Make sure you keep your cell phone with you, okay?"

"No problem. Oh, by the way, a gentleman by the name of Jake Carberry called you. He left his number. You want it?"

Why would Mickey's brother be calling me? Shit, I hope Mickey's okay.

"Yeah, give me the number."

⁓

Once Bobby threatened to sue Dr. John Dunne—Trisha's primary care physician—it took less than five minutes to convince the doctor's receptionist to divulge all necessary information.

"Your mother came in here yesterday morning. She complained of feeling run down, and we took a number of tests. This morning, we received confirmation that she has an extremely aggressive infection. Gone untreated,

122

it is potentially fatal. While I don't want to over dramatize this situation, we do need to start her on a cycle of antibiotics."

"How soon?"

"As soon as possible. It can affect people in a variety of ways. The common denominator is that when it hits, it hits quickly and can incapacitate someone. We need her to start on the antibiotics right away … today … *this morning,* if possible."

"I need to figure out a way to contact her—"

"Excuse me, Mr. Barron, but is your mother on vacation? The reason I ask is that Dr. Dunne can reach out to police departments to pay a visit to a patient who is unknowingly in need of service. Things like this happen more often than you think."

"No," Bobby said, thinking, *I wish she was on vacation.* "I can contact people who know where she is." *Not that they'll care. Hey, wait a minute, of course they'll care. No hostage, no leverage. Okay, but how do I get in touch with them?*

Bobby grabbed a pen. "Let me have your number. I'll have my mother get in touch with you as soon as possible."

༼ঞ

"Thanks for taking care of my brother, Davey," Mickey yelled after slipping in the door.

Jake's information on his brother Mickey's whereabouts led him to King's Tavern during his lunch break. One city block and a lifetime away from last evening's meeting spot at O'Bannion's, King's Tavern was one of many new high-end restaurant-bars catering to South Boston's young professionals.

"No problem, Mick," the bartender responded.

Jake turned to face his younger brother. "You've got these guys trained."

"Hey, it's not always a social visit when people come in here looking for me, you know what I mean? You want a drink or something?"

"Actually, I was wondering if you could take a ride over the job with me. Arthur wants to talk to you—"

"Oh, man, don't start Jake. I *can't* take the fucking job." Mickey rolled his eyes for emphasis.

Mickey was an unquestionably tough kid. In Jake's eyes, however, he would always be just that, a kid. While Mickey could turn on the intimidation with the best of them, he knew it would get him nowhere with his oldest brother.

Jake's widened glare afforded Mickey a front-row seat to a potential explosion.

Mickey attempted to neutralize his brother. He couldn't afford the backlash of being backed down in front of the people who reveled in his reputation for toughness. "I'm sorry Jake. I don't mean to be a fresh prick."

Jake took a deep breath. He bit his lower lip, but the glare lingered.

Mickey went into damage control. "You remember seeing Bobby Barron last night?"

"Yeah?" a still angry Jake answered.

"He's got problems. He's in a bind and I promised to help him. I can't help him if I'm working all day. Once I get this straightened out—"

Jake placed his hand on his brother's shoulder and cut him off. "Look, you don't want the job, *don't* take the job. Arthur wants to talk to you about something else. I already told him you weren't interested. *After* I told him, he asked me to reach out to you. He said he needed to talk to you. Come on, take a ride over the job, and we can talk in the truck. I'll drop you off back here afterwards."

"Whatever." Unable to resist re-testing Jake's patience, Mickey joked, "Maybe Arthur wants me to take his daughter out."

"You go near Kaitlyn, and he'll cut your balls off with a deck saw."

Mickey shivered at that thought. He yelled to the bartender, "Davey, I'll be back if anyone's looking for me."

Jake popped the lock of the passenger side door for his brother. "So what are you doing for Bobby?"

"I can't get into it."

"Don't give me that shit. It's the *lawyer* who can't divulge information, not the client."

"For once, I'm not the client, but you don't want to know, trust me."

"I'm a big boy. Trust *me*. What's going on?"

They were heading down Summer Street. Mickey explained the previous evening's events as they passed the power plant on East First Street, concluding with "… So once Bobby found out his mother was kidnapped, he asked me to meet him at O'Bannion's to see if I had any ideas."

"Are you shitting me? *Kidnapped?* Like ransom notes and all that?"

"Well, he got a phone call, actually, a couple of phone calls, about a previous case Bobby was involved in. They think Bobby bagged the case. Some heavy-hitting lawyer ended up going to the can. You remember? The guy's name was Dunlap. Bobby caught a break and ended up putting him away. It was all over the newspapers. It's how he became famous."

"Yeah, yeah, I remember. Are you saying the *lawyer* had Bobby's mother kidnapped?"

Mickey suddenly hesitated. He was getting in too deep. "I've got no idea. I guess she went out for a walk and they grabbed her off the street—"

Jake snatched Mickey's left wrist, squeezing it tightly. "Where was she walking? Was she out by Columbia Point? I was out walking yesterday, and I saw some maggot messing with a woman who was walking behind me. What's Bobby's mother look like?"

Jake released Mickey's arm and jerked the truck over to the curb on Summer Street. He stared at Mickey. "Listen. I was out walking around UMass after work yesterday. Right over by the Teachers' Union Hall. There was this guy standing there with a ski coat on—beige coat, bushy eyebrows, he looked like he was up to no good. I eyeballed him when I walked by, but he wouldn't look at me. Still, something about him bothered me."

Mickey maintained his silence.

Jake's story flowed out, "There was this woman walking behind me. As soon as I passed him, he started walking in her direction…."

స

"What are you talking about?" Pick Piccorino was pissed.

Attorney Carl "The Shadow" Bionda had a prepared response for the inevitable explosion. "I sent our friend to Barron's house, just like you said. The cops showed up while he was trying to get the information out of him—"

"What?" Piccorino cut him off mid sentence. "The fucking cops showed up that quick?" Springing from his chair, he got up into Shadow's face. "You think I'm a fucking idiot? How long does it take to beat information out of a guy? You guys can't do anything right."

"Pick, I'm telling you—"

Pick's tirade continued. "I give you a simple fucking job and you can't even do that. Tell me something, Shadow. Do you really expect me to believe that the cops would ever show up that quick? Come on. I know I've been locked up for a while, but if I couldn't coax the information out of this kid within five minutes, I'll give you a million fucking dollars. How could the cops be there that quick? It don't add up."

Shadow's attempted response was equally futile.

"Now, tell me what *really* happened." Pick said, walking briskly to the other end of the room. He ran his fingers through his hair, vigorously massaging his face, then his temples, before turning to face his long-time attorney. The disdainful look on his face said it all.

Embarrassed, Shadow shook his head and mumbled, "It gets *worse.*"

"How can it *possibly* get any worse?"

"I just got word from Willie that the fucking broad is sick. Puking all over the place, fever, the whole bit."

Pick walked away again. When he turned back in Shadow's direction, he tempered his response. His sudden lack of aggressiveness shocked the attorney.

Speaking barely above a whisper, Pick said, "What do we do now? Take her to the hospital? Yeah, that's what we'll do. Call an ambulance. Tell them we have a *kidnap* victim who's not feeling well. Make sure they understand that. We don't want to be stuck there all night. You know what I mean? We can probably jump right up to the top of the list. I mean, she's a *kidnap* victim, right? What the hell, maybe we can order a police escort."

A stoic Shadow sat still. What could he possibly say to appease his client? Pick's cynicism was on point and indefensible.

Pick continued, sarcasm dripping from his voice. "You writing this down, Shadow? Come on, we've got a lot of work to do here."

℃

Mickey's mind raced after hearing Jake's detailed report of what he'd witnessed while out walking. *Why did I open my mouth? What are the chances of my own brother witnessing this incident? Yet, he's describing the chain of events perfectly.* Mickey chose the isolated spot, and had even followed Trisha there on four separate occasions. *She was a creature of habit, as she was never more than ten minutes apart in arriving at that general area. There was never anyone around. What were the chances?*

"So, what do you think? This had to be her, right?" Jake asked.

"No, couldn't have been. That's not where she got grabbed."

"You sure?" Jake was simultaneously relieved to think that he wasn't responsible for his lack of intervention, yet upset that he hadn't unearthed a significant clue.

"Yeah. She was nowhere near there," Mickey reassured him.

Jake wasn't giving up easily. "Are you *sure?* What does his mother look like? This woman was a little younger than me, good shape ... dark hair. She was good looking. Tall ... what's his mother look like?"

"I don't know. She looks like Bobby's mother."

Jake persisted. "And you're sure she wasn't out near UMass? I'm telling you, Mick. How do you know?"

"Bobby told me."

"Where was she?"

"I don't want to get into it." Mickey needed to change the subject. He reminded Jake of his earlier advice. "I told you that you didn't want to get into this. Look, I've got stuff to do, if you want me to meet up with Arthur we've got to get moving."

Jake pulled the truck back out onto Summer Street. He was not satisfied with his brother's answers.

Mickey was right about one thing, however. He did have to get back to work.

24

Willie Marcus had spent the last several hours escorting his prisoner back and forth to the bathroom. Because Trisha was shackled to the bed, he didn't always release her in time.

The residual effect was obvious.

You can't fake being this sick, he thought.

Trisha had concentrated on using her cell phone to facilitate her rescue once the initial shock of her kidnapping had worn off. Her adrenaline diminished once that possibility was dashed. As the reality of her dire situation set in, her health took a sudden and dramatic turn for the worse. Her initial requests to use the bathroom went ignored due to her previous antics.

Now, they were all paying the price.

Profuse sweating, vomiting, and acute diarrhea were indicators that she wasn't getting any better as a long and uncomfortable night gave way to a new day.

☙

While Mickey reassured Arthur there was nothing to worry about, Jake walked over to the general contractor's trailer.

He called information to retrieve Bobby Barron's phone number. He was uncomfortable with Mickey's evasive answers, and he wanted to make sure that Bobby knew what he had witnessed. He left his contact information with Bobby's secretary.

He and Mickey headed back to Southie after exiting the construction site.

Mickey explained that Arthur's son, Sean, and several of his friends had gotten into a recent skirmish with a group of Southie kids over the territorial rights to several attractive young ladies. Back channel conversations and threats followed in the ensuing weeks, and someone alluded that the Southie youths were connected with Mickey Carberry and his crew.

Sean went to his father after one of his friends was beaten.

Arthur was now seeking Mickey's advice and some sort of closure to this bad blood.

Instead of broaching the subject with Jake, Arthur wanted to deal directly with Mickey to iron out any potential problems and impress upon him—face-to-face—how important this was to him.

Jake dropped Mickey off at King's Tavern and banged a U-turn in the middle of East Broadway.

He passed through K Street, still dwelling on their conversation. *I could have saved Arthur a lot of aggravation. I wonder why he didn't tell me?*

A stunning redhead appeared in front of a double-parked white Dodge Durango.

Jake was suddenly mindful of the state's rule of yielding to pedestrians. That she was seventy-five feet from any crosswalk was irrelevant. She was heading in the direction of the Mt. Washington Bank, and despite having to get back to work, Jake abruptly decided he was in no particular hurry.

Jake couldn't help but peek into the Durango once she'd crossed in front of his truck.

Bobby Barron sat behind the steering wheel.

Jake pulled in front of the Durango and slammed the gearshift into park. He hopped from the vehicle and headed straight toward Bobby.

Bobby lowered his window. "Jake, what's up? Hey, I got a message from my office. Did you call me?"

Jake was unsure whether to bring up his conversation with Mickey. He considered the consequences and thought, *Ah, what the hell. If nothing else, he would get a close-up of Bobby's lady friend upon her return.* "Yeah. Look, Bobby, I try not to stick my nose in other people's business, but I just left Mickey and he gave me a brief rundown of your problem."

"How much did he tell you?" a wary Bobby asked, doing his best to mask his piqued interest.

"Well, he told me about your mother."

You've got to be kidding me, Bobby thought. He immediately analyzed the ramifications as Jake continued speaking.

"... and the crazy thing is, I saw this woman being hassled yesterday while I was out walking. I was telling Mickey about it, but he said that wasn't anywhere near the area where your mother was taken."

Bobby's eyes narrowed. "I'm a little confused, Jake. What are you talking about?"

"You know how your mother got grabbed while she was out walking?"

"Who told you she got grabbed while she was out walking?"

"Mickey. Well, actually, I was telling Mickey a story about my seeing a woman getting hassled when I was walking around UMass yesterday afternoon."

"Jake, I really don't know what you're talking about. I mean—"

"I thought I witnessed something, but Mickey told me that your mother was nowhere near the area I was talking about when she was grabbed."

"How does *Mickey* know where she was?"

Jake hesitated. He was suddenly uncomfortable with where this conversation was heading. "He told me that you told him."

The redhead returned. She gave Jake a killer smile as she slid back into the passenger seat.

Bobby introduced the pair.

She's even more stunning up close, Jake thought.

"I've got to jump out for a second," Bobby said to Jill.

Bobby steered Jake toward the back of the vehicle.

Jake said, "Jesus, Bobby, I shouldn't have even brought it up. Don't be pissed at Mickey, I kind of forced it out of him."

"Tell me one more time what you saw."

Jake reiterated the entire story.

Bobby said, "What I don't understand is how Mickey knows where she got grabbed?"

"Like I said, he claims you told him."

"I have no idea where she was grabbed. How could I have told him?"

Jake's uneasiness increased as Bobby continued. "The one thing that *does* make sense is my mother does walk around Harbor Point every day. Now you're saying you saw this happen out in that area and around the time that she usually walks. It all sounds plausible."

Nodding, Jake asked, "What does your mother look like?"

"I don't know, dark hair, tall. She's very attractive. She's fifty-three, but she looks a lot younger."

"Do you know what she wears when she walks? This woman was tall and attractive …" Jake answered his own question. "She was wearing black pants, a white windbreaker, and one of those white visors. You know, a baseball hat with a brim but no top?"

"That's *her*. I mean, everything you're saying is right on the money. She walks around Harbor Point. She fits that description. She's tall, has dark hair, and she wears a white windbreaker and a visor. The only thing that *doesn't* fit is nobody ever told me how—or *where*—they grabbed her. Just why."

Jake stood there as Bobby asked him the very question he so wanted to ask Bobby.

"How does Mickey know all this?"

ॐ

"Listen, we've got to get a doctor in here. She's got a fever, and she's fucking puking and shitting all over the place. She's getting worse by the hour. She ain't going to last. Plus, how do I know that it's not contagious."

132

Mickey squeezed the cell phone, signifying his aggravation. "Willie, how are we going take her to a doctor? Wake the fuck up, will you?" After uttering the words, a thought came to him. "Hey, what's that doctor's name over in Brookline? You know. The guy we used to get the Oxys from?"

"McGlinty, right? Dr. McGlinty," Willie said.

"McGlinty, yeah. He could be the answer. Pick me up in an hour. Make sure Sammy stays there to keep his eyes on her."

"Don't worry about Sammy. He fucks up again and I'm going to shackle *him* to the fucking bed with her. It doesn't matter anyway. She's not going anywhere. Christ, she couldn't escape if I left the front door open and the van running. I'm telling you, Mick, she's in tough shape."

"Yeah, yeah, I hear you. Just make sure Sammy stays there. Tell him to get his head out of his ass and keep his eyes on her."

"All right, I'll pick you up."

"One hour. Meet me inside the bar."

25

Jake stared at Bobby and shrugged. "I was just going to ask you the same question. I mean, Mickey's my brother, but you've got to understand, this guy has no conscience. At first, his story sounded believable. Now that we've spoken, it's got more holes in it than a piece of Swiss cheese."

"We've been best friends since we were kids, Jake. I know what you mean, but I'm still having a hard time believing he would kidnap my mother."

"Piece it together. What else could it be?"

A woman exiting the Cranberry Café called out in their direction. "Excuse me, is that your truck?"

Jake shook his head in acknowledgement. "I'll move it for you." Turning back to Bobby, he said, "Look, we've got to talk. Can you take a ride down the beach?"

"How much time have you got? Can you swing by my house for a few minutes instead? I need to show you something."

"Yeah, I'll follow you." Jake jumped back into the front of Arthur Williams's truck to extricate still another unwitting victim of the neighborhood's double-parking epidemic.

❧

Trisha could barely hold her head up to vomit. Her captors had cleaned up as best they could—admittedly, for their own benefit as much as hers—as they, too, were captives.

I'm going to die and nobody will ever know, Trisha thought.

The sweating was diminishing. Severe dehydration was rapidly setting in. Unable to hold anything down, and losing additional body fluids with every passing minute, she was entering the initial stages of fever-induced hallucinations.

જી

"Look Shadow, I need you to work with me here. Willie and Mickey need to be pointed in the right direction."

The attorney nodded.

"I want you to set up a meeting with this Barron kid. Make it clear that his mother's going to die if he doesn't straighten this shit out. Did you bring the phone?"

Here we go again, thought Shadow. He prepared himself for another detonation of Pick's hair-trigger temper. "I brought it, but they made me leave it with all my other stuff before I came in here. They won't allow us to carry anything in, Pick."

"Yeah, yeah, don't worry about it. Your load will be a little lighter on the way out. The phone's being delivered to me as soon as I get back to my cell. Did you do what I told you with the number, you know, write it down?"

"I set it up just like you said. All you have to do is flip it open, and it's all set to go. Everything's set on vibrate, and the battery's fully charged."

"You guys better get the point across to this fucking Barron kid! And from what I'm hearing you better do it soon."

જી

Bobby yanked the vibrating BlackBerry from its holder on his right hip. Its illuminated screen read *Work.* He braced it against his right ear. "What's up, Marie?"

"Bobby, I have a couple of things for you. A woman named Krissy called a couple of times. She works for a Dr. Dunne, and she's calling about—"

"It's okay, Marie. I already spoke with her."

"Is everything all right, Bobby? She seemed pretty concerned."

"Yeah, it's all set. My mother has some type of blood infection. I'm going to take her over to the hospital. Everything's all set."

"Are you sure? Is there anything I can do?"

"I just need you to hang tight and keep doing what you're doing, okay?"

"Speaking of calls, I got another one of those disturbing calls. Very abrupt and unprofessional. When I told the man you were unavailable, he said, 'He better make himself available. He's not working on anything more important than what I have to talk to him about.'"

"I don't suppose he left a number?"

"Actually, he left his name *and* his number. He's an attorney. I looked him up on the Mass Bar database. He's licensed to practice in Massachusetts and Florida, but he's not associated with any firm. He seems to be a sole practitioner, and he was very anxious to speak with you.

With Bobby deep in thought, Marie continued, "His name is Carl Bionda. You want his number?"

露

Jake surveyed the damage. "Wow, what a mess. When did this happen?"

"Last night. This is what I walked into when I got home. My mother's place on the first floor looks the same way. Cellar too. Someone hiding in the house nailed me from behind with a baseball bat. Luckily, Jill and my neighbor Larry came to my rescue, and it spooked him off."

Just thinking about the incident made Bobby's ribs ache.

A quick trip to his medicine cabinet found its contents intact. Bobby popped a couple of Ibuprofen. He washed them down by drinking a mouthful of water directly from the sink's spigot. Despite a lifetime of hydrating in this fashion, whenever he did it, he would hear his mother's voice—be it real or imagined—resonating in his head. "Get a glass. You know what kind of germs live on those faucets?"

Wouldn't it be great to hear those words right now? Bobby thought. He twisted the faucet shut and headed back to his newly deputized sleuths.

露

"What's up, Jake?"

Jake had been able to reach his boss through a little job networking.

Arthur Williams was on the other end of a co-worker's cell phone. The hardened and cynical man's massive and dirty hands dwarfed the slim cell phone. "Where the hell are you?" he bellowed.

"I ran into some trouble after I dropped Mickey off. It's a long story."

"Hey Jake, you know the old saying: I don't mind a little *tale*, but I hate a long story."

Jake couldn't help but laugh at his boss's oft-used and gender-sensitive joke. "Listen, I got myself involved in something I need to follow through on."

"Everything all right? Anything I can help you with?"

"I'm all set. I'm just calling to let you know that I may not have time to get your truck back to you by quitting time. If I don't make it back, I'll leave it in front of my house. Think you can get a ride over there?"

"What the hell's going on? I can come over right now—"

"No, no, I ran into a friend who's in a jam. He needs some help, that's all."

"If you ain't back, I'll get a ride over there. Make sure you leave the keys in the glovie. I don't have another set with me."

The trio surveyed the mess before deciding to walk up the street and grab some take-out food at Sal's Ristorante & Pizzeria.

They returned to Bobby's house and pieced together the events of the past eighteen hours while they ate. Mickey's involvement was clear to the three of them.

Bobby rehashed Mickey's questioning at O'Bannion's under the harsh light of this newfound realization. He concluded that the emphasis that these kidnappers were the wrong people to mess with was infinitely more self-serving than had he ever imagined. This thought manifested itself in Mickey's thinly veiled advice that Bobby come clean. The sooner, the better.

Mickey telling Jake about Trisha's abduction, when Bobby had not offered—nor did he possess—any information to that end, was a particularly damning piece of evidence. It was also a severe cause for concern.

At a certain point, Jake had heard enough. "I'm going to the bar right now to confront him."

Knowing Mickey's volatility and the impact such an accusation could have on his behavior, Bobby said, "I don't think that's a good idea."

"I know he's your friend," Jake said, before the absurdity of that statement struck him. "Well ... he's *supposed* to be your friend. But this simply isn't adding up. I know Mickey better than anybody knows him. I don't need you to go with me. I'll take care of it myself, and then I'll get back to you."

"You can't do that Jake. I need to go with you. We can leave Jill here in case we need her to do something after we talk with him."

Jill suppressed her journalistic curiosity and agreed with Jake's initial assertion that he should go alone. "You should listen to Jake, Bobby, but if you're going, we should *all* go. We can take my car. I'll drive, and I'll wait outside with the car running while the two of you go in."

"What's it going to be?" Jake asked. "I'm going, and I still think I should go alone, but Jill's got a good idea about having the car running outside, just in case."

"Yeah, let's do that," Bobby said.

Jake stepped in Bobby's direction. With a steely-eyed look, he said, "That's fine, as long as we're clear on *one* thing. *I'm* doing all the talking."

❧

Bobby pulled out his BlackBerry after entering the front passenger seat of Jill's red Volvo. He typed the number Marie had e-mailed to him after their last phone conversation.

"Hello," said a tentative voice on the other end.

"Yeah, this is Bobby Barron. I'm looking for a Carl Bionda."

"Not on the phone. Where and when can you meet?"

"Look, pal, first off, I don't know what you're calling about. Second, I have no idea who you are. Why would I want to meet with you?"

"You're a smart kid; figure it out. You got my number. *Where* and *when?* I'll wait for your call."

The line went dead.

"Who was that?" Jill asked.

"It's a long story," Bobby mumbled with a resigned shake of his head.

Jill was fortunate that Jake's boss wasn't there to supply his favorite off-color punch line.

ري

Willie entered the bar. He was fifteen minutes early. *Might as well have a drink.* He grabbed a seat in front of a giant plasma television. A CNN Headline News talking head blabbered on as Willie ordered a double Jack and Coke. He peeked around the corner into a separate dining area.

Mickey was in his customary spot, his back to the wall and as far from the entrance as possible.

Willie caught Mickey's eye to let him know he was there before heading for the men's room. He found Mickey occupying the seat next to his when he returned.

Mickey pointed at the glass. "A little early, brother. Go easy on the booze, huh? I don't need you making a punching bag out of McGlinty."

"Listen to you. The fucking ambassador of peace and good will."

"How bad is she?" Mickey asked.

"It's bad, man. Puking, shitting, the whole works. We've got to get McGlinty over there to help her. She's sick, man."

"Yeah, yeah, finish your drink. Come on, let's get this done."

Willie tossed the drink back with several quick mouthfuls, leaped from the stool, and threw a five-dollar bill on the bar. "Let's go."

Mickey followed Willie. He fingered the five and turned to his right to see if Davey the bartender was watching. He stuffed it into the right front pocket of his jeans.

Fortunately—for the bartender, not Mickey—he was preoccupied with another customer.

"Thanks, Davey," Mickey yelled before exiting the bar.

ↅ

Jill turned left on East Broadway. She passed through K Street before braking to allow an old woman pushing a metal grocery basket to cross the street.

Jake sat in the back seat. His mind raced as he calculated the possible ramifications of pursuing the matter with his younger brother.

Bobby noticed Mickey and Willie crossing Broadway first. "Shit, there he is!"

Jake slid to the middle of the backseat and lunged forward for a better look. His brother didn't catch his attention, but the person crossing East Broadway with him did. Despite being hoodless, Jake recognized those bushy eyebrows and the beige ski coat he was still wearing as belonging to the same person he had seen at Harbor Point.

It suddenly became clear to him—if not yet the others—that this intervention with his brother was nothing more than a fool's errand.

26

Jake couldn't contain himself. He was sickened to see his brother moseying across Broadway—seemingly without a care in the world—but the story now fit together seamlessly. "I don't frigging believe it," he yelled.

He startled Jill, who peeked in the rearview mirror and witnessed them enter a double-parked white van.

Jake squeezed Bobby's left shoulder and shook him. "That's the guy I was telling you about! The guy with Mickey. I saw that same guy yesterday. You remember?"

"Turn the car around," Bobby said. "Don't let them get away"

As Jill completed a U-turn, Bobby said, "They're taking a right down K."

Jill slid her car to the right but the white van suddenly reversed direction, banging a reckless U-turn in the middle of the intersection.

Jill could not duplicate the maneuver because several cars were now passing them on their left.

"You've got to pull out," Bobby urged. "We can't let them get out of our sight."

Jill finally swung around. She was now heading down East Broadway. Only a gold Ford Taurus stood between them and their prey.

Bobby hit W on his BlackBerry, his speed dialing default for work.

"Marie, I need you to stay on the line. I'm going to give you a license plate number. Call Jerry Driscoll over at police headquarters, and ask him to run the plate for me."

"I'm not sure I have his number."

"It's in my computer."

"Jerry Driscoll," Marie repeated, scribbling his name on a note pad.

They got their first break at I Street when the Taurus veered right, disappearing down Emerson Street.

Passing Dr. Wissard's office on the left, they ascended Pill Hill. Bobby said, "It's a Mass plate, Marie. One one four two A Z H. Got it? Eleven forty two, A as in Apple, Z as in zebra, and H as in … I don't know, H … H as in *hurry up!*

"Got it."

"Have Jerry run it for me, then call me back, okay?"

❧

Dr. Eugene McGlinty was a first-class physician. He was also an avid—albeit unlucky—gambler. His inability to choose winners led to a growing arrearage. This eventually led to an introduction to Mickey Carberry and Willie Marcus. The duo explained that they would gladly accept other tangible products of value to settle the debts of the cash-starved doctor.

The commodity they agreed upon was OxyContin. This highly effective, but controversial pain relief medication, it contained oxycodone, a potent narcotic with morphine-like properties. Legitimate users, following carefully crafted directions, swallowed it whole, after which it would be time-released over a twelve-hour period.

Mickey and Willie's customers were more apt to crush up the pills before swallowing, snorting, or injecting the drug.

This usually initiated an insidious downward spiral.

The pills resold for thirty to forty times their market value in the free market supply and demand economy of the illegal drug world. This was particularly fortuitous for the gang's sales force, but eventually far too expensive for young kids or adults caught up in its clutches. Most robbed, conned, or stole to feed their habit. Many invariably turned to the much cheaper but equally insidious alternative of heroin.

The gang's street-corner sales department didn't care. They had their grimy fingers buried in that pie, too.

Over the next twelve months, the doctor supplied them with falsified prescriptions for thousands of Oxys. The product never hit the street until the gang imposed cost-prohibitive street taxes.

And so it went, until an investigation was launched against Dr. McGlinty.

The daughter of the chairwoman of the Massachusetts State Senate's Law Enforcement Committee, and ranking member of the Mental Health and Substance Abuse Committee, nearly died after ingesting the poison emanating from one of McGlinty's prescription pads.

His propensity for dispensing inordinate amounts of the drug was eventually uncovered. The layers of street dealers provided him a certain amount of insulation. His attorney convinced the jury that brutal intimidation tactics and falsified documents forged without the doctor's knowledge were the root cause, and his client was a *victim,* not a criminal or a drug dealer.

McGlinty utilized one of Boston's most accomplished attorneys and prevailed in a photo-finish victory. This allowed him to maintain his medical license, but little else. When he aggregated his substantial gambling losses and the huge legal bill, a balance of which he still owed, it was a pyrrhic victory at best.

Ironically, his attorney had ended up in the throes of his own legal mess. McGlinty had not seen a bill from Tim Dunlap in quite some time. He wasn't about to complain.

When Mickey and Willie sauntered through the office door, the scowl on the face of Dr. McGlinty's secretary said it all.

"The doctor's not here," she whispered. She stared blankly at her appointment book as dreadful memories reemerged in her mind.

Mickey leaned over the counter and whispered, "Listen, Paula, this is a one-doctor office." He pointed at the waiting room. "There are *three* people sitting over there waiting to be treated. The doc's BMW is in the fucking parking lot, and you're going to tell us he's not here?" Mickey cocked his head to the right, widened his eyes, and issued a wry grin at the absurdity of her statement.

The receptionist sprung out of her brown leather chair. She pushed open a door marked Private and disappeared from view. Returning thirty seconds later, she quickly ushered her unwanted visitors into an adjacent examination room, shutting the door from the inside.

"He'll be right in," she whispered, before pleading, "but he *can't* give you prescriptions. He'll lose his license."

Mickey stared hungrily at her ample breasts. She smelled good, and he smiled as he rubbed her right shoulder. "Don't worry, Paula, we don't need any medication. We're feeling just fine. We need the doc's help on another matter."

The shaken receptionist was unsure how to proceed, but she did know one thing; she didn't want to spend another second with these two psychopaths.

Mickey grabbed her right wrist when she reached for the doorknob. He jerked her back in his direction. With their faces inches apart, he said, "Those patients out there have to be rescheduled. Don't wait for the doctor to tell you, as you'll only be wasting their time. He's coming with us."

℥

Apportioned to Boston farmers as excess land in the 1600s, the rural land known as Muddy River Hamlet eventually rejected Boston's domineering rule. Initially, they petitioned for exemption from tax payments before finally seeking their complete independence. It took three attempts, but upon the official signatures of thirty-two of its freeholders on November 13, 1705, the Muddy River Hamlet formally incorporated into the Town of Brookline.

Brookline would become the birthplace of President John F. Kennedy and the hometown of former Massachusetts Governor and former United States presidential candidate, Michael Dukakis.

It was also home base for Dr. Eugene McGlinty.

Moreover, it was Brookline where Jill, Bobby, and Jake now found themselves. They had followed Mickey and Willie here and were now debating their next move.

"What if I walk in there and look around?" Jill said; staring at the massive brownstone building the duo had entered several minutes earlier.

They stationed themselves across the street to maintain a clear view of any activity adjacent to the front door. Their problem was what if they were holding Bobby's mother inside? It would certainly be helpful to narrow down where they had gone.

"It's too late," Jake said. "They went in a few minutes ago. They're not going to be standing in the lobby waiting for us to tail them."

"Plus, we may have to move quickly and we don't want to leave you behind," Bobby added.

"You guys can drive. If you have to go, just go. I'll grab a cab back to Bobby's house and wait for your call. They have no idea who I am. I can walk right in there, and they'd never recognize me. I'll need the key to your house just in case."

Bobby reflected on Jill's idea as he removed his house key. He looked at Jake and said, "Jill's right. They have no idea who she is. It might be worth a shot."

"What does your Mom look like?" Jill asked.

"She's tall, dark hair ... shoulder length ... she's a good-looking woman. She's fifty-three, but doesn't look it."

Jake cut in, "She's wearing a white nylon coat with black pants. She had on a white visor, at least she did. I know you can't count on that, but how could they get rid of the jogging suit?"

It dawned on Bobby that he had a photo of him and his mother at a recent family wedding. He retrieved it from his wallet and gave it to Jill. Jake describing what his mother was wearing unnerved him. It also reemphasized Mickey's betrayal.

Jill held the photo up to the window for one last peek. She took the key from Bobby. "I'm going in there to see what I can find out."

જી

Dr. McGlinty stared into Mickey's eyes. He knew who made the calls in this duo. "Listen, I can't do it. I don't even know what you guys want, but you've got to understand that I'm lucky to still have a practice—"

Mickey cut him off. "Doc, you're telling us you can't do it, and you don't even know what we want done."

"Okay. What do you want?"

"We've got a sick woman. She's so sick she couldn't come with us."

"What's wrong with her?"

Mickey's eyes widened. He took a step toward the doctor. "Come *on,* doc. If we knew that we wouldn't need you, now would we?"

"Where's the woman?"

"Couple of miles away."

"I'll follow you," McGlinty offered.

Willie laughed. "That sweet-looking quarter-of-eight wouldn't last long where we're going."

McGlinty had no idea that a quarter-of-eight was street lingo for his BMW 745. He continued to protest. "Look, I've got patients—"

Mickey took command. "Fuck the patients! You're coming with us. I already told Paula to reschedule them. It's as simple as that."

Resigned to his fate, McGlinty asked, "What are the woman's symptoms?"

Mickey deferred to Willie for his diagnosis.

"She's shitting, puking, and sweating. She's fucking out of it."

"How old is she?"

"She's *old.* Forty? Forty-five?" Willie said, looking at Mickey for corroboration.

"And her symptoms are dysentery, vomiting, fever, and a general malaise?"

Willie looked at the doctor bewilderedly. "Like I told you, she's shitting, puking, and sweating. I don't know if she got any of that other stuff."

ભ

146

Jill didn't need much time to investigate. After a cursory survey of the lobby, she turned to see Mickey and Willie approaching her in full exit mode.

A trim, distinguished looking man with a shock of white hair and dressed in a gray suit walked alongside them. He was carrying a large stainless steel-handled rectangular black leather case in his right hand.

Mickey was the only one to pay any attention to Jill as they breezed past her. He winked and smiled at the attractive redhead who, given the fact that her eyes were locked in on him, was undoubtedly attracted to his roguish good looks.

Well, that isn't Bobby's mother, Jill deduced. She paused, before casually heading for the door they'd just exited. She stepped from the curb and briskly traversed Beacon Street, never removing her eyes from the three men.

She noticed Bobby was in the driver's seat as she approached her car.

He reached across the passenger seat, popped open the door, and pulled away the moment Jill settled in.

"Who's the guy in the suit?" Bobby asked.

"No idea. When I walked in, they were walking out. I didn't have time to look around. Mickey's the one with the blue coat, right?

Bobby nodded.

"He winked at me as he was passing. Can you believe that?"

A disgusted Jake Carberry sat silently in the backseat. He believed her. There were few things left he wouldn't believe about his brother, and that list was rapidly diminishing.

27

"I spoke with Jerry Driscoll. The license plate you gave me came back as a stolen vehicle," Marie explained to Bobby. "He said it belongs to a white van. If you know where it is he'll have it impounded."

"I'll call you back. Ask Jerry not to do anything right now. Better yet, tell him I'll call him in an hour and explain what's going on."

The trio had followed the stolen white van down Beacon Street to Park Drive. They were now heading down the Riverway, baffled where this joyride was taking them.

Willie's maniacal driving tendencies exacerbated their elevated level of confusion.

Staying hidden behind them was becoming increasingly difficult, especially when Willie whipped the van into a last-second turn onto Brookline Avenue.

☙

"Look at that red car behind us," Willie yelled, peering into his rearview mirror before twisting his head around for a better look. "I'm telling you, they're following us."

"You're fucking paranoid. Watch the road," Mickey said.

"There's no way they were making that turn. I made it at the last minute. All of a sudden, *boom* ... they make the turn too? No way!"

"Pull over," Mickey said. "If they pull over with you, we'll know something's up."

Pulling sharply to the right, Willie brought the van to an abrupt stop in front of the Deaconess Hospital.

☙

Larry Fitzgerald peered through his living room window. "You've got to be shitting me," he mumbled. *Who the hell is that?*

He headed out his front door to find out. The destruction of Bobby and Trisha Barron's house had been disconcerting. Its proximity to his house left him no alternative but to maintain additional vigilance against any unusual activity in the neighborhood. He walked down his front stairs, a collapsible metal police baton stuffed strategically in the back of his jeans.

Larry was dismayed that the guy he'd seen peering in the window of Trisha's first-floor apartment was nowhere in sight.

Did he go inside the house? Man, this shit's getting out of hand, Larry thought as he walked up the driveway and into the dark side alley adjacent to the Barron's home.

The steady crunching of the two-inch layer of dried-out leaves beneath Larry's feet precluded him from hearing the guy closing in on him from behind.

☙

"Keep going, Bobby," Jake said, slinking down in the backseat to avoid detection. "We can't let them see our faces when we drive by."

Bobby regained his bearings. He turned his head to the left as he passed the van, shielding his face.

Jill rummaged mindlessly through her pocketbook on the car's console. This hid her identity equally well.

"Take a left here," Jake said, pulling himself forward for a better view.

"Slow down, Bobby, there's a little side street up ahead. Take a right there."

Slumping backward, Jake twisted around, focusing his eyes on Brookline Avenue to see if the white van was moving again.

Bobby made the left turn onto Francis Street.

"Slow down," Jake said, refocusing on the front windshield. "There's a small side street just up ahead. Take that right."

Bobby followed Jake's instructions. They were now heading down Binney Street.

"Go to the end and take a right. Another right will bring you back out to Brookline Ave. When we get up to the corner, we can take a right and see if they're still sitting there. If they're moving we can fall back in behind them."

Second-guessing himself—or perhaps just looking for support—Jake shrugged and looked at Jill. "I mean, what else can we do?"

"*Slow down*, Bobby," Jake repeated. "You're going to draw too much attention going this fast."

Bobby stared in the rearview mirror in search of the white van as he approached the intersection. He slowed the car down, but not quite enough.

He never saw the woman emerge from behind an illegally parked car adjacent to the intersection's crosswalk prior to hitting her.

 crossing

"What do you think?" Willie asked.

"I already told you. You're fucking paranoid." Looking at McGlinty, Mickey sought consensus. "What do you think, doc? Is my boy paranoid, or what?'"

"That's not my field, sorry," was all the doctor would offer.

"I'm telling you, Mick. I was watching them for a while. They were right up our ass all the way from Beacon Street. I banged that turn at the last second and they did the same thing. They never planned on making that turn!"

"We'll soon find out," Mickey said. "You've got to take the next left, and that's where they went. Let's go. If they're parked down that street, then we'll know you're on to something. What kind of car was it?"

"A red Volvo. Two people in the front. Couldn't make much out, but there was definitely two people in the car. Looked like a woman in the passenger seat. You think we ought to go another way?" Hesitating and lowering his voice, he repeated his warning, "I'm telling you, Mick, they were following us."

"What other way are we going to go? This is the way. If we see the car, we'll drag them the fuck out and see what their problem is. Relax, will you?" Turning to McGlinty, he said, "You got anything in that bag to relax this guy, Doc? He's fucking paranoid. Give him a shot of something."

"I'll give you a fucking shot." Willie mumbled under his breath.

Willie whipped away from the curb. A cacophony of car horns blared harmonically in the background in response to his insensitive driving habits. He turned left on Francis Street, convinced that the red Volvo would be lurking in the shadows.

Neither he, nor his passengers, noticed the activity off to their right, one short block down Binney Street.

They didn't yet know it, but the likelihood of the occupants of the red Volvo wreaking additional havoc was no longer an issue.

∾

It was arguable who reacted to the presence of the poor old woman first. When Bobby's gaze refocused from the rearview mirror to the windshield, he instinctively slammed on the car's brakes. The resulting screech of rubber tires burning into the asphalt, Jake's scream, and Jill's shrill, ear-splitting shriek seamlessly fused together.

Angela Lyons, a ninth grade English teacher at Thayer Academy in Braintree, never completed her mission of visiting her daughter, Marylou, and her new grandson, Jack. Instead, she ended up in the Brigham & Women's Emergency Room where she was treated infinitely better than the guy who hit her.

He was locked up in a nearby Boston Police holding cell.

Hitting pedestrians is a universally frowned upon practice. When that pedestrian is the mother of the Boston Police Commissioner—as was the case here—the offending driver's troubles multiply exponentially.

❧

Jill and Jake's paradox was that the now inaccessible Bobby was the only one of them equipped to handle the chaos that resulted from the accident.

Jill worked the desk sergeant for information. She was not averse to using her physical attributes to obtain information. She forged ahead, flashing her press credentials, but her misguided ploy was never going to bear fruit.

The sergeant was hardly impressed.

Jake contemplated their next logical move. He took a seat in the lobby of Boston Police's District B-2 station on Dudley Street in Roxbury.

Earlier, after the police whisked Bobby away and towed Jill's car as evidence, Jill and Jake had crossed Francis Street and entered the hospital emergency room to check on the injured woman. It would have been difficult to imagine more police presence at the seventh game of a World Series at nearby Fenway Park.

When Jake encountered a patrolman friend from Southie who explained the relationship between the victim and Boston's top cop, the added presence made sense.

Police quickly cordoned off the emergency room, making it impossible to ascertain any information regarding the woman's condition.

Jake's pal recommended they head over to the station in Roxbury where Bobby remained locked up.

After Jake convinced him to call Jill's cell phone if he received any new information, they headed to District B-2.

❧

"Excuse me—"

Fear engulfed Larry Fitzgerald. Every hair on his body stood on end. He screamed, and the temporary paralysis morphed into an intuitive need to defend himself. Pulling the police baton from its holding area in the backside of his jeans, he went on the offensive. He approached his foe with the club raised menacingly over his right shoulder. Larry reacted with a maniacal scream, yelling "Whaaaat! … What the fuck are you doing?"

A frightened Dr. Joseph Wissard backpedaled away, flailing his hands awkwardly in front of his face.

Continuing to backup, the shaken doctor blurted out, "I'm looking for Robert Barron."

ᘓ

Jill asked Jake, "What do you think?" as they headed up Francis Street toward Tremont in the backseat of a taxi that had commandeered outside the emergency room door.

"I don't think she was hurt too bad, do you?"

"But she's the *mother* of the police commissioner. That can't be good, right?"

Jake shook his head in agreement and changed the subject. He was suddenly mindful that he'd never checked in at home, and asked, "Do you mind if I use your phone to call my house?"

Jill walked him through the dialing process.

He smiled ruefully and said, "This ought to go over well."

He was significantly more subdued when his wife answered his call.

28

Edward "Ted" Lyons was an icon within the Boston Police Department and beyond. His steady rise and laudable successes at every level, and from virtually all perspectives, were a direct result of his possessing the most important of all personal traits—he never forgot where he came from.

While previous commissioners shied away from hiring supremely qualified former opponents out of some inner fear of losing control, the potential threat of such an action never entered his mind. Lyons subscribed to a Lincolnesque theory that had served our country's sixteenth president well.

Lyons's department flourished through the open promotions of a number of previously ardent, albeit supremely talented, competitors.

While many of his peers took advantage of the Police Career Incentive Pay Program to further their education, he already possessed a college degree. Lyons took it to the next level and put himself through Boston College Law School.

Despite a ten-year age gap, one of his law school classmates and close friends during that period was Bobby Barron, a fellow South Bostonian.

Commissioner Ted Lyons entered District B-2 surrounded by a phalanx of uniformed police officers and plain-clothes detectives. The group disappeared from Jill and Jake's view as quickly as they had appeared.

While Jill stood with her mouth agape, Jake couldn't dispose of the notion that a pending beating—akin to something one might witness on a security camera from Bourbon Street in New Orleans—was in the offing.

One would have had to suspend all rational thinking to envision what actually transpired over the next several minutes. Knowing that his mother was just badly bruised and a bit shaken up—and fortified by the fact that his old pal probably still had no idea who it was that he'd hit—he turned the corner and headed down the corridor toward Bobby's cell.

"All right, where's the guy who ran over my mother?" Lyons barked in mock furor.

Bobby stood in disbelief. It took him several seconds to begin piecing the puzzle together.

A patrolman rattled a huge metal ring of keys, unlocking the cell door.

Lyons burst through the opening, bellowing, "What kind of an asshole runs over his friend's mother? You better have a good lawyer, pal."

Muted laughter surrounded a sheepish and still silent Bobby Barron.

What could he possibly say in his defense?

℘

"What's going on? Where are you?" Barbie Carberry asked from the other end of the phone.

"Barbie, if I told you, you wouldn't believe me," Jake began. He had no idea where their conversation was heading.

"Try me."

"I was helping out one of Mickey's buddies—"

"You're tied up with Mickey and his buddies?" Barbie asked, fully aware of her husband's disdain for his younger brother's lifestyle, never mind his acquaintances.

"This guy's a lawyer. You remember I told you about that attorney Bobby Barron being a close friend of Mickey's. You didn't believe me ... remember?"

"Yeah, but what's he got to do with it?"

"Like I said, if I told you, you wouldn't believe me."

"Is Mickey with you?"

"Actually, we were following him when Bobby got into an accident. He hit a woman with his car ... actually with a friend's car."

"Are you all right? Were you with him when he hit her?"

"Yeah, we were following Mickey—"

"Where were you going?"

Here we go, Jake thought. "I don't know."

"You don't *know*? Where's this guy Bobby now?"

"They locked him up," Jake said. "I left out one key component. The woman we hit was Ted Lyons's mother."

"The police commissioner?" Barbie gasped. She'd heard enough. When it came to her heretofore-responsible, trustworthy, and usually reliable husband, there could be only one excuse.

"Are you drunk?"

༄

Willie exited Francis Street onto Tremont. "Which way, chief?"

"Straight," Mickey replied, putting them on Malcolm X Boulevard. "This'll take you to Dudley, and that'll take us to Columbia Road."

"Near the courthouse?"

"Yeah, up Dudley, then take a right on Columbia."

As the trio approached Columbia Road, Mickey said, "Slow down. You've got to turn right up ahead."

The van turned onto Columbia Road and again on Quincy Street.

As they approached Sacomma Street, Willie said, "Home sweet home. What do you think, doc?"

Willie banged a left, then another onto a small side street that housed the opening of a driveway. He engineered another vigorous left turn to complete the mission.

"Pull right up to the door," Mickey ordered. "Close as you can get, I don't want any nosy neighbors wondering what we're doing."

෴

Enough was enough. Larry Fitzgerald was not a patient of Dr. Wissard.

This was unfortunate for the good doctor.

Larry was unwilling to back off. He screamed again, "I'm going to ask you one more time. Why are you looking for Bobby Barron?"

Wissard pleaded, "Relax, sir. Please. Robert's mother works for me. She called in sick, and I couldn't get through to her on the phone, so I figured I would stop by to see how she was doing after work. When I got no answer, I peeked through the window next to the front door. I was shocked to see the furniture and belongings strewn about. It looks like somebody tore the place apart."

Larry lowered the club, but not his guard. "Your office is up on East Broadway, right?"

"Yes—"

"Yeah, yeah. Anyway, I saw you from my window," Larry said, pointing to his house. "By the time I got to my door, and then over here, you had disappeared."

"Well, I got in my car," the doctor said, pointing toward his vehicle, its driver's side door still slightly ajar. "I was going to call the police, you know, the mess and all. However, Trisha has been telling me that Robert's doing work on the house, so I wasn't sure whether I wanted to cause a fuss. When I first saw you walk up the driveway, I thought you were Robert and I followed you." The doctor glanced at the club still tightly wrapped in Fitzgerald's right hand and said, "I suppose that wasn't the wisest move."

The doctor's stare caused Larry to gaze down. Redirecting his attention on the doctor, he said, "Yeah, you scared me pretty good, too. Look, you've got to understand, it's been pretty crazy around here the last few days...."

෴

A huge grin encompassed Ted Lyons's face. "What the hell were you thinking about? If you wanted to see me, all you had to do was give me a call. What happened?"

Embarrassed, Bobby said, "I was looking in my rearview mirror, and when I looked back, she was right there. That was your *mother*?"

"My one and only."

"Is she all right?"

"She's shook up, but they say she's going to be okay. They're going to keep her overnight for observation, but it doesn't appear to be anything serious."

That's the first bit of good news I've had today, Bobby thought. He wondered where Jill and Jake were.

"My younger sister, Marylou, just had a baby at Brigham & Woman's. That's why my mother was there."

"Jesus, Ted, I'm so sorry. What should I do?"

"You're kidding right? Get your ass back in the cell," Lyons said. His grin disappeared, and then reappeared just as quickly. "Just kidding. I pulled a few strings and called to have them bring the car back. It should be outside by now. Come on."

Lyons escorted Bobby out of the holding area. He stopped for a word with the previously impenetrable desk sergeant in the lobby. "I'm taking this one home with me, Sarge. If any reporters start nosing around, just tell them I'm dishing out some maternal justice."

The desk sergeant's surprise paled in comparison to the incredulous looks plastered on the faces of Jill and Jake.

෨෩

"This woman needs to go to a hospital immediately."

Mickey approached Dr. McGlinty. "Listen, you fucking moron, I don't know how many ways I can explain this to you. She *can't* go to a hospital. She *ain't* going to a hospital. This is *why* you're here. Now, get the fuck to work."

When Willie relieved the doctor of his cell phone, wallet, and cash, it dawned on McGlinty that he might not get out of there alive, or, at the very least, any time soon.

Willie had removed the handcuffs from Trisha's wrists prior to his arrival in the room. Despite that, the doctor immediately diagnosed the woman's severely chafed wrists the result of some type of restraint mechanism.

McGlinty felt powerless. He stepped out of the room and offered Mickey some advice. "I don't know what's going on here, and I don't *need* to know what's going on here, but you've got to listen to me. I'm limited in what I can do." He pointed his right index finger in Trisha's direction. "That woman needs *serious* medical attention. She needs things that only emergency rooms are equipped to provide."

Mickey gave the doctor an unbelieving glare. The screaming obviously hadn't worked. As Mickey walked in his direction, he tried a more muted tone, "Which part of what I said didn't you understand?"

McGlinty continued reasoning with Mickey, purposely emphasizing Trisha's grave condition. "This woman could *die* if she isn't provided the proper treatment."

❧

Trisha had been lapsing in and out of consciousness for the past few hours.

The animated voices outside the half-open door increased her level of awareness. *Did he say I could die if I'm not taken to a hospital? Who is that talking?*

The argument raged on.

Mickey amplified his rebuttal. "I don't know what I've got to say to make this completely clear in that thick fucking head of yours doc, but the only person going to a hospital is you. No, check that, you ain't going to a hospital, you're going to the fucking city morgue in a body bag. You hear what I'm saying? What's it going to be? You want to be a *doctor* or a fucking *victim*?"

Willie edged in behind McGlinty.

The doctor decided to buy some time. He walked into Trisha's room, clicked open his large medical bag, and began sorting through the material. *Maybe he could do something,* he reasoned, pulling several instruments from his bag. "I'm going to need some space to lay this stuff out."

Willie obliged. He swatted several objects from a nearby night table and dragged it over to McGlinty.

With the required deference, McGlinty said to Willie, "I'm going to need some space. It's not going to do you or her any good to be breathing down my neck."

"Did you hear what my boy said, doc?" Willie asked. "You don't want to end up in a body bag, now do you?"

As Dr. McGlinty went to work on Trisha Barron, he now wondered if either of them would survive.

29

Bobby stood with Ted Lyons in a quiet corner of the hospital lobby. "Should I visit your mother?" Bobby asked.

Lyons shook his head, indicating that was not a good idea. "She's still shook up. They want her to get as much rest as possible. Call me in a couple of days, and I'll arrange something." He pulled a small notebook and a pen from the inside left breast pocket of his suit coat and scribbled something. He ripped the sheet of paper from the notebook and handed it to Bobby. "Here's my cell number. Now remember, I'm trusting that you'll keep this number to yourself. Call me in a few days and we'll set something up."

Bobby stuck the paper into his pants pocket. After taking and exhaling a deep breath, he said, "Ted, I've got a problem, and I might need your help. I'm just not sure I should get into it right now."

"What's the problem?"

Standing fifty feet away, Jill and Jake observed Boston's Police Commissioner clutching Bobby's elbow and turning him back in his direction to continue their conversation.

Was Bobby filling him in on his dilemma?

☙

McGlinty could not extract an intelligible response from Trisha. *Some type of infection is obviously ravaging her.* Taking the requisite initial precautions, he said to Willie, "We're going to need some ice. We have to lower her body temperature."

Willie quickly returned with a plastic bag filled with ice and its top tightly knotted. He handed it to the doctor.

"Do you have any terry-cloth towels? You know … heavy towels?"

Willie hesitated.

McGlinty sensed his reticence. "Willie, you and Mickey want me to help this woman. I can only help her if you are willing to pitch in."

The doctor looked around for Mickey's assistance. He was unaware that Mickey remaining conveniently out of sight was a necessity.

A consciousness Trisha Barron could easily identify him.

ↄ

Larry Fitzgerald slowly pieced the evidence together. *Trisha's apartment is wrecked. So is Bobby's. Trisha's allegedly at home sick, yet he'd walked every inch of the house with Bobby and Jill and he had not seen her. Yet, harkening back to the words of Trisha's boss, "She didn't go to work due to an illness." That was straight from her boss's mouth to his ears. What the hell was going on?*

His brother-in-law Danny was a Boston Police lieutenant and close confidante—some would even say protégé—of the police commissioner. With his heretofore-quiet neighborhood in disarray, it was time to call in some chips.

Larry picked up the phone.

ↄ

The words wafted through Trisha's fever-ravaged brain. Dreamlike, yet simultaneously realistic, she replayed the conversation in her mind.

"Willie, you and Mickey want me to help this woman. I can only help her if you are willing to pitch in." *Who was speaking? Not Willie? Not Mickey? Who were Willie and Mickey?*

In spite of her confusion, the steady rubbing of ice on her forehead, wrists, ankles, knees, and armpits felt wonderful. What was disconcerting—not to mention confusing—was the person doing the rubbing kept calling her Mary, the predictably instantaneous pseudonym her captors chose when McGlinty asked her name.

❧

Bobby broke away from Ted Lyons before returning for additional discussion. He made a beeline for Jill and Jake once the conversation concluded. He looked over each shoulder several times to ensure that he couldn't be overheard. A sheepish grin morphed out of his serious façade. "Do you believe this? The woman I hit was the police commissioner's mother."

"Yeah, we knew," Jake said. "Jerry Watts was one of the cops that responded. Do you know Jerry? He's from Southie."

"No, but luckily I know Ted Lyons. We went to law school together. I mean, what are the chances?"

"Did you tell him what was going on?" Jake asked.

"I told him I was dealing with a problem and there was a possibility that I was going to need his assistance. He gave me his cell phone number," producing the small sheet of paper as verification. "I wanted to talk to you guys first, you know, see what *you* think. I mean, these guys made it clear that if I got the cops involved they would kill my mother."

Without hesitation, Jill said, "I think you should get him involved. What are we going to accomplish? We couldn't even tail them. I mean, we don't have the experience to handle something like this; we have no weapons—"

Jake interrupted Jill, "It's *your* call."

❧

"Hello?" Willie said.

"Mickey?" replied the voice on the other end of Willie's cell phone.

"Who's this?"

Pick Piccorino's first venture with his new cell phone was not going well. "I'm looking for Mickey Carberry. I was given this number—"

"I don't know no Mickey Carberry," Willie said, stealing a furtive glance toward Mickey. "And I still don't know who this is."

In his haste to please his ex-boss, attorney Carl "The Shadow" Bionda had transposed Willie's number with Mickey's when programming the phone.

Pick terminated the call. Enraged, he punched the number in again, convinced he had dialed it wrong.

Mickey reacted instantly when the phone rang again. "Let me answer that," he said, grabbing the phone from Willie.

☙

Jill maneuvered her recently recovered car past a labyrinth of intermittently double-parked vehicles on either side of East Sixth Street. She headed east, through K Street, pulled over to her left, and double-parked in front of Jake's house. *When in Rome ...*

Jake opened the backdoor but remained in the car. "You're going to call me, right Bobby?"

"Look Jake, I'm not going to do anything without you. You've got my word."

"We'll get this squared away." Jake said, slapping Bobby on the shoulder before bounding out of Jill's car.

When Jill reached Hardy Street, she pulled in close to the curb to allow Bobby's exit.

Bobby assumed she was coming in.

Jill had other thoughts. She was looking forward to a hot shower and, more importantly, a change of clothes.

She explained her intentions to Bobby, and he apologized. "I wasn't even thinking, Jill. Look, I don't want this to come out the wrong way, because you've been really helpful, but if you want to bail out now, I totally understand."

"You're not getting rid of me that fast, pal. You know the old saying—in for a penny, in for a pound ... I'm *in,* buster. And you better not sneak off with Jake and leave me behind either. I'm going home to shower, put some comfortable clothes on—maybe a pair of sneakers—then I'll be back. If you guys leave me behind, *I'll* call the cops."

"Do you really think I made the wrong decision not letting Ted Lyons know?"

164

"You can always call him, so I understand your hesitance. Jake was right; it's your call. I should have kept my opinion to myself."

"No, it's important that you tell me what's on your mind. Seriously—"

"Well, right now, grabbing a shower and a change of clothes is the only thing on my mind. I'm going to take care of that, and then I'll be back." She stared at Bobby, wanting a similar commitment to the one he had given Jake.

Bobby threw his left arm across her shoulder blades. "I can't thank you enough." Giving her a hug, he said, "Hurry back, I'm going to need your help," as he climbed out of the Volvo.

His recognition of her role energized Jill as she pulled out of the driveway.

Bobby followed her out to the edge of the sidewalk. He observed the tail end of her vehicle until she turned right and disappeared from his view.

Bobby walked up his front stairs. After he took a quick peek through his mother's first-floor window, he found a note attached to the stainless-steel door handle on his front door. He snapped it off and read it as he fumbled with his keys.

Bobby,

Dr. Wissard was by looking for your mother. He wants you to call him ASAP (says you have his number). I also need to talk to you when you get a chance. Knock on my door or give me a call.

Larry F.

617-555-2344

This is the last thing I need right now, Bobby thought. He glanced over his shoulder to see if his neighbor was observing him before wading through his front door and the stairs.

He wasn't sure what to do once he reached the second floor. His mother's diary caught his eye. It was right where he'd left it after removing it from Jill's grasp the previous evening.

Bobby flopped onto the couch and was pleasantly surprised to find the scent of Jill's hair on the couch's throw pillow. He took a deep whiff before opening the diary. *Better than nothing.*

Once again, Bobby perused his mother's thoughts from a bygone era.

30

"Be careful, we don't want him to see us."

Mickey had no idea they were following him as he jumped in his Jeep. He was on a little side trip to meet an acquaintance and look over a stash of stolen watches. He slowed down at a stop sign at the intersection of Farragut Road and East Broadway, turned left, and drove an additional two-and-a-half blocks. He pulled in behind the vehicle housing his prospective business partner.

The trailing car's occupants watched as Mickey leaped from his car and approached the driver's side window of the other vehicle. They pulled over to avoid detection.

It mattered little. Mickey was oblivious to their presence.

❧

"What have you got?" Mickey asked when the driver opened his door.

"Let's walk," the thief said, heading down a ten-foot wide paved hill without waiting for Mickey's response.

The emergency access road was a boundary between the Joseph Evans Little League field on its left, and South Boston's Murphy ice skating rink on its right.

Mickey's aggravation surfaced as he fell in behind. "Where the fuck are you going? It's too dark down here to see anything. If you want to move these watches, I've got to be able to look them over."

A stealth figure stepped out from behind an adjacent steel cargo container that housed the various South Boston Pop Warner teams' football equipment.

A voice sang out behind Mickey, startling him.

"Don't worry about looking over the watches. You've got bigger problems than that."

Mickey turned and found himself staring down the four-inch barrel of a bead-blasted stainless steel Ruger MK II. That it was purposely equipped with a sealed silencer escaped Mickey's immediate attention.

"Who the fuck are you?" Mickey asked. His usual bravado was noticeably absent. He turned back to face his drug-addicted acquaintance whose squinted eyes represented windows of confusion.

"Yo, what the fuck's going on here?" Mickey asked. He spun back around to face the gun-toting assailant.

"It's over, you piece of shit. There are no watches. This is what you get for dealing with fucking junkies. You're going to die just like him." He fired two bullets into the center of the junkie's chest. The successive blasts drove him back ten feet, leveling him to the ground.

The gunman had convinced the junkie into luring Mickey to this spot with a promise of one hundred dollars, fifty of which he already paid as a show of good faith.

"What's your problem?" Mickey gasped, regretfully mindful that his gun was sitting a short distance away, under the front seat of his Jeep.

"You almost beat my kid and his friend to death on K Street last night. You're a fucking tough guy, right? You don't think twice about shit like that, do you? Well, you're not so fucking tough now, are you?"

Mickey begged for time. "What do I got to do to make this good? I'll pay you whatever you want." His mind temporarily wandered back to the beatings he had administered to the two punks the previous evening.

When Mickey attempted to reach into the right front pocket of his jeans, the gunman pointed the weapon toward the center of his face. "Don't even fucking think about it!"

"Easy, man." Mickey said, removing and raising his hands. "I was meeting this guy to buy some watches. You can have the watches *and* the money I was going to pay him," pointing at his pocket with his right index finger.

"What part of this don't you get, asshole? There *are* no watches. You can get these junkies to do anything for a few bucks." He then gave Mickey the impression that his curiosity was piqued. "How much money were you willing to spend?"

"I've got a couple a grand on me now," Mickey responded quickly. "But I can get more. Whatever it takes."

"Show me the money, nice and slow," said the gunman. He lowered his weapon slightly.

Mickey reached into his pocket slowly. He produced a substantial wad of cash. Nodding at the dead victim on the ground, Mickey said, "I didn't see a fucking thing. I'll never say a word." He then handed the money to the gunman.

"I know you won't say anything, that's the furthest thing from my mind. And, as far as you paying me any more money, this is enough," he said, waving the stash of cash in Mickey's face before jamming it into his pocket. "Now, as far as me giving you a break? Too fucking late. You didn't give my kid a break, and you ain't getting one either—"

Mickey charged the gunman with every fiber of strength he could muster.

The first bullet obliterated the center of Mickey's face.

Mickey's forward momentum left him lying face down in the grass.

The job was quickly finished with two amazingly quiet shots to the back of Mickey's head, and another in the center of his back.

The gunman then pumped a couple of more shots into the upper torso of the junkie, who lay perpendicular to Mickey—face up—about fifteen feet away.

The gunman reached into the junkie's coat pocket. He removed a plastic bag of drugs and some related paraphernalia and tossed it onto the ground near Mickey's body. It would lend credence to a drug deal gone wrong.

His night's work done, Jack Bradshaw tucked the gun in the backside of his pants and walked briskly back up the short hill where his son sat waiting in the car. When he opened the passenger-side door of his car, he was greeted by his son's battered face and blackened eyes.

"Everything okay?" a worried Bryan Bradshaw asked, as he looked his father over for any evidence of a struggle.

"I told you, you've got nothing to worry about. Those two scumbags were in the middle of some type of drug deal with a couple of other guys. I was glad to get out of there, but it was important to address this, the sooner the better. It's a good thing I know Mickey. He said words to the effect that Scott's mouth is what caused the problem. He admitted that even *you* were trying to get him to shut up."

"That's the truth. I told you—"

"Now I'm sure. His story pretty much mirrored yours. Anyway, now there's nothing to worry about as far as *you're* concerned, but I told you before, that kid Scott's nothing but trouble. This shit ends up happening whenever you hang around with people like him. I hope you learned your lesson."

"No doubt."

"Good, because this guy Carberry is still pissed at him, but that's not my problem. If you're smart, it won't be *yours* either.

"I hear you. I'm done with him."

"Good. Listen, swing by the house and jump out. I've got to run a couple of errands."

Errand number one, which he just accomplished, was disassociating his son from his dirt bag friend. Jack Bradshaw's second errand was a return to the Pleasure Bay area and a brisk walk out the manmade causeway toward Castle Island. He reached the Sugar Bowl, a circular precast structure and popular fishing area approximately halfway out the causeway. After looking around to ensure he was alone, he tossed the weapon into the ocean.

His third errand was the disposal of the latex gloves he had worn during his mission. He deposited them in a dumpster he had located earlier in the day behind a bustling new pizza shop on West Broadway. They were identical to those used by the deli counter employees during food preparation.

After a cursory investigation, Boston Police investigators would categorize the death of Mickey Carberry and the other low-life as little more than addition by subtraction.

ↀ

Jake Carberry was able to calm his wife after proving his absolute sobriety. He proceeded to fill her in on the abject madness he, Bobby, and Jill had experienced.

Barbie Carberry sat in amazement. She pieced things together with a series of rapid-fire questions that culminated in what was more an incredulous statement than a question: "Mickey *kidnapped* his friend's mother."

Jake nodded. "Listen, Barb, you can't tell anybody what I'm telling you."

"Tell me again about following them in the car."

Jake knew this informal inquisition would never end. He decided to visit his mother at a local nursing home. "I've got to run up the Manor and see my mother."

"Whoa, whoa, I have more questions to ask."

"What do you think this is, *CSI?*" Jake said with a laugh. "We'll talk about it when I get back. I've got to run up and see my mother. I never made it up there last night because I was out looking for Mickey."

Jake grabbed his coat off the hallway hook and headed for the door.

ↀ

Jill's mind began clearing the moment the hot water contacted her body. She might have remained in the shower forever if her phone hadn't rang.

She didn't want to miss a call from Bobby, so she jumped out, barely covering herself with a towel as she headed for the phone in her living room. Her lack of adequate cover was compounded by the fact that various house lights were on and she had never lowered her window shades in her haste to cleanse herself.

She hoisted the phone to her ear, but waged a losing battle in keeping her taut and well-proportioned body covered by the towel. Tethered to the phone

171

line, she crouched down like a baseball catcher and used her couch as a shield to avoid detection by any nosy neighbors.

"Hello?"

"Jill?

"Yeah."

"Mickey's dead."

ↄ

Jake Carberry exited the Marian Manor elevator on 5-East. He mouthed hellos to the familiar crew assembled behind the nurses' station before continuing on to his mother's room.

A wide smile spread across Stella Carberry's face as soon as he entered.

He bent over for the inevitable hugs and kisses that accompanied his every visit. "How you doing, Mom?"

"I'm doing great, love. They're spoiling me rotten. How about you, how are you doing?"

Jake's almost daily trips to the Manor were a virtual overlay of each other: Same questions, same answers, and same familiar faces walking up and down the sky-blue and white vinyl tiled corridor.

Thirty minutes later, Jake encountered two of his brothers, Jimmy and Eddie, and his sister Eileen as he exited his mother's room.

The three of them had just gotten off the elevator. The somber looks affixed to their respective faces were an ominous sign that a visit to their beloved mother was not on their agenda.

ↄ

Jill got dressed and left her Marina Bay condominium almost as quickly as she had arrived.

Bobby had asked her to meet him back at his house.

She was mentally reconciling the shocking news as she headed there. *It was only a few hours earlier when Mickey Carberry had been leering at her as he and his sidekick led the guy out of the building in Brookline. Now he was dead?*

172

Jill arrived at Hardy Street. With parking at a premium, she blocked in Bobby's Durango.

Bobby was waiting at the door. "Can you believe this?" he asked, pecking Jill on her left cheek and giving her an abbreviated hug.

"He's *really* dead? I mean—"

"It's on the radio. He's dead."

"Is that how you found out? The *radio?*"

"Jake called me. He's actually coming here. He said there's something he wants to talk to me about."

Jill pointed at the diary dangling from his hand. "Have you been catching up on your reading?"

"Not really. Like I was saying earlier, I feel kind of creepy reading it. Do you know what I mean? I feel like I'm violating my mother's privacy."

"How recent is it? Is there anything in there that could shed some light on what happened? You know, *why* they kidnapped her?"

"I actually haven't read too much. I've been flipping through it, but it ends years ago. She ran out of pages, at least in this one. Maybe there's another edition, you know, a sequel." He laughed, then answered Jill's original question. "We already know *why* they kidnapped her."

"Just a thought."

Bobby handed her the diary. "Here, you figure it out. You hungry?"

"What have you got in mind?"

"I don't know. Something light. I'm not too hungry, but I should probably eat something. How about you, what are you in the mood for?"

"Surprise me," Jill said, entering the still messy living room and flopping on Bobby's couch with his mother's diary clutched in her hand.

Jill opened it. Once again, she began reading passages penned by the once young mother of a man she was rapidly falling for.

⌘

173

Jimmy Carberry guided Jake into a small common area of Marian Manor's East Building, adjacent to the fifth floor elevator bank.

Their brother and sister followed, forming a huddle around Jake.

Jimmy whispered, "I just got a call from a cop friend of mine, Tommy Nolan. They found Mickey shot to death down Marine Park, you know, behind the rink. Him and another guy, I didn't recognize the other name. Ricky MacDonald?"

"*McDonough*," Eileen corrected him.

"McDonough, McDonough, yeah. Ever hear of him?"

Jake shook his head. "I tried not to get too close to any of Mickey's friends unless they were iron workers."

Nodding, Jimmy said, "I hear that. Should we go in and tell Ma now, or should we wait?"

A bitter and seething Eddie Carberry mumbled under his breath before piping in, "He never visited Mom unless he needed something."

Jake regained control. He directed a bit of anger at Eddie to make a larger point to the group. "Look, first of all, this is our *brother* we're talking about and somebody killed him! That's enough of that noise!"

Eddie didn't dare rebut his older brother.

Jake then alternated his gaze among the three of them. "We're in Southie. We all know the networking never stops. It's only a matter of time before someone sticks their head in Ma's room to offer their condolences. Think about it."

The trio acknowledged Jake's thought in various manners.

"Plus, it's going to be in the newspaper. We're talking about two murders in Marine Park. We've *got* to tell her; the sooner the better." Jake paused, and then asked, "Has anybody got a phone I can use?"

Eddie handed his cell phone to Jake.

"Take a walk with me, Eddie," Jake said, pulling out a slip of paper and walking out next to the elevator doors. He handed the phone back to his brother. "I don't know how to use these things. Can you dial this number for me?"

Looking at the piece of paper, Jake recited Bobby's number as Eddie punched it into his phone. He then handed his phone to Jake.

Jake apprised Bobby of Mickey's death. He then said, "Look, I'd like to swing by your house and see you as soon as possible. I have something I want to discuss, and I don't want to do it over the phone."

A shocked and confused Bobby readily agreed.

Jake handed the phone back to Eddie, took a deep breath, and marched down the hall.

His siblings fell in behind.

They turned right and entered their mother's room.

☙

Jill was profoundly moved by the eloquence which Bobby's mother detailed her early life. Moreover, she remained impressed with her exquisite handwriting— kudos to the Sisters of Saint Joseph and the Palmer Method.

At a certain juncture, however, what started as little more than an adolescent rant took a sudden and wildly unexpected turn. Its graphic nature forced Jill to the boundaries of voyeurism.

Having worked her way through the winter of 1969, Jill originally chuckled at various samplings of Trisha's boy-crazy tendencies. She now understood why Bobby felt so uncomfortable in reading his mother's thoughts. Nonetheless, Jill persevered and she was now at the point where Trisha Barron introduced Jill—albeit inadvertently—to a '... gorgeous guy named Tad....'

Years of cover-ups, half-truths, hidden secrets, revisionist history, and a healthy dose of denial collided; splintered by the weight of a handwritten account of what *really* transpired on May 10, 1970.

31

The content of Trisha's diary shocked Jill.

A seemed adolescent crush quickly spun into something far more insidious. Sunday, May 10, 1970, may have started like most other days in Trisha Barron's universe, but…

> … Everyone was celebrating the Bruins winning the Stanley Cup and I was stuck in work. It was all worthwhile when this gorgeous guy named Tad came into the store around nine to buy something. How was I to know that this gorgeous guy was a rapist????….

She did not highlight the word *rapist*. It was not underlined, nor bolded. Arguably, the four question marks following it could have been the cause, but whatever the reason, the word *rapist* ingrained itself in Jill's eyes. She read on:

> …He was in the PBL, with some friends (at least that's what he said), and he returned there after flirting with me for about a half-hour. When I was leaving work, he offered me a ride. <u>Whatever possessed me to get in his car</u>? He was so cute I simply couldn't resist the temptation and then I couldn't get out! It was like a movie; he was really drunk

> *and never stopped the car until we got out*
> *past the MDC police station. By then it was*
> *too late. When I grabbed the steering wheel*
> *to keep him from heading out Morrissey*
> *Boulevard he drove into Columbia Point....*

It raged on. Trisha chronicled the entire ordeal. The assault ... the rape ... the kick to Tad's face ... and her fears—real and imagined—available to anyone with access to the diary.

Jill found it improbable that Bobby had gotten this far into its content. It detailed the heroic role of Tommy Carr getting her home safely and the juxtaposition of her parents' lingering suspicion of Carr's potential involvement in her pregnancy.

As a professional journalist, Jill found Trisha's detailed explanation of her abject loneliness at the home for unwed mothers at Saint Margaret's Hospital particularly moving.

She read of the subsequent cover-up, vis-à-vis keeping "Tad" anonymous when, in fact, Trisha had recognized him through a newspaper story related to his college hockey exploits.

Finally, she read of the birth of Robert Gordon Barron—named, not for a boyfriend who succumbed to the war in Vietnam; but after Boston Bruins sensation and, irony of ironies, the legend of May 10, 1970—Robert Gordon *"Bobby"* Orr.

Jill couldn't help but wonder: *Did Bobby know he was the progeny of this ill-fated encounter?* She doubted he knew as she headed for the kitchen; unsure of the appropriate way—or, for that matter, if there *was* an appropriate way—to broach such a sensitive subject.

இ

Tears flowed down Stella Carberry's face. Her "kids"—albeit full grown adults—doted over her, showering her with hugs and kisses, condolences, Kleenex, and personal remembrances of her youngest son.

Jake hid his internal fury. He knew that Mickey's final act—save for dying alongside some junkie—was kidnapping the mother of his lifelong friend. *I've got to get over Bobby's house and touch base with him,* he thought. Jake grabbed his brother Jimmy's arm and whispered, "I've got to talk to you outside."

When they were safely out of anyone's earshot, Jimmy asked, "What's up?"

"I've got to go meet someone. It's connected to Mickey. Can you hold down the fort here?"

"Yeah."

"Okay. I'll meet you tomorrow morning at O'Brien's to make the funeral arrangements. Pick a time and spread the word. Oh yeah, and make sure you let Billy, Joey, Eric, and Katie know," referring to their remaining siblings. "Whoever wants to be there can just meet us."

Jimmy nodded.

"Okay? I'll call Jackie to let him know to expect a call from you. Just call my house and let me know what time we're going to meet once you've touched bases with everyone."

"No problem, I'll call you later. Hey, one other thing. After Tommy Nolan called me, I took a ride down to where it happened, you know, down behind the rink. Mickey's car was parked up above the Little League field on Farragut Road. Its doors were unlocked, so I peeked inside to see if anything of value might be stolen. One of the few things worth taking was this."

He held up Mickey's cell phone.

Jake stared at his brother, unsure of where the conversation was heading.

Jimmy continued, "Look, I know you hate these things, but I was thinking maybe you should hang on to it for the time being so we can reach you if we need to."

Jimmy handed Jake the phone and a slip of paper with the phone's number. "Just for a few days."

Jake stared at the piece of paper, then back at his brother, before slipping the paper and phone into his coat pocket. He headed for the elevator.

"Whoa, there's one other thing before you go," Jimmy said.

Jimmy coaxed Jake in the direction of a vacant sitting room adjacent to the nurses' station. He reached into the pouch of his hooded sweatshirt and looked around nervously before pulling out a white plastic bag and removing its content. Turning his back to the door, he pulled the item out of the bag. "I found this under the front seat of Mickey's car."

Jake stared at the gun in his brother's hand.

"It's a forty-five. He probably should have taken it with him when he left the car," Jimmy said before stuffing it back into the bag.

"Maybe he was forced out of the car," Jake responded.

Jimmy held the bag out and Jake accepted it. After everything he had experienced today, he was far more comfortable with the gun than the cell phone. He headed toward the elevator, intent on meeting with Bobby. He had to assure himself that Bobby had not been part of any plan to kill Mickey.

In this particular respect, Southie was no different from most areas around the country. Blood usually proved to be thicker than water.

32

Jill walked into the kitchen, startling Bobby.

Too busy in front of his grill to notice her entrance, his body went rigid. "What are you trying to give me a heart attack?"

"I couldn't resist the smell any longer. What are you making?"

"You haven't eaten until you've had a world famous Bobby Barron Panini."

"If it tastes as good as it smells it should be 'world famous.'"

Jill sat at his kitchen counter and began wrapping up the left over cold cuts and cheese. "I know I asked you before, but just how much of the diary did you read?"

Bobby was too preoccupied to turn around. "Why, did you find something good?"

"Depends. Can I ask you a few questions?"

The abrupt change in her demeanor gave Bobby pause. He turned to face her. "What's the matter?"

"I don't know where to start. That's why I need to ask you some questions. It may be nothing, yet it could be earth shattering. I guess it depends on your answers."

❧

"Look, Pick, I've been giving this a lot of thought, and I just don't feel comfortable. I just want to finish my time and get out."

Tim Dunlap felt prepared for the vitriol that would undoubtedly follow. He totally underestimated Pick's reaction.

They were meeting in a heretofore-unrecognizable area of Riverfork.

Clearly off-limits to prisoners, Pick was sitting in a chair that resembled a royal throne. Wrapped in crimson red velour with shiny gold beading, the back legs of the chair rose almost six feet from the floor, where they were finished with opulent gold medallions. The legs were connected two-thirds of the way to the top by a horizontal support that held an intricately detailed engraved gold crown. When someone sat on the throne, the crown seemed affixed to his or her head if viewed from a certain perspective.

That was exactly how it looked to Tim Dunlap.

Shiny gold tassels hung from the chair's thickly padded arms. A sparkling gold accent stripe lined its periphery, enhancing its three-dimensional appearance.

An apoplectic Pick leaped from the throne. "You just want to finish your time and get out, huh? I spent all this time putting the wheels in motion to get this thing going and now you want out?"

"When I get out, I'll help you. I just don't want to do anything in the meantime to jeopardize my getting out."

"You fucking piece of shit." Pick strode toward the far corner of the room and ripped open a bejeweled trunk. It resembled a treasure chest, and its intricate detailing closely resembled that of the royal throne.

Why would a prison house a throne and a treasure chest? Christ, is there anything this guy can't access?

Pick reversed direction, moving quickly toward Dunlap. He was clutching a sword reminiscent of the weapon of choice in the old pirate movies Dunlap had so enjoyed in his youth. More disconcerting, however, was that the sword-wielding assailant was no longer Pick Piccorino, but Blackbeard the Pirate.

Blackbeard's intended victim screamed.

A sweat-soaked Dunlap snapped upright, smashing his head on the solid aluminum frame on the underside of the cell's top bunk.

"What the fuck?" yelled his cellmate, who leaped to the floor from above, spun around, and backed toward the cell door. He never took his eyes off Dunlap.

Cell #24 of Building H-C of the Riverfork Institute of Correction was home to two completely confused individuals.

The only one more confused than Tim Dunlap's cellmate was Tim Dunlap. His recurring dream of pending doom was becoming more and more lifelike with each day of Pick Piccorino's involvement in his affairs.

৩

"Earth shattering, huh?" Bobby said. "Sounds pretty heavy. Let's have it."

Jill took a deep breath. "Tell me about your father."

"Never had one," Bobby said, before reconsidering the biological impossibility of such a statement. "Let me rephrase that. I never *knew* my dad. He died in Vietnam."

Bobby recited—chapter and verse—straight from his mother's playbook. He regaled Jill with the story of a young Bobby Gordon, and his tragic death alongside his sergeant at the Battle of the Rock.

He doesn't know the truth, Jill thought.

She doesn't need to know the truth, Bobby thought.

Bobby's doorbell rang.

"Saved by the bell," Bobby said, heading for the door.

An agitated Jake Carberry stood in the doorway.

৩

Willie Marcus was overburdened.

Dr. McGlinty was slowly bringing Trisha around, but Willie's unwillingness to embrace or even consider his logic had him stymied.

He explained the situation again. "Between the ice, the cold cloths, and an introduction of some basic antibiotics I happened to have with me, she's *temporarily* stabilized. Absent my introducing a more powerful medicine,

182

however, she will slip back where she was and eventually her condition will worsen from there. What do you want to do?"

"About what?"

This guy's as dumb as a box of rocks. With limited options, McGlinty kept his opinion to himself and forged ahead. "About what I just said. Can you drive me to a drug store to get the proper medication?"

"I can't do it unless Mickey says it's okay. He was supposed to be back by now."

Sammy had driven Mickey back to Southie a few hours earlier to take care of some business.

Willie never imagined they would be gone this long.

"Can you call him?"

"I've been calling him for the past hour. I keep getting his voicemail."

Exasperated, McGlinty said, "Willie, if we wait for Mickey and he doesn't come back soon, we'll be right back where we started. All the work we have done will be for naught."

"*Not* what?"

McGlinty shook his head in despair.

"Let me try him one more time. If I don't get him we'll hit a drug store." Pulling out his cell phone, Willie dialed Mickey again.

Mickey Carberry's bullet-ridden corpse would not be answering—never mind returning—any phone calls.

༄

"I need to talk to you," Jake said.

"Sure," Bobby said, unsure how to react to Jake's hostile attitude. He climbed the stairs.

Jake was right on his heels.

When Jake saw Jill he whispered, "*Alone!* I need to see you alone."

Jill sensed the obvious uneasiness and said, "I'm going to run out and grab some soda."

The moment Jill departed, Jake said, "Like I told you, Mickey's dead. They found him down behind Murphy rink. He was shot to death."

Bobby's legal skills kicked in. The other shoe—and the purpose for this trip—was about to fall. He maintained his silence.

"Here's what I've got to know Bobby. Did you have anything to do with this?"

"Are you *serious?* I mean, Jake, I would never—"

"You and I know the whole story, Bobby. What I've got to know—right now, no bullshit—is did *you* have anything to do with killing Mickey?"

Jake's allegation rocked Bobby. "Absolutely not. When Jill and I dropped you off, we came straight here. Jill went home to clean up and pick up a few things. I was poking around the house, you know, I made a few calls—"

"So you were alone?"

"I was alone, but I *never* left the house." Bobby snatched his cordless phone from its base. He began pressing buttons. He showed Jake the screen and said, "Here, you can see the calls I made, and what time I made them. Do they know what time Mickey was shot?"

"All I know is that my brother's dead."

"And all I know is my *mother's* still missing," Bobby reminded him with just enough cynicism in his voice to drive his point home.

❧

"You've got to be kidding me." Jill fixated on Jake as he filled her and Bobby in on the details of Mickey's murder.

The two "world famous" Panini sandwiches Bobby had carefully prepared and cut into quarters sat untouched atop his kitchen's granite center island. The recently purchased bottles of soda sat unopened next to them.

"How did you find out?" Bobby asked, still shaken and wary of Jake's earlier insinuations.

"I was visiting my mother up Marian Manor. Two of my brothers and my sister Eileen showed up to tell me."

"Does your mother know?" Jill asked.

"We talked it over and decided we had to tell her. You know you can't keep a secret like this in Southie. We were afraid she would receive condolences from someone who assumed she knew."

Both Jill and Jake nodded.

"What do we do now?" Jake asked.

"I understand if you need to back out," Bobby said. "I know you've got a full plate."

"What did I tell you earlier? I'm *in*. My brother made a mess and I'm not walking away until we straighten it out. We need to find that guy we saw him with on Broadway. Once we ID him—"

"Yeah, he's the key to the puzzle at this point," Bobby agreed, finishing Jake's thought.

"But, where do we start?" Jill asked.

"What about up at King's Tavern?" Bobby said.

"That's as good a spot as any," Jake replied.

ɕ

"Jake! What the hell are you doing here?" asked a large young man when the trio entered King's Tavern.

Kevin Maguire was an apprentice ironworker on Jake's job, but he moonlighted as a bar-back, or what Jake's generation called a bouncer.

"You work here?"

"Yeah, Doreen and I are trying buy a condo, but I'm not going to swing it working broken time."

"Yeah, it gets tough this time of year. Listen. Let me ask you a question. You know my brother Mickey, right?"

"Sure. He's in here all the time. I'm surprised he's not in here now."

Jake glanced around the half-empty bar. He guided Maguire over to a vacant stool in the corner.

"Kevin, they found Mickey shot to death behind the rink down Marine Park a few hours ago."

Maguire's eyes bulged open. "You've got to be shitting me? They know who did it?"

"No. That's why I'm here. Tell me something. I was here earlier today and Mickey was with this other guy. Tall, thin, bushy eyebrows? Beige coat. Kind of a dirty-looking bastard. You know him?"

"Yeah, he comes in once in a while, always with Mickey, or to meet Mickey. Never says much—"

"Is there anyone here who might know him?"

"Let me ask around." Maguire said, slipping off his stool.

"Whoa, whoa, come here," Jake said. "Don't say anything to anyone about Mickey. I need you to wait until the word hits the street, okay? I'm counting on you to keep this quiet."

"You got my word, Jake. I won't say a thing."

"Good. In the meantime, see what you can find out."

Maguire headed toward the other end of the establishment.

☙

Dr. McGlinty urged Willie once again. "We can't wait. Her body is going to quickly immunize itself against these antibiotics. If we don't introduce something more powerful, we'll be right back where we started. We have to go fill a prescription."

A defiant glare emanated from Willie's eyes. "How many times you going to tell me?"

A set of headlights suddenly lit up the kitchen. Willie bounded out of his chair to the window, hoping Mickey was back to take charge and get McGlinty off his back.

Unfortunately, it was just Sammy.

Willie headed to the door as Sammy approached the stairs.

Willie's rapid-fire questions rattled him. "Where the fuck is Mickey, dude? We need him back here now!"

"What do I look like, his fucking babysitter."

"Don't be a fucking wiseass. He left with you. Where did you drop him off?"

"At his house."

"That's it? You haven't seen him since?"

"He told me to pick him back up there, but he never showed up."

"Where were you supposed to meet him?"

"I just told you, at his house."

"You have to go find him. Don't come back without him."

Sammy shrugged his shoulders and nonchalantly turned back toward his car.

"Are you hearing me? Hurry up!" Willie screamed.

33

Jake stood up. He stretched his arms above his head and gave an exaggerated grunt. "I've got to get going. We're making funeral arrangements at O'Brien's in the morning."

The thought of Mickey's betrayal and subsequent demise was occupying too much real estate in Bobby's head.

A high-pitched tone rang out as Bobby walked Jake toward the stairs.

Jake stared at Bobby, and then Jill, figuring one of their cell phones was ringing.

The duo stared back at him, as the ring was obviously coming from Jake's direction.

Silence followed the three loud rings.

Jake finally realized what was happening and retrieved Mickey's cell phone from his pocket. He nearly dropped it when it vibrated in his hand. A more subdued beep then emitted from the unit.

He looked at Bobby and Jill for guidance. "I forgot. This was Mickey's phone. My brother Jimmy found it in Mickey's car. He thought I should hang on to it for a couple of days, but what the hell am I going to do with it? I don't even know how to answer it."

"It's pretty simple. Just push the green button—"

Bobby cut Jill short. "Are you *kidding* me? We've got to check the messages."

"All we have to do is hit redial and we can speak with anyone who has phoned him," Jill added, quickly catching on to Bobby's thoughts.

"Better than that. We can check the messages and cherry-pick who we call back. Everyone Mickey has spoken with will have their number stored in here." Bobby manipulated the buttons as he walked back into the kitchen. He reached into a cabinet and produced a pad of paper and a pen. He placed them on the table and said, "Let me see if I can access his voicemail first," pushing a series of buttons.

"Shit, we need his password." Bobby said, pulling the phone from his ear. He stared at the screen. "Here take these numbers down, Jill. Six one seven, five five five, nine eight five seven." Turning to Jake, he asked, "Do you know if Mickey had any lucky numbers? Probably four digits."

"No idea. Sorry."

"Okay, here's the next one, Jill. Five oh eight, five oh nine—"

The phone rang again.

Time was of the essence. Unable to get into Mickey's voicemail, this might be the best chance to unravel his mother's location, not to mention the identity of her captors. Bobby held the ringing phone out toward Jake

"Answer it. Keep it simple. Let *them* do the talking."

Jake reacted as if Bobby was handing him a bomb. He refused to accept it.

The phone continued ringing.

Bobby took a deep breath. He pushed the green button, accepting the call on behalf of the late Mickey Carberry.

∽

"Dude, what the fuck is wrong with you?" Tim Dunlap's cellmate asked.

"Sorry, Paulie." Dunlap was soaked in sweat. His recurring dream left him shaken.

"Man, you've got to get down and see the doc, get yourself some kind of sleeping pills. This is getting worse."

"Yeah, you're right. I've got to do something, but it's not seeing the doctor. I've got to go over his head. I need to see the man."

Dunlap's cellmate nodded. He knew their wily warden "Wild" Bill Harvey wasn't 'the man' he was talking about.

℘

Jill and Jake stared as Bobby morphed into Mickey Carberry.

"Yeah," he mumbled.

"Mickey?"

"Yeah."

"Mickey, it's Pick. What's going on with that broad? Shadow says she's fucked up. What's going on?"

Bobby's classic Boston accent, coupled with his unmistakable South Boston dialect, convinced Pick that he was speaking to Mickey Carberry.

Bobby had no way of knowing that, however, and he couldn't take a chance. He baby-stepped his way along, mumbling, "What did he tell you?"

Pick's voice rose in proportion to his frustration. "I just told you, he said, 'The broad is fucked up. Shitting, puking, unconscious,' you know, fucking out of it."

He's talking about my mother, Bobby thought. He removed the phone from his ear and motioned to Jill, mimicking the act of writing and pointing to the pad of paper and pen on the table.

Jill positioned the pad of paper and pen in front of Bobby.

"Is that doctor still there?" Pick asked.

"Who?"

"Mickey, I ain't got time to play little-kid games. What the fuck is going on?"

"Where do you want to start?"

This was not what Pick wanted to hear. He squeezed the phone tight. Their inability and utter incompetence in implementing such a simple

190

plan stupefied the longtime gangster. "How about at the *beginning?* Yeah, that sounds good," Pick said, cynically agreeing with his own assessment so wholeheartedly that he repeated himself. "Yeah, let's start at the fucking beginning.

Bobby began taking notes.

"You fucking morons took a simple job and made a mess out of it. *Willie* picks up the broad and she gets sick. *You* get some doctor involved, which simply creates another eyewitness. You found nothing in her house. Your *sidekick* gets chased out of the house like a fucking coward when I sent him back there to straighten out that prick Barron. And now you've got the balls to ask me where do I want to start? You've got to be shitting me?"

"We'll get it straightened out," Bobby promised.

"Are you in Dorchester now?"

As he developed a list of ostensible clues, a preoccupied Bobby missed Pick's question. "What?"

"Are you at the house in Dorchester?"

"No—" Bobby answered, scribbling as Pick went off on him again.

"Then who the fuck is watching Barron's mother? Is the doctor still there? Jesus Christ, what the fuck is going on here?"

Unsure of the answers and overwhelmed by the reference to his surname, Bobby needed time to evaluate the situation. "You're starting to break up … I think I'm going to lose you." Moving the phone away from his mouth, he repeated, "I think I'm losing you."

Bobby terminated the call and handed Mickey's phone back to Jake.

ↄ

"Who was it?" Jake asked,

"All he said was 'it's Pick.' You think—"

"Pick Piccorino," Jake answered.

"He's that gangster, right?" Jill asked.

191

Jake nodded. "He's originally from the South End. He picked up a lot of friends and took over a lot of business in Southie when Whitey Bulger took off."

Even Jill knew the history of that well documented and sordid story: James J. "Whitey" Bulger had ruled South Boston's underworld with an iron hand for decades. Nothing happened in Southie without his sanction and the attachment of his unilaterally administered street tariffs. Bulger proved especially adept at maneuvering and manipulating diverse segments of society. Providing law enforcement agents with information on fellow criminals—while simultaneously profiting from relationships with the same mob factions he was exposing—was one tangible example of the legitimacy of his genius.

Eventually, his carefully crafted house of cards imploded and Whitey Bulger—under the pseudonym Thomas Baxter—slipped out of Boston with his girlfriend Catherine Grieg on the evening of December 23, 1994.

Pick Piccorino subsequently enhanced his foothold into Southie's lucrative underworld activities in the ensuing years until he became the latest victim of the far-reaching tentacles of the law.

ↁ

"Did you know this Bulger guy?" Jill asked, alternating her glance from Jake to Bobby.

"I didn't," Jake said, "but I know Mickey did. I've seen them together before."

"Yeah, he definitely knew him," Bobby said with a nod.

"What else did he say?" Jill asked, "You were on the phone for quite awhile."

Bobby looked at the contemporaneous notes in his lap. "He asked, what was up with the broad? Said something about Shadow; something about a doctor." Bobby looked at the notes. "He said something about Dorchester." After additional reflection Bobby said, "He said that the broad was sick, you know, throwing up, the whole bit. He got really upset when I didn't give him the answers he wanted."

"Anything else?" Jill asked.

192

Bobby re-created Pick's words in his head. "He was just really pissed off. I don't know." Looking at the notes again, he said, "Wait, he asked me if I was in Dorchester?"

Jake peeked at the notes over Bobby's shoulder. "Who's Willie?"

"Yeah, yeah, he said, 'ever since Willie picked the broad up;' that's my mother, right? 'Ever since Willie picked the broad up, things were going wrong.' He was upset that some 'doctor' was involved. He said he was 'just another eyewitness who could identify people.'"

Jill gasped as it all sunk in. "That has to be the two guys we saw with Mickey over in Brookline. That was a doctor's office—well, a bunch of doctors—and Willie has to be the guy that was with Mickey; and the guy with the briefcase in the suit must be the doctor."

"Willie's the same guy I saw hassling your mother out Harbor Point." Jake said.

"And then on Broadway," Bobby added.

Mickey's cell phone rang again.

☙

Pick grabbed Dunlap and led him to a private area of the prison. His conversation with "Mickey" disturbed him. He placed a hand on each of Dunlap's shoulders. In a solemn whisper, he said, "Look, there's been a little development. Once I get you out, I'm going to give you a list of people to shoot. I want you to take care of that immediately. Now, I'm talking *immediately*. Start at the top of the list and work your way down."

He paused, detecting the confusion in Dunlap's eyes. He then continued the enjoyable proceedings. "Just so we're crystal clear here; I'm talking about doing this *before* you even begin working on getting my case tossed."

Dunlap continued to stare blankly at Pick.

Pick burst out laughing. He released Dunlap's shoulders and said, "I'm just fucking with you. I've got to vent a little. I'm telling you, I've got to have some of the dumbest fucking people in the world working for me. Of course, what's that say about *me*? I'm in here and they are out there. I'm telling you, they're too stupid to get arrested."

Dunlap smiled at the juxtaposition of Pick's incongruous conclusion.

Though insignificant, his smile empowered Pick, who raised his rant several decibels. "You know the old saying that truth is stranger than fiction, because the truth has to make sense? That's my crew. They defy logic. The cops can't catch them because they never consider the possibility of such illogical behavior. You give them the simplest of tasks and they can't get it done. But, not to worry. We're going to get you out of here."

"Listen, Pick—"

Pick suddenly jumped and reached into his pants' pocket. He produced a cell phone and immediately eyeballed the only guard in the area, giving him gave a quick nod with his head as he pointed at the phone.

The guard winked before sauntering off in the opposite direction.

"Stand right where you are and just act like I'm talking to you," Pick whispered. He cocked his head slightly and placed the phone over his right ear.

⁋

Jake handed the phone back to Bobby.

Bobby pushed the green button to accept the call and mumbled, "Yeah?"

"Mickey?"

"Yeah."

"It's Willie, man, where are you?"

"Where are *you*?" Bobby mumbled, thinking *Willie?* He prepared to take more notes.

"I'm in Dorchester, where else would I be? You coming back? I just sent Sammy to find you. He said you were supposed to meet him at your house and you never showed. We need to take the doctor to a drugstore to fill some 'scripts and I didn't want to do it without your okay. Doc says she'll end up back where she was if he don't get some stronger medicine. What do you want to do?"

Combining his best Mickey Carberry impersonation with some quick thinking, Bobby said, "Put the doctor on the phone."

⁂

"Hello."

"Doctor, do not overreact," Bobby warned, "This is *not* Mickey Carberry. I need to ask you some questions. *Yes* or *no* answers, that's it. Do *not* let that other guy hear what I'm saying under *any* circumstances. Hang up if you have to. It's vital that you give me as much information as possible. Now, are you a medical doctor?"

"Yes."

"Are you being held against your will?"

"Yes."

"Is your office in Brookline?"

"Yes."

"Are you treating a woman about fifty years old?"

"Yes."

The rigidness of the doctor's answers made Bobby uncomfortable. He slightly altered his instructions. "Listen, you've got to loosen up a little. Say, 'Okay Mickey.' Act like you know who I am and you understand everything I'm saying; you know, like we're making a plan and you're talking to a guy named Mickey."

"Okay, Mickey."

"Good. Is the woman okay? Tell me as much as you can without Willie getting suspicious."

"She's got a serious infection, but we've stabilized it. We must purchase stronger antibiotics to keep her from slipping back."

"Doctor, can you think of a way to describe where you are without Willie figuring out what you're doing?"

"I'm not sure, hold on."

Turning to Willie, McGlinty said, "Mickey wants to know what drugstore we're going to use. I don't know where we are. What's the name of this street?

I have a digest in my bag that lists all of the drugstores in Massachusetts. If you give me the address—"

Brilliant, thought Bobby from the other end of the phone. His exuberance was short-lived, however, as he heard Willie cut in, "Give me the fucking phone. What do you think, I'm stupid? I know where the nearest drugstore is."

"Willie wants to talk to you, Mickey. What's that?" The doctor bluffed, acting out an argument on Bobby's behalf. "I know, but he wants to talk to you."

Turning toward Willie, he withdrew the phone from his reach. "Mickey said to hold on. He says he needs to ask me a few more questions."

Willie backed off.

The intimations continued.

"Can Willie hear me?"

"No."

"Great job. All right, now, listen. I need to figure out where you are. It's in Dorchester, right."

"Yeah. I'm not familiar with the area, but Willie says he knows where the drugstore is so don't worry about it." Ad-libbing, the doctor paused and said to Willie, "Mickey wants to know if you're talking about the Walgreens?"

"Yeah."

Wanting him to say no, then tell him what store he meant, Willie's response temporarily stymied McGlinty.

"Mickey wants to know which Walgreens?"

"Corner of Quincy and Warren, man. It's right down Quincy Street."

Bobby dropped into an adjacent chair and began punching keys on his laptop.

"Keep talking," he implored the doctor. "I'm bringing up a map on my computer to narrow down your location."

Jill and Jake fell in behind Bobby as he brought up MapQuest from his list of favorites. He clicked on Maps, then punched in *quincy street,* then *dorchester ma.* Without a street number, the initial map showed the closest main intersection as Columbia Road. He clicked on the default choice of 294–327 Quincy Street—the fifth of ten choices—figuring he would start in the middle of the street and work his way out.

"Ask him if there isn't something closer on Columbia Road."

Bobby listened to the doctor relay his request while he expanded the coverage by zooming out one level on the map. Warren Street was still not visible.

Willie was berating the doctor in the background, giving Bobby time to hit the west button on the left side of the map. He could now see the intersection of Quincy and Warren. Double-clicking on the intersection centered it on the map.

Bobby said, "Don't let him have that phone, doctor. Do whatever you have to do to stay on the line. Explain the medicine you need to purchase. I need time to look at the map and ask you some questions."

McGlinty filibustered about the medication.

Bobby cut him off. "If I said the name of the street would you know it?"

"Uh, no."

"Is it an apartment?"

"No."

"Three-decker?"

"No."

"Single-family house?"

"I believe so."

"Big yard?"

"Yes."

"Remember, call me *Mickey.* Driveway?"

"Yeah, Mickey."

"Is it attached to any other house … you know, a duplex?"

"No."

"Color … color. Is it gray?"

The doctor sneaked a peek out the window to double-check. His recollection of the house was spot on. The house's exterior was white. "Not quite."

"Not quite gray? Is it black?"

"Absolutely not," said the doctor.

"Absolutely not black? You mean it's white?"

"Yes."

Bobby scribbled furiously. He summarized his notes and read them back to the doctor. "So, it's a single family, white house on a street off of Quincy between Warren Street and Columbia Road. It has a large yard and a driveway?"

"Yes."

"What else can you add, doc? Anything?"

"No, it'll be all uphill from there Mickey. At least I think so."

"It's on a hill?" Bobby said. "Are you saying the house is on a hill?"

"Yes."

"If I find the hill and I go up it, do I go right—?"

McGlinty cut him off, "No, that won't work."

"So I've got to find the hill, go up, and take a *left*, correct?"

"Yeah, that will work if you do it right away."

"So I go up the hill and I have to take the *first* left, correct?"

"Yes."

"Then what?"

"Then you would do it *again*. You know, you'll have to keep giving her the medicine."

"Do it *again*, right?" Bobby referred to his notes. "So I go up the hill … take the first left, and then take another left. Is that what you're saying?"

"Exactly."

"Then what?"

"I don't understand."

Frustrated, Bobby stared at his notes and reiterated their conversation. "I go up the hill … take the first left and then take another left. Will I be at the house?"

"More or less. It'll be all downhill from there."

Bobby said, "So a left off Quincy, then another left. Then a third left will put me in the driveway, and then I go down a hill to the house, right?"

"Yeah, I am pretty sure that that will do it, Mickey."

"Doctor, real quick. Is my mother going to be all right?"

"Once we get this new medicine into her, everything should be fine."

"What's your name, Doctor? How can you let me know your name without drawing suspicion?"

Without missing a beat, McGlinty said casually, "Mickey, the only way this can be ordered is under my name." Pausing, he continued, "Yeah, you can try, but I don't think it will work." He paused again and seemed resigned to Mickey's course of action. "Okay, if you say so. If not, you have to use McGlinty. It's capital M, small C, capital G—"

Bingo, thought Bobby. "Dr. *McGlinty*," he half-whispered as he wrote his name on the paper.

"What the fuck are you doing?" Willie screamed. "He knows your fucking name. Give me that phone."

Bobby could hear Willie screaming. "Act like you're having a hard time hearing me, you know, like the phone is breaking up, then hang up." Bobby terminated the call.

"You're starting to break up Mickey ... Mickey? It's all broken up. I can't make out what you're saying ... Mickey?"

Turning to Willie, a seemingly frustrated McGlinty said, "I lost him."

34

Bobby drew a series of lines representing a map of their destination. He alternated his focus between the computer screen and the notes gleaned from the doctor. "This Dr. McGlinty said that I've got to go down Quincy Street, take a left, a left, and a left, and I'll end up in the driveway of the house where my mother is being held."

Jake asked, "Did he say which end of Quincy Street to come in from? I know a little bit about that area. We built a health unit over there a couple of years ago. If you are coming from Warren Street, all those lefts will put you in one area. If you're coming in from the Columbia Road end it's a whole different ballgame."

"But we can do both, right?" Bobby responded. "We'll start on the Columbia Road side. If that doesn't work, we'll try coming in from the other end. What do you think?"

Jake checked his watch. "That's a rough neighborhood Bobby. Plus, we're going to stick out like a sore thumb. I mean, three white people driving around in a car in that area, especially at this time of night, is not a common sight."

Bobby didn't hesitate. "I'm *going*. I understand if you guys don't want to go, but I've got no choice."

The three of them headed for Jill's Volvo.

❧

Willie ripped the phone from McGlinty's hand. "What's that shit all about? Spelling your name? What's up with that?"

McGlinty backed off. "What's the problem?"

"What the fuck would Mickey need you to spell your name for? That wasn't even Mickey on the phone, was it?" Willie snatched up an old wooden chair, spun one-hundred-and-eighty-degrees, and hurled it in the general direction of McGlinty's head.

The doctor ducked, avoiding the brunt of the blow.

The dried-out chair hit the wall and splintered into a half-dozen potential weapons.

℘

Jake directed Jill through Uphams Corner from the backseat of her car.

A light rain began to fall.

Bobby sat next to her in the front passenger seat. His eyes were fixated on the computer generated street map as Jill navigated Columbia Road.

"You want to stay over to this side," Bobby said, adding, "You'll be taking a right up ahead."

Bobby replayed Dr. McGlinty's instructions in his head as Jill slowed down to make the right turn on to Quincy Street. He reminded Jill, "We'll be taking a left, and then going up a hill … first left … another left … and then supposedly we'll be in the driveway. Then down the hill to the house."

They headed down Quincy Street.

"You want me to take this left?" Jill asked.

"We're going to have to try them all," Bobby reasoned.

The first left on Conley Street produced no tangible evidence. Worn out and graffiti clad pre-engineered metal buildings stood aside long-neglected masonry structures. There were no houses anywhere in sight.

A similar result awaited them after their second left-turn. Jake said, "Maybe we should have started up on the other end of Quincy Street."

Jill made a U-turn and headed back.

Their third left was infinitely more promising. They drove up a hill with an abundance of residential properties.

Bobby mumbled the doctor's instructions: "Up a hill … first left … another left … and supposedly we'll be in the driveway. Then it's down the hill to the house." He looked to his left and paraphrased the doctor again. "A white house. Left, left, left, down the driveway to a white house. I asked him if the house was black. He said absolutely not. I said, absolutely not black, you mean the house was white? And he said yes." Bobby pointed down the driveway. "That's the house!"

Unequivocal proof that they had the correct house hit Bobby like a brick in the face.

As the light rain turned heavier, he pointed through the increasingly large droplets gathering on the windshield. The house no longer held his attention. "Remember the *van* we were following when we got in the accident? That's *it!*"

"Unbelievable," Jill whispered.

Bobby's analytical skills kicked in. "Dr. McGlinty was the guy I talked to on the phone. He must have been brought here by Mickey and that Willie guy to tend to my mother. Remember, she has some type of infection. Her doctor's office was trying to locate her. It all adds up!" He paused, and then added, "He also told me they were holding him against his will. I'm telling you, she's in *that* house!"

Jill said, "What should we do?"

Jake chimed in from the back seat. "We can't just rush in there; and we certainly can't walk around the neighborhood and case things out."

Pausing, he added, "We might want to call the cops."

❧

Willie retrieved a leg of the splintered chair. His tirade continued. "Who the fuck were you talking to?" he screamed. He moved in on McGlinty, his weapon positioned for optimal damage.

"It was *Mickey*," the doctor assured Willie, before trying to change the subject. "Willie, the longer we wait to treat this woman, the longer it will take for her to get better. If we wait too long, you're going to have a dead body on your hands. Mickey is concerned that doesn't happen. He was very clear about that and wanted my assurances that she was going to receive the appropriate treatment. Whether or not she does depends on what you do."

Willie re-dialed Mickey's number.

Bobby—sitting just outside the Sacomma Street house in Jill's car—took the phone from Jake. He reviewed the caller ID and chose not to answer. *He already knew what he needed to know.*

Willie terminated the call when he was transferred to Mickey's voicemail. He waved the makeshift weapon in the doctor's face and said, "I don't know what the fuck is going on around here, but I'm telling you, I'm going to cave your fucking head in if I find out you're playing games with me."

McGlinty stayed on message, "We need to get the medicine, Willie; the sooner, the better."

ↇ

"I'd rather not call the cops," Bobby said in response to Jake's idea. "All I can picture in my head is one of those hostage scenes you see on TV. Flood lights, bullhorns, you know, the whole ball of wax." What he really envisioned—and which deeply troubled him—was the thought of a weapon being held to his mother's head; or her being injured or as seriously ill as all the evidence led him to believe.

"What *choice* do you have?" Jake argued. "Take a look around, Bobby. Do you feel comfortable walking up to that door and asking if you can see your mother?"

"I agree with Jake, Bobby," Jill added. "You can't get close enough to the house. You'd have to walk fifty feet just to reach the door and they could be watching you from one of those windows."

Jill barely finished her thought before the door to the house burst open and two men appeared.

They were headed for the white van.

ↇ

"Shit, we've got to get out of here Jill."

Jill's squealing tires further ripped up the unkempt pavement.

This drew the immediate attention of the two men at the bottom of the driveway.

From the back seat, Jake stared into the bushy eyes of the same guy he had seen hassling Bobby's mother out at out at Harbor Point; and then crossing East Broadway with his brother Mickey. As they sped up the street he said, "Well, at least we know we've got the right house."

They reached the end of the block, and were out of sight of the two men.

Bobby sat upright and said, "Pull over Jill, I'm getting out."

❧

"That's the same fucking car that was following us when we picked you up," Willie said.

Dr. McGlinty did not respond but he knew his information had worked.

"Come on, get back in the house; we're going to Plan B. I *told* Mickey that car was following us. But no, he knows everything!" Mimicking his now deceased friend, he said, "Willie's just a fucking dummy."

He whipped out his cell phone and called Mickey again.

He was greeted by the same voicemail message.

❧

"You can't get out, Bobby," Jake said. "What are you possibly going to do?"

"All I know is my mother's in that house and this may be my only chance to get her out of there." Mickey's cell phone rang again. Bobby grabbed it off the console and terminated the ring before tossing it next to his phone.

"There must be other people inside. I mean, they wouldn't leave her in there alone, would they?" Jake asked.

"What else are we going to do? We can't follow them in the van; they'll be expecting that."

"Whatever we're going to do, we've got to get out of here," Jake said. "They could be heading this way any second. Look, we know where the house is. It's the *same* van that we followed earlier, and we know that guy is the same guy we saw with Mickey."

Bobby absorbed Jake's thoughts.

Jake continued, "It *all* adds up. We're simply not prepared to take them on. They're probably armed. If we rush in, any number of bad things could happen. Take a left Jill, we've got to get out of here for the time being and think this through."

Before she could act, Bobby ripped open the passenger door and vaulted into the rain. He ran toward the white house and—he hoped—to his mother.

☙

Willie was in a quandary. *He didn't want to let the doctor out of his sight, yet he couldn't leave him here while he went for the medicine. What if the people in the Volvo were waiting for him to leave? Where the fuck was Mickey when he needed him most? If he stayed, the woman's condition would deteriorate. He couldn't let the doctor go alone, as he might never come back. I never should have sent Sammy after Mickey.*

McGlinty interrupted Willie's thoughts, "You said the drugstore's right down the street, right?

"Yeah?"

"Let's go get the medicine. You have no choice. I hate to sound like a broken record, but keeping the woman alive is the most important thing you have to do. Where's that young kid that was here earlier? What was his name, Sammy? Can't you get him back here?"

"I sent him to get Mickey and told him not to come back without him. He's Mickey's guy. I don't have his cell phone number. Fuck, I've got to get ahold of Mickey."

"We *have* to get to the drugstore," McGlinty persisted.

An overwhelmed Willie walked down the hall. He muttered, "I've got to check on that bitch first."

McGlinty fell in behind him, buoyed by the phone call with Bobby and the possibility that help seemed to be nearby.

206

Getting Willie out of the house is key, McGlinty thought.

℀

"What should I do?" Jill asked Jake from the driver's seat.

When she did not receive a response, Jill turned and discovered Jake was gone too.

He had catapulted from the back seat the moment Bobby exited the vehicle.

"You've got to be kidding me," she mumbled, repeatedly checking her side and rearview mirrors. She concluded the most prudent course of action was to drive around the block in hopes of coaxing them back in the vehicle. When she reached Quincy Street, she turned left. She had to make a decision whether to turn back up Sacomma, knowing that by doing so she could be heading directly toward the white van.

When she reached Sacomma, she continued driving down Quincy Street—confident that was the appropriate move—yet equally unsure of what she should do next.

℀

Despite having a twenty-foot head start on Jake, Bobby was moving tentatively. His emotions and common sense created internal conflict in his mind, and the increasing rainfall limited his vision. He came to a sudden stop and Jake quickly caught up to him.

Bobby was momentarily startled. "Where's Jill?" he gasped.

"You're making a huge mistake," Jake said. "Jill took off. I have no idea where she went, but she can't be driving around this area by herself while we're out here playing detective."

"If I walk away without trying something I may never see my mother again. We're here. We should at least scope things out."

They neared the top of the driveway and slipped down the right side of the property and behind the first of the two massive oak trees. The empty white van sat to their left, less than twenty feet away.

Bobby whispered, "What if we disable the van—you know, flatten the tires—would that help us or hurt us?"

"We don't want to do that," Jake said. "Remember, it looked like they were getting ready to leave when they saw our car. Jill's gone now, and hopefully she knows enough to stay out of the area. We *want* them to leave. We should call her and have her pull the car over until we get back to her."

"My cell phone's in the console of her car," Bobby said, shaking his head and lamenting, "It's right next to Mickey's." Shaking his head again, he said, "I don't *believe* this."

"I have Mickey's phone." Jake said, pulling it from his coat pocket and handing it to Bobby. "I grabbed it before jumping out of the car. Can we call her on this?"

Bobby's momentary elation quickly evolved into despair. "Only if you've got her number. I don't know it; I have her on speed dial on my phone."

"They got Information for these things? You know, can you call an operator to get a number?"

"I'm not sure, but I've got a better idea."

Bobby punched in numbers as a sudden burst of bright light radiated from the entrance to the house. The two individuals they had seen minutes earlier exited again. They warily headed toward the white van as they looked around for Jill's car, or any other suspicious activity.

Bobby closed the phone. He shoved Jake behind the trunk of the oak tree and nestled in as tightly as he could next to him.

The bushy-eyed guy they had come to know as Willie climbed behind the steering wheel and fired up the van. The guy with the gray suit and the briefcase climbed into the front passenger seat.

"That has to be the doctor," Bobby whispered.

The van reached the top of the driveway, turned right, and headed toward and eventually down Sacomma Street toward Quincy.

"I hope Jill's not parked down there," Jake said. "She'll be a sitting duck."

Bobby finished punching in the phone number.

❧

Willie burst into the room to check on Trisha, tugging at the handcuffs that tethered each of her hands to the steel bedposts, somehow managing to tighten the left one an additional notch. He crossed the hall and looked out the window to see if the Volvo was still there.

It was gone. *Was that good news or bad news?*

Willie turned to McGlinty. "C'mon, we're going to get the medicine. We may have to move her to another location and it'll be easier if she's able to get around on her own."

Willie and McGlinty left the house for the second time, still spooked by the ubiquitous red Volvo. He fired up the van and kept his head on a swivel, searching for any unusual activity.

His inability to see Bobby and Jake huddled together behind the trunk of the adjacent oak tree would ultimately prove problematic.

∽

"Yeah?" Pick said quietly into the cell phone as he moved slightly to his right to optimize Tim Dunlap as a shield. While having a cell phone was a huge perk, Riverfork was loaded with rats who would leverage the tiniest shard of information to gain any personal advantage or edge.

Pick's body went rigid. "What the fuck are you *talking* about, I just talked to him. *What!* How reliable is he? No fucking way! I'm *telling* you, I talked to him within the past hour." Following an exaggerated pause, Pick said, "Shadow, if it wasn't Mickey Carberry I was talking to, then who the fuck was it?"

Pick processed additional information from the other end. He hissed, "You're fucking right I want you to follow up. I've got to know what's going on. Don't stop digging until you get to the bottom of this, you hear me? Start with Willie. Get back to me as soon as you hear any more information."

∽

Bobby called Marie to retrieve Jill's phone number.

After some rudimentary banter, he fended off Marie's insistence to bring her up to speed by promising to call her back.

He dialed the acquired number. He needed Jill to answer.

Willie headed northwest on Quincy, his eyes moving steadily from window to window as well as back and forth between the vehicle's mirrors in search of the red Volvo.

Dr. McGlinty had barely settled in when Willie pulled the van into a parking lot at the intersection of Warren Street. They were less than a half-mile from the white house.

McGlinty had already written out the necessary prescription for "Mary Smith." It dawned on him that this falsification would undoubtedly result in the revocation of his medical license, given his previous problems. Ironically, it was Willie and Mickey who originally placed him in this untenable position. They now seemed poised to finish the job. What was *more* ironic was it was the least of his problems.

Willie's cell phone rang as he was exiting the van. He signaled with his forefinger for McGlinty to stay put, pointing at the passenger seat he was preparing to vacate.

"Willie, it's Shadow. They found Mickey shot to death over in Southie."

"What are you talking about? I talked to him less than a half-hour ago."

McGlinty stiffened. He surmised the worst after hearing Willie's reaction. *This can't be good.*

Shadow didn't pay Willie the same homage as Pick. "Well, you must have a special connection," Shadow responded. "If he calls you back maybe you can find out what color suit he wants to be laid out in, because the cops found his body over two hours ago."

ↄ⟋ↄ

The vibrating phone startled Jill. She didn't recognize the number but answered anyway.

"Jill, where are you?"

She recognized Bobby's voice instantly. "I'm not quite sure. I was going to go around the block, but I figured they might come out and identify the car. I went past that street we went up earlier and took the next right to get out of sight."

"Good thinking, because they did take off in the van. The two guys came back out and they went down that street. Where are you now?"

"Hold on, I'm coming up to an intersection." She stared through the rain swept windshield at the fluorescent green street signs with the white lettering sitting perpendicular—one atop the other—on a pole. "*Dudley* Street? I'm on a smaller street called Howard Avenue, right where it intersects with Dudley."

Bobby gave her general directions back toward the house. "Get close, but not too close, then stash the car as best you can. Keep it running and keep your eyes open. We don't know where they went. When we call, we need you to get here as quickly as possible. Make sure all the doors are unlocked when you pull up"

"What are you going to do?"

"We don't have time to discuss it. Please, just do what I ask, and don't tie up your phone."

ᥴᕪᗄ

Willie went berserk on McGlinty. "I fucking told you that wasn't Mickey on the phone. He's been dead for hours. How the fuck were you talking to a dead man?"

"What are you talking about?"

"You know just what I'm talking about, Mickey's dead! He has been for hours. If he was dead for hours, then how the fuck were you talking to him on the phone?"

"Willie, *you* handed *me* the phone. Didn't *you* speak to Mickey?"

Willie nullified any minimal level of reasoning he might possess when he responded, "How could it have been Mickey? I just told you, he's *dead.*" He stared contemptuously at the doctor, thinking, *He has to be beyond stupid. I have it all figured out.*

"Willie, you've got a sick woman who needs medicine. We're here," McGlinty said, pointing at the front door of Walgreen's. "Let's get the medicine."

ᥴᕪᗄ

Bobby slid down the perimeter of the property.

Jake fell in behind.

When they passed the second large oak tree, they entered an open area and possible sighting from within the confines of the house.

Fortuitously, the ominous rain clouds and the resulting rain darkened the surrounding area.

As they neared the house, Jake said, "Maybe we should go around back. Maybe we can peek through a window. Who knows, maybe we'll find one that's unlocked. If we smash the door in they'll know we were here as soon as they get back."

Bobby nodded and took off.

Bobby moved quickly around the corner to the rear of the building. He stopped at the first of the house's old six-over-six paned windows. Bobby got on his tiptoes and stuck his nose up against it to ascertain any noticeable activity inside. He tried mightily to shove it open, to no avail. Stopping at successive windows, the results were the same until he reached the fourth one.

An errant baseball from a neighborhood pick-up game from long-ago had smashed out a middle pane of the bottom sash. Bobby's cursory investigation revealed that the window led to a walk-in closet. The door to the closet was slightly ajar and led to what looked like a hallway.

A sheet of quarter-inch plywood replaced the pane of glass after the accident. The eight brad nails holding it in place had gradually corroded over time. It quickly succumbed to a rapid thrust of the base of Bobby's half-open right palm.

The pair waited several seconds to see if the noise drew any discernable attention from inside the house. When no reaction occurred, an emboldened Bobby reached inside and unhooked the window's lock. He quickly shoved the lower portion of the window up.

Jake located a discarded milk crate and tossed it at Bobby's feet. He then assisted him in climbing through the window.

Once inside, Bobby turned to face Jake. "Wait out here," he whispered.

"No way, pal." Jake hopped onto the crate and managed to pull himself through the window with the assistance of a healthy tug from Bobby.

Bobby approached the closet door. He had no idea what awaited them. He paused to listen for any activity before opening the door.

Jake followed him and they moved tentatively down the hallway.

Their respective hearts hammered double-time and their senses heightened considerably.

Bobby stopped when he encountered a padlocked door, rationalizing that this was why nobody was guarding the room or approaching them from another area of the house.

While Bobby considered the significance of the padlock—and what they might encounter on the other side of the door—Jake noticed the ring of keys hanging from the nail on the opposite wall.

Jake poked Bobby on the back and gestured toward the keys.

Bobby grabbed the ring and reached for the padlock. He tried to match the appropriate key to the lock, a standard Master Lock. His hands were shaking, but he managed to pop the shackle on his second attempt. The loud click and the resultant clang against the similarly heavy metal hasp allowed Bobby to remove the lock.

Bobby pulled the door open and found his mother handcuffed to a bed.

Trisha's eyes sprung open in surprise. "Bobby," she mouthed weakly.

"Save your strength," he whispered. "We've got to get you out of here."

Bobby turned to Jake. "We have to free these handcuffs and we probably don't have much time. See if you can find something that might help us."

"What about the other keys on the ring?"

Bobby was embarrassed he hadn't thought of that possibility. He fumbled with the remaining keys while simultaneously assessing his mother's physical condition.

The handcuff key was not on the ring.

Jake left, frantically searching for any tool or instrument that might be of assistance. He couldn't help but think of how many tools he worked with each day that could easily assist them. He pulled open kitchen drawers and cabinet doors but was unable to locate anything of value. As he considered the inherent danger of extending his search outside to the yard, bright lights suddenly bathed the kitchen walls.

Jake dropped down, sneaked up against the side of the window, and peered out.

The white van was rumbling down the driveway.

Jake stayed low to avoid detection. He hurried down the hallway to the padlocked room. "We've got to get out of here, Bobby. The van is back."

Bobby couldn't believe their misfortune. He ran into a room across the hall, giving him a view of the top end of the driveway. While he couldn't see the vehicle, he also couldn't mistake the sound of the van's doors opening and subsequently slamming shut.

Bobby had to make a split-second decision. He ran back to Trisha's room and said, "Don't say a word, Ma. And don't worry, I'll be back to get you. I promise."

Bobby padlocked the door and placed the key ring back on the nail.

He and Jake quickly retraced their steps.

"In here," Bobby whispered, guiding Jake into the closet. "Hurry up," he implored, before backtracking and sticking his head out the slightly ajar closet door to monitor the approach of his mother's captors. He heard voices from the other end of the house. Mindful that any physical confrontation would be a foolish option given the likelihood that Willie was probably armed, Bobby gently closed the closet door and headed for the window.

"Watch the milk crate," Jake warned.

Bobby lowered himself out the window as Jake guided his feet toward the added height of the crate, facilitating an easier exit.

Bobby stood on the crate, lowered the window, and took the time to lock it. He remained mindful that there was no way, nor enough time, to reinsert the piece of plywood.

With a watchful eye on the front door, Jake whispered, "Come on, we're going to need some reinforcements."

35

"How quickly will this medicine work?" Willie asked, as he and McGlinty shed their wet coats.

"There will be incremental improvement."

"What do you mean by incredimental?"

"*Incremental*," McGlinty corrected, retrospectively unsure why he bothered. Dumbing-down his explanation, he said, "It's going to take time. It's not like we give her the medicine and she'll miraculously stand up and be all better. What's important is that the sooner we *start* the cycle, the sooner she'll get well."

Willie nodded. He activated the light switch and they headed down the hall.

McGlinty fell in behind, assuming they were going to administer the medicine, only to crash into Willie's back when he came to an abrupt stop.

"What the *fuck!*" Willie yelled, looking around the adjacent area before grabbing at the padlock. It was in place and locked, just as they had left it.

He's spooked about something, McGlinty thought. The doctor's first instinct was that the keys were missing. He looked up and they were hanging from the nail where Willie placed them earlier.

"What's the matter?"

"Look at the floor," Willie yelled. He pushed the doctor back toward the kitchen and pulled out a gun.

Wet and muddy footprints led from the locked room down the hall, well past where Willie and McGlinty had just stopped.

Willie strode back down the hall, grabbed the keys, and popped the lock.

His first obligation was ensuring Trisha was still locked in the room.

❧

Was it a dream? If so, it was unbelievably real. Trisha could feel her son's rain soaked head when she ran her fingers through his hair. Her palms remained resultantly wet. *But why did he leave so soon? But he did say he would be back, didn't he?*

An agitated Willie burst through the door, brandishing a gun. He breathed a sigh of relief when he found Trisha still tethered to the bedpost.

He then used McGlinty as a shield, searching room-by-room for any intruders.

❧

Jill hung up from Bobby and headed toward Quincy Street to retrieve him and Jake. She spotted them sprinting in her direction as soon as she turned the corner.

Bobby pulled the door open and said breathlessly, "I *saw* her—"

"We can't sit here. You've got to go!" Jake yelled from the backseat.

The car's tires squealed before gaining traction on the wet road. "What should I do?" Jill asked.

"Just keep moving," Bobby said. The residual effect of the soaking rain dripping down his face could not wash away his despair.

A half-mile later, they found themselves on Dudley Street.

It was decision time.

❧

"Is this some kind of joke?" Carl "the Shadow" Bionda screamed at Willie through the phone. His glass eye stared aimlessly in the opposite direction of the good one. The good one seemed in grave danger of popping out of its socket.

"All we did was go to the drugstore. We couldn't have been gone more than ten minutes. When we got back, we were getting ready to give Barron's mother the medicine when I noticed the wet footprints."

"Weren't *you* guys out in the rain? How do you know—"

"Yeah, we were out in the rain, but when we came back we never walked that far down the hall. When I noticed the footprints, I stopped. I then followed them. They led into a closet across the hall from where we're holding Barron's mother."

"Yeah, but—"

"The closet has a window in it. Someone punched out a pane of glass. Actually, they punched out a small piece of plywood that must have replaced a pane of glass. There was no broken glass—"

"Willie, I don't care about the closet or any broken glass—"

"Shadow, there was a fucking milk crate right under the window. They used it to climb in the window. When we tried to leave earlier, we spotted a red Volvo. That same car was following Mickey and me yesterday. I'm telling you, they know we're here and it ain't safe. We've got to get her out of here."

☙

Shadow ordered an Amaretto Sour from an attractive young female bartender in an upscale West Broadway bar. Her colorful tattoos and multiple body piercings would have normally intrigued him and undoubtedly provoked conversation. Unfortunately, his curiosity of why she would mar such a beautiful body quickly transitioned into his racking his brain for a solution to *his* problem. *This plan was a non-starter from the beginning. The only chance of succeeding was having Mickey Carberry at the helm, and Mickey was dead.*

He eventually resorted to the teachings of an old law professor who drummed into generations of his students' heads that analytical solutions often require one to resort to ideas that are initially categorized as absurd.

With that as his guide—and several additional servings of the almond-flavored liqueur relieving some of his tension—he paid his bill and headed out the door in search of his automobile.

⟡

"Are you out of your mind?" Pick whispered into the cell phone.

"It's the only choice we have," Shadow said. "Mickey's dead, and Willie can't handle this. You have no other choice. Trust me; it's a cluster fuck over there."

"I've got to think this over. I'll get back to you."

"You better get back to me soon; we don't have much time."

Pick reconsidered his position. Lockdown was approaching, and cell phone reception was a hit-or-miss proposition from the bowels of his cell. "Okay, you may be right, but I need you to work with me on this. Once she's gone, our leverage is gone with her, no?"

"That's not the point. She's useless to us either way, Pick. Trust me, it's the only choice."

"Call Buddy Curran and have him take care of it. Tell Willie I want him out of there. He's fucked everything up and I can't trust him on this. Sammy too! I want them both out of there."

Pausing, he added, "You better move quickly. Like you said, it doesn't sound like we've got much time."

⟡

Bobby reached into his pants' pocket. "Can you put the light on?"

Jill powered up her car's interior lighting system.

Bobby rummaged through a mishmash of currency and receipts, eventually finding what he was looking for.

Who better to call at this moment than his good friend and former fellow law student, Boston Police Commissioner Ted Lyons? He must have forgiven my running his mother over by now, Bobby thought.

He punched Lyons's number into his cell phone.

⟡

"Why didn't you tell me this when we were at the hospital?" an incredulous Ted Lyons asked.

Bobby was unable to reach him on the cell phone. After several maneuvers and an impassioned explanation that Lyons would be wildly upset were he not contacted, Bobby convinced a police dispatcher to contact the commissioner to verify Bobby's veracity.

Lyons was attending a retirement celebration for a Boston Police sergeant and longtime friend at the Elks' Hall in West Roxbury. The commissioner had shut off his cell phone to participate in the roasting of the evening's guest of honor.

When the dispatcher called him back with the commissioner's whereabouts, Bobby—accompanied by his two intrepid partners—made the trip to meet him face-to-face.

Lyons pulled out his cell phone and activated it. While he waited for it to power up, he turned to one of his men. "Jimmy, get me Richie Flynn, will you?" before changing his mind. "You know what? Just give me the radio." He accepted it and turned to Bobby. "Richie Flynn heads up a special strike force for us." He hit a button on the side of the unit emitting a sonar-like noise followed by a loud beep. "Richie, it's Ted Lyons."

"Commissioner. What can I do for you?"

"I need you to mobilize your crew and get over to Sacomma Street in Dorchester. It's right off Quincy Street. We have a potential hostage situation." Pausing to field an inquiry, he said, "I don't have the house number. Hold on." He turned to Bobby and Jake, "Do you have an address?"

When both of them shook their head, Lyons said, "You said it was a *white* house?"

Bobby nodded. "If you go up Columbia Road you go right on Quincy. Go down two—"

Jake cut him off, completing the directions. "*Three* ... *Third* left off Columbia Road and the house will be on your left. You go up a hill take a left—"

Lyons turned away and pulled the radio up to his mouth. "Hold on, Richie." Turning again he said, "Jimmy, get my car. We're going to Dorchester. Pull it up to the door." He pointed at Bobby and said, "You're coming with me."

Lyons looked at Jake and Jill, then back at Bobby. "We can't take your friends."

"We'll follow you," Jake said.

"No, you won't. We're going to be moving too fast." Pausing, he spoke into the radio again. "Richie I'll get back to you in a minute." He then turned to Jill and Jake and repeated his order. "I'm very serious, do *not* follow us." He waved over another officer and took him aside for several moments, intermittently pointing in Jill and Jake's direction as he spoke to him.

Within minutes, flashing blue and white lights conjoined with the rain droplets on the establishment's glass doors, projecting a kaleidoscopic light show on the interior walls of the private club's foyer.

Lyons barked, "Let's go."

A half-dozen Boston Police officials fell in behind their leader as he and Bobby moved toward the entrance and the police cars that idled just beyond it.

❧

Fairly Sawyer Curran, better known as "Buddy," never reached the high hopes his parents probably had in mind when they attached that moniker to their bouncing nine-pound bundle of joy in 1954.

Nevertheless, he was one tough and nasty son of a bitch. That was irrefutable.

Christ's Apostles cornered the market when it came to the name game in South Boston. James became Jim, Jimmy, or Jimbo; while John was Jack, Johnny, Jay, or Jake. When it came to Thomas, Tom or Tommy fit. Andrew was Andy or Drew; Peter, Pete; and Philip was Phil and there were plenty of them too, as were there Matthews and Mattys. There were less Simons; and while there were Barts and Bartleys, strangely, there were no Bartholomews—at least admittedly.

But Fairly? Often purposely changed to Fairy as a source of youthful aggravation—it was less common than Thaddaeus, and more akin to Judas (of which there were none, for all of the obvious reasons)—and thus began the plight of young Fairly Sawyer Curran.

While there are no quantifiable statistics, it was inarguable that his life could have been infinitely easier had his parents followed traditional neighborhood form and named him after an Apostle—*perhaps* even Judas.

The rigidity of the Sisters of Saint Joseph—who ran "Buddy" Curran's South Boston grammar school with iron fists, whippet-like blackboard pointers, and large wooden paddles—precluded the use of nicknames in the 1960s. Thus, daily battles resulting from the mere mention of his name were commonplace. Many students unwittingly made the mistake of coupling Fairly's odd name with some sense of entitlement to belittle or punish the average-sized youth.

Not one of them ever made that mistake twice.

In a nutshell, the best way to describe Fairly Sawyer "Buddy" Curran was a physically smaller Mickey Carberry in a semi-consistent psychotic rage.

Pick Piccorino had originally excluded him from the plan to leverage Bobby Barron **by** kidnapping his mother for that very reason.

He hadn't wanted it to get too messy.

Now he had no choice but to utilize Curran to straighten things out. Avoiding a potentially messy problem was a distant memory.

∓

Jill repeatedly checked her rearview mirror as she drove through Franklin Park. The marked police car remained affixed to her rear bumper, per order of Commissioner Ted Lyons. When they crossed Blue Hill Avenue and veered left on Old Road, they soon found themselves heading down Columbia Road toward Quincy Street, and the scene of the pending police action.

"What do you think will happen?" Jill asked.

"Who knows, I can't help but think that Bobby should have done this earlier," Jake responded. "Twenty-twenty hindsight, right? But they probably know we were there by now, and they might do something irrational as a result."

"Yeah," Jill agreed.

"I mean, they saw us when they came out of the house the first time, right? Then Bobby punched out a window so we could get into the house. Who knows what they're going to do."

"Well, hopefully it will be over shortly."

☙

"Leave the keys," Shadow instructed. "We're going to need that van. Sammy's on his way over to drop Buddy off and pick you up. As soon as they get there, Pick wants you and Sammy gone. Buddy will take care of the rest."

Sounds good to me, Willie thought. *They should have given that sick fuck the job in the beginning.* "Does Sammy know?"

"What did I just *say?*" Shadow's exasperation emerged. "He's on his way there now with Buddy. As soon as they get there, Pick wants you and Sammy to take off. Buddy will handle it from there."

☙

By the time Bobby tracked down Ted Lyons, Buddy Curran had all the time he needed. He would complete his task long before any reinforcements arrived.

Sammy pulled into the driveway. Willie stepped outside and stopped Buddy as soon as he stepped out of the car. Pointing at the front door, he said, "Go in the front door and down the hall. The room is on the right. There's a nail in the wall on the left with a key hanging off it. I took all the other keys off. That'll open the padlock—"

"What the fuck happened to Mickey?" Buddy growled.

"I've got no idea, I've been here the whole time," Willie said, before continuing his explanation. "The keys to the van are on the floor just outside the padlocked door. I undid one of her handcuffs and used it to handcuff the doctor to the bed. Here's the handcuff key."

Curran accepted the key. His hands were clad in latex gloves. He shook his head disgustedly, produced a gun from his coat pocket, and headed for the front door.

"Let's get the fuck out of here," Willie said as soon as he jumped in Sammy's car.

A like-minded Sammy had the car in reverse and screeching back up the driveway hill before Willie even shut the door, and well before Buddy Curran had reached the front door of the house.

☙

"Should we go to Bobby's house?" Jill asked.

"Let's stop there anyway, huh?"

"Yeah." Jill's mind focused on the diary. She thought of the information she had never passed on to Bobby regarding his mother's past, and the sordid origin of his existence. She turned toward Southie.

As they drove along Day Boulevard, Jake said, "I'm a little surprised they let Bobby go with them."

"Being a good friend of the commissioner didn't hurt."

"Yeah, plus he knew exactly where the house was."

"I never thought of that ... that's a good point."

The police escort dutifully hugged their bumper as they turned right at Mirisola's Restaurant at the corner of L and East Eighth Streets.

They were seconds from Bobby's house.

When they reached Hardy Street, they turned right. They had no idea what to expect.

The infamous white van—parked slightly askew and directly in front of Bobby and Trisha Barron's house—was probably the last item on that list of expectations.

Nevertheless, there it sat.

☙

Various police units set up systematic perimeter protection in the area adjacent to Sacomma Street. Static-laced voices squawked back and forth over the Boston Police internal communications system.

Bobby sat in the back seat of the commissioner's vehicle. He was mentally exhausted and totally scared.

A large police officer sat at the wheel and the commissioner sat next to him in the front passenger seat. Lyons was monitoring each stage of the plan through a computer affixed to the car's dashboard, and from the walkie-talkie in his right hand.

"Take a ride by the house, I want to get a look at it before they go in," Lyons ordered.

Bobby's cell phone rang as they exited Quincy Street onto Sacomma.

Almost simultaneously, a staticky voice echoed from the dashboard: "We found a white van containing the Barron woman. It's parked on Hardy Street in South Boston. Repeat—we've found the Barron woman and an unidentified man inside a van in front of the Barron home on Hardy Street in South Boston."

Bobby answered his phone. "Hello," he said frantically.

"Bobby, it's Jill. I'm at your house. You're not going to believe—"

"Is she *alive*, Jill? Oh Jesus, tell me she's alive!" Bobby screamed.

36

You've got to be shitting me, Larry Fitzgerald thought.

A fleet of police cars and several ambulances rolling up within minutes of each other created an ever-increasing symphony of sirens. In addition to the noise, his Hardy Street neighborhood was awash in a hypnotic display of flashing lights.

Larry never even made it to the sidewalk before one of the police officers ordered him back up his front stairs. He watched the action unfold from his front porch.

It was now an official Boston Police crime scene.

໑

Commissioner Ted Lyons hit a button to silence the vehicle's intercom system. This transferred the communication directly to the earpiece of his handheld unit. He leaped from the vehicle, took a deep breath, pushed a button, and said, "Come in, Mike."

Michael Luce was the police officer Lyons had assigned to follow Jill and Jake back to South Boston. He quickly responded, "Yes, commissioner?"

"What do you have? Did you say the woman was in a van in front of her house?"

"That's correct, sir. She—"

Lyons cut him off. "Is she alive?"

෪

Bobby's heart was racing. While part of him was unsure whether he wanted to hear the answer, he was simultaneously unwilling or unable to wait any longer for Jill's response.

"She's *alive*, Bobby."

Bobby exhaled. Tears of joy quickly welled up in his eyes and rolled down his face. "Is she *okay?*"

"The EMT's are working on her. The guy we saw Mickey and his friend take out of the building in Brookline was arguing with the police. He kept saying he was a doctor, but the cops were having none of it. They had to remove handcuffs to get him out the van—both he *and* your mother were handcuffed—it all happened so fast. Anyway, they removed his handcuffs then put a different set of handcuffs on him and locked him in the back seat of a police car."

"But he *is* a doctor. At least we think he is. You've got to let them know. He may be able to help!"

"I'll try, but there's a lot of paranoia around here. They're still trying to sort out what's going on. They're putting up that yellow crime scene tape. I mean, you'd have to see it to believe it. It looks like they're filming a movie."

෪

Buddy Curran crossed onto the beach road near a row of yacht clubs along the southeastern corner of South Boston. His initial sprint had slowed considerably. When he was finally convinced that nobody was following him, he stopped running and walked into a horseshoe-shaped portion of land just west of the yacht clubs. After a thorough look around the area, he tossed the van keys into the water then peeled the rubber gloves from his hands and tossed them into the surf too. He then reached into his coat pocked for his cell phone and placed a call.

Once he was picked up, he'd get back to Shadow and let him know that the job had been taken care of. He was unaware that Shadow—at the behest of Pick Piccorino—still had some unfinished business they wanted him to complete.

This worked well for Curran. He was always looking for a good job.

⅌

Dr. Eugene McGlinty was explaining his plight to a disinterested patrolman when a police captain approached.

"Are you a doctor?"

McGlinty stifled a laugh. His story had gone ignored for the past ten minutes. "I've been trying to explain—"

"Are you a *doctor?*" the captain repeated, his voice louder and his obvious intolerance for a long explanation unmistakable.

"Yes."

"I've got someone who wants to speak with you." He handed the doctor a cell phone.

Looking a tad confused, McGlinty placed the cell phone over his right ear. "Hello?"

"Yeah, this is Bobby Barron. Are you the person I spoke with earlier regarding your location?"

"Yes."

"What did we discuss?" Bobby asked. "Be as *thorough* as possible so I'll know it was you."

He had his cell phone set on speaker mode so Ted Lyons could listen to the conversation.

McGlinty paused, and then recalled the phone conversation as best he could. "We talked about what type of house it was … you know, single family, two-family. Ah, let me think … we … oh, you asked me what color the house was? No, you asked me if it was gray, and I said, not quite. You then asked me if it was black, and I said, absolutely not."

Bobby had heard enough.

Ted Lyons signaled with a roll of his hands to let McGlinty keep talking.

The doctor continued. "We spoke about the location of the drugstore, the Walgreens on the corner of Quincy and, ah … I think it was Warren Street."

Bobby covered the phone tightly. He took it off speakerphone and buried it between his legs. "Ted, this is definitely the guy I spoke with. They took him from his office in Brookline. We watched them take him out of there—Mickey Carberry and some guy Willie—watch this." Bobby uncovered the phone and asked the doctor, "Where's your office located, and who took you from there?"

"My office is in the Cunniff Building on Beacon Street in Brookline. It was Mickey Carberry and Willie Marcus who picked me up. I know them because—"

Bobby had heard enough. He pulled the phone away from his head and muffled it with his left hand. "Christ, Ted, this guy's a doctor and he could be helping the EMTs with my mother."

Lyons took the phone from Bobby. He said, "Doctor, could you please put the captain back on the phone?"

"Sure."

"Hello?"

"Captain? This is Ted Lyons. We believe this gentleman is a doctor. Please escort him over to the woman they found in the van and allow him to assist the EMTs. Keep your eye on him until I arrive there. I want our guys to check out this house in Dorchester while we're here, and then we're heading over there. If the ambulance leaves with the woman, assign someone to stay with the doctor. I don't want him out of our sight for a second. At the very least, he's a key witness."

♥

The trip to South Boston took an eternity.

Ted Lyons's mobile command center fit neatly amidst the phalanx of wailing sirens and flashing blue lights. When they turned left on N Street, the roadblock along East 8th Street suddenly parted, allowing the commissioner's car to make it all the way to the corner of East 8th and Hardy Street.

Bobby jumped from the vehicle before it came to a complete stop.

He was initially intercepted by a pair of patrolmen before being escorted the last few steps by the officer who had followed Jill and Jake back to South

Boston. The assisting officer understood the backdrop of circumstances and stood by while Bobby peered into the ambulance.

Two brown-uniformed EMTs—a man and a woman—were receiving advice and assistance from a seemingly knowledgeable gentleman in a gray suit.

Bobby was unable to get a good look at his mother due to the oxygen mask affixed to her face. He surveyed the chaos surrounding them and his eyes suddenly locked on Jake, then Jill. It was hard to believe that the madness epitomizing their recent existence had ended so abruptly.

Jake and Jill walked toward Bobby. Jake shook his hand, but their handshake quickly turned into a bear hug.

Once they released each other, Bobby turned to Jill. They skipped the handshake in lieu of a long embrace. Bobby buried his face into her neck. The embrace ended when Bobby kissed the left side of Jill's neck softly, whispering, "How can I ever thank you guys?" Tears rolled down his reddened cheeks.

"You're off to a good start," Jill said.

"Mr. Barron? I'm Dr. McGlinty."

"Doctor!" said Bobby, shaking his hand. "How's my mother? Is she going to be okay?" Bobby peered back toward the ambulance and noticed the female EMT was closing one of the rear doors.

"She's going to be fine—"

A preoccupied Bobby was already in full stride, running toward the back of the ambulance.

McGlinty quickly fell in behind him, his police escort right on his heels, as were Jill and Jake.

"That's my mother," Bobby yelled to the woman as she attempted to close the second door of the ambulance.

The ubiquitous Ted Lyons *suggested* to the EMTs that Bobby ride in the ambulance with Trisha.

Police investigators caught up to Dr. McGlinty and explained they would need information from him for background as to what had transpired.

Bobby interrupted them to thank the doctor for all he had done. He climbed into the back of the ambulance after promising Jake and Jill he would keep them updated. Settling in, he drew in several deep and calming breaths as he watched his exhausted and dehydrated mother lapse in and out of consciousness.

Bobby took hold of his mother's hand and mentally reconciled the bizarre chain of events. As he looked down at Trisha, one overriding thought continued reverberating through his mind.

Why would Mickey Carberry kidnap my mother?

37

Bobby was unsure of what had happened to his cell phone in all the excitement. He exited the emergency room and headed toward the main lobby in search of a pay phone.

Pulling out a pocketful of coins, he was about to dial his secretary Marie when a breathless voice behind him said, "What's up?"

Turning, Bobby hugged Jill tightly. In that moment, nothing else in the world existed. In a perverse twist of fate, the incongruity of their entire ordeal was now manifesting itself in a positive manner.

Grudgingly separating, they stepped back from each other. Each of them mindful, adamant, and independently confident that they would share many more intimate moments.

Jill bit when Bobby laughed. "What are you laughing at?"

Bobby pointed to his left and said, "Isn't this how our little adventure began, at a bank of pay phones?"

38

Over the years, Jackie O'Brien had partaken in a disproportionate amount of mourning on behalf of his friends and neighbors from Southie and beyond. His business consisted of burying friends and neighbors and consoling survivors since taking over the John F. O'Brien Funeral Home from his father.

His sympathy was especially sincere at present. He counted a number of the Carberry clan as close friends.

The funeral home sat just a couple of doors down from the Marian Manor, allowing the family to pull double-duty on this damp and chilly November morning. Five of Stella Carberry's kids had paid her a visit before ducking up the alley and into O'Brien's backdoor to plan the final services of their youngest brother.

" … and we're going to Cedar Grove?" O'Brien asked Jake, scribbling the specifics on a lined yellow legal pad.

"My parents have a double plot. You know, enough to fit four."

"You have the deed?"

A pile of multi-colored paperwork sat in a manila folder on Jake's lap.

His sister Eileen popped out of her chair to assist him. "It's the light-green paper. Way down the bottom."

She took the pile from Jake, dug it out, and handed it to O'Brien.

O'Brien sat opposite the family members at a large oak conference table. The requisite wear-and-tear of years of families facing the inevitable mortalities of loved ones had disfigured its once lustrous surface.

"Limos? We'll need one for the coffin, another for the flowers. How do you want to handle the family?"

On it went, until they ironed out all matters related to an appropriate memorial service for Mickey.

"One final question," the funeral director said. "Are you going to have any type of get-together after the burial? We usually announce that at the gravesite."

It was customary in South Boston to rent a function hall for a post-burial gathering. This allowed family and friends to continue their commiseration in a less formal setting.

The Carberrys had not considered this aspect.

"What do you think?" Jake asked to nobody in particular.

They eventually settled on a few hours to exchange appropriate updates with distant family members and friends from long-ago. In reality, this was the only time that many of these participants' paths crossed. Invariably, discussions would result and empty promises would be made for relatives to congregate for purposes other than a funeral. These thoughts rarely bore fruit. It was an Irish thing.

Jake said, "Let's stop down and see Bobo at the Bayside and see if his function room's available."

"Seapoint," Katie said.

Jake's confusion was obvious. "What?"

"It's called the *Seapoint*," his younger sister said. "You're showing your age.

Jimmy Carberry piped in, "Seapoint—Bayside—what about the Social Club?" rattling off an even earlier appellation of the longtime Covington Street establishment.

Jake laughed, adding, "Don't forget the German Club."

Katie played the always-reliable age card. "Well, you're a lot older than *us*, Jake. I barely remember it being the Bayside."

Now the youngest living Carberry, Katie's good-natured ribbing provided momentary relief in what was an otherwise somber time for the tight-knit family.

ↅ

Pick Piccorino was disgusted. A deep-seeded need for revenge consumed him once Shadow assured him that Buddy Curran had successfully removed Barron's mother from the safe house.

I should have used Buddy from the beginning, Pick thought. He knew he had grossly misjudged the situation. In retrospect, the possibility of having an attorney of Tim Dunlap's caliber in his corner was too important to cut corners.

Regardless, it was now Buddy Curran's job to put his plan back on track.

ↅ

Bobby awoke to a sliver of autumn sun sneaking through an unintended crack between his bedroom's room darkening honeycomb shades and the window frame. *Had this all been a dream?* he thought.

He snapped upright, mentally revisiting the abject craziness of the previous evening.

"Are you all right?" asked a soft voice. A sleepy-eyed Jill propped her head up by doubling up her pillow. She pushed aside a large lock of hair to focus on Bobby.

A nagging of Bobby's sub-conscious suddenly came clear. She was Nicole Kidman. No. While bordering on doppelganger status—her hair was redder, thicker, but not quite as curly. She also lacked the neurotically skeletal look that seemed necessary to appear normal in the lens of a Hollywood movie camera. Her body had just enough meat in just the right places. Nevertheless, the distinct resemblance was unmistakable.

"Yeah." Bobby said, a satisfying smile plastered on his face.

He and Jill had gone to the hospital the previous evening only to find a heavily sedated Trisha sound asleep. Bobby encountered a pair of detectives

234

and agreed to meet them for a follow-up meeting the next morning. Once Ted Lyons appointed a patrolman for around-the-clock protection, *Now what?* became the only remaining question.

Jill stopped at Bobby's house under the pretense of picking up a few things.

Identical thoughts permeated their respective minds: *She wasn't going anywhere.*

Once inside, several awkward moments preceded an embrace and a long-anticipated kiss.

Two hot showers followed additional kissing and snuggling and a few cold beers. Eventually, the two hot showers morphed into one particularly hot shower involving the two of them.

Bobby stretched. He had forgotten how satisfying a good night's sleep could be as he arched his elbows backwards and extended his body with an exaggerated grunt. He then placed his head on Jill's taut and warm stomach, grabbed the remote to the bedroom's television, and turned on the TV.

Jill rubbed her fingers through his hair.

Ironically, *Dead Calm*, a 1989 movie starring Nicole Kidman, was playing. When a key scene appeared where Kidman has sex with fellow actor Billy Zane to entrap him and affect revenge, Bobby couldn't help but think *She's better looking than Kidman.*

He rolled his eyes up at Jill and motioned toward the television. Suppressing a grin, he said, "That looks like fun."

Jill agreed.

Their second foray was less rushed and more fulfilling than the previous evening.

∽

Jackie O'Brien closed Mickey's memorial service folder. After he placed it on a shelf, he turned to Jake and said, "I need to speak with you in private for a second."

Jake followed him into another room and O'Brien shut the door behind them.

Boston Police Commissioner Ted Lyons sat in a corner of the room. He was reading a newspaper, his right foot propped up on his left knee. He uncrossed his legs, tossed the newspaper on a table, and stood up.

"Jake, you know Ted Lyons? O'Brien asked.

"Sure … well, I know who you *are*," Jake said, staring the commissioner in the eyes.

Lyons stepped forward and shook Jake's hand. "We're hearing a lot of rumblings that this isn't over. I don't think I need to tell you that your brother Mickey was a bad actor. With all due respect to you and your family over your loss, I assume you know that?"

"He was no saint … but he *was* my brother."

Lyons held his palms up in a defensive manner. "We have a lot of mutual friends, Jake. I checked you out and I've heard nothing but good things about you. The problem we have is that we're uncomfortable with what we're hearing from several informants. Do you know Willie Marcus?"

"I don't think so," Jake lied.

Lyons slipped his hand inside his suit coat and produced a picture. He handed it to Jake. "Does this guy look familiar?"

Jake stared at the picture. "Yeah, yeah…he was the other guy with Mickey." He suddenly became animated.

Ted Lyons lowered himself into the upholstered chair he'd vacated upon Bobby's arrival.

Jackie O'Brien fell into a chair opposite the Commissioner.

A spigot opened and out flowed Jake's story: "I was out walking the other day. That was when I first saw this guy. I actually saw him *before* Bobby. He was hassling Bobby's mother … but I had no idea it was his mother. Then when Bobby and I … oh yeah and Jill, were up on Broadway we saw him come out of King's Tavern…."

Jake's lengthy eyewitness account stitched together many key points.

When Lyons coupled his existing information with this newfound knowledge, the story fell neatly in place.

Or so he thought.

ભ્ર

"Your mother being sick saved *her* ass, but you're not going to be so lucky you prick," hissed the voice on the other end of Bobby's BlackBerry. "Don't think for a moment that this is over."

"Who—?"

"Shut the fuck up!" the voice bellowed.

Jill sensed the stiffening in Bobby's body language. She whispered, "What's the matter?"

Bobby shook his head, placing his left index finger over his lips.

"You're going to straighten this out or *you're* fucking dead. You're not dealing with those morons they sent to do the job the first time. When you least expect it, *bang!*" The caller's voice rose significantly when he said 'bang.'

"You got one last chance to do the right thing. Otherwise, start looking over your shoulder, pal. And don't think your mother's out of the woods either."

ભ્ર

Buddy Curran looked at Shadow. "What do you want me to do?"

"Pick's pissed off. He's pushing me hard, but things are red-hot with the law. Barron's mother has a 24-hour police guard on her hospital door for Christ's sake."

"Yeah, but she's not the target anymore," Curran reminded him.

"They know something's going on. Remember, she can identify Willie and Sammy. Lyons is sharp. Working with his people, they'll connect the dots. You've got to stay as far away from Willie and Sammy as possible. I'm talking no contact whatsoever."

"No problem there," Curran grunted. Although he had been tight with Mickey Carberry, he had little use for his two minions. He fortified his dislike for the duo by forwarding an idea that would throw them under the proverbial bus. "We've got to convince Willie ... Sammy, too ... to go to Mickey's wake.

That will go a long way towards telling us how much they've pieced together, you know, how much Barron's mother remembers."

"It ain't just the mother," Shadow reminded him. "What about *McGlinty*—you know, the *doctor*—he knows Willie and Mickey from previous business dealings. *He's* the one I'm really worried about. He can easily ID both of them."

"Don't worry about him. I'll take care of that problem."

⁒

Bobby didn't know what to expect insofar as his mother's physical condition. He exited the elevator on the sixth floor with Jill hard on his heels. The pair headed toward Trisha's room.

They had replaced the on-duty police officer from the previous evening.

Trisha's grilling of Bobby was still underway a full five minutes after they entered: What had happened? Who was the lovely woman? What was Mickey's involvement? How soon before she could go home?

Trisha rattled off a scattershot of questions, interspersing the queries with various comments.

Her rapid recovery amazed Bobby.

A nurse suddenly appeared. "The doctor will be in this afternoon. He thinks that you may be able to go home. Naturally, you'll have to promise to take it slow."

Once the nurse completed taking Trisha's latest vital signs, Bobby followed her out of the room. He was intent on convincing her that Trisha going home was unhealthy.

As Bobby headed down the hall to catch up with her, he noticed Ted Lyons walking in his direction.

Several confidantes surrounded him, as usual.

⁒

Bobby, Jake, and Jill's relief at finding Trisha safe and relatively unharmed paralleled, and perhaps even paled in comparison to that of Dr. Eugene McGlinty.

The doctor was driven back to retrieve his car after intense questioning by police investigators the previous evening. Upon returning to his Brookline home, his wife subjected him to a comparably uncomfortable level of questioning. It took several hours to convince her that he had not suffered a gambling relapse.

He eventually succumbed to the physical and mental exhaustion he had endured and begged off to bed.

He was still asleep the next morning when a Boston Police detective phoned to schedule a follow-up interview.

Mrs. McGlinty answered the phone and breathed an additional sigh of relief as the call corroborated her husband's story. Although the police were vague, she was able to get them to verify several key components of her husband's account of what had transpired. When she turned on the TV and saw the news stations carrying related activity about the story, she felt a tinge of guilt and headed out to pick up coffee and pastries before he woke up.

Buddy Curran watched her pull out of her driveway. He and Shadow were staking out the house from the corner of the curved street. Buddy jumped out of car and headed up the opposite sidewalk, about a half-block from the McGlinty home, as soon as she exited the driveway. He was dressed in a blue, gray, and black nylon-jogging suit and blended in as a typical middle-aged neighbor out for his daily walk.

A preoccupied Mrs. McGlinty paid him no mind when she passed him. Even if she had observed him closely, the bulkiness of his outfit and its deep recessed pockets were more than adequate to hide the 9-milimeter Beretta clutched tightly in his right hand.

Despite their planning, neither Curran nor Shadow had considered a contingency plan to offset the Brookline Police car sitting directly across the street from the McGlinty's driveway.

The radical curvature of the street had precluded them from noticing it sooner.

ᴄᴐ

Ted Lyons's aggravation surfaced as he glared at Bobby. Armed with the additional information provided by Jake, he said, "How many phone numbers do I have to give you? Listen to me; you're playing with fire here. You, your *mother*, your *friends*, you better start taking this seriously. You're dealing with bad people here. Don't minimize the lengths to which they'll go; and *don't* underestimate their resolve."

He grabbed Bobby's elbow and led him to the corner of a family waiting room. He stopped and said to a young, poker-faced police officer, "Don't let anyone in here."

Lyons pointed to a chair. "Sit down and tell me exactly what the guy said to you."

Bobby rehashed the story.

Lyons systematically broke it down in his mind. Once he was comfortable he had gleaned all the necessary information, he said, "I'm going to talk to some people. We're going to keep your mother here for a few more days. Have you got a problem with that?"

"I don't, but she might."

"I'll just have to convince somebody in power to temporarily downgrade her condition," Lyons said with a sly smile and a wink. "Just don't be too alarmed when you hear her next prognosis."

❦

Ted Lyons contacted a close friend from the Brookline Police Department. He explained the potential danger Dr. McGlinty might encounter as a witness to the activity related to Trisha, and requested that his friend's people keep a close eye on the McGlinty home.

The police chief absorbed the severity of Lyons's story and immediately dispatched a cruiser to conduct twenty-four hour surveillance at the McGlinty home.

Despite Lyons's prescience, and his friend's willingness to help, Buddy Curran was not easily deterred.

Once McGlinty's wife left—and Shadow remained in place to keep an eye out for any premature return—Buddy conducted a cursory survey of the ground floor rooms, ultimately entering through the rear of the McGlinty home.

The police presence initially shook him, but, as a youth, Buddy cut his teeth on breaking and entering jobs, or "B and Es" in police jargon. It was like riding a bike and in this case, the bike was equipped with training wheels.

The door under the McGlinty's backyard deck was unlocked and Curran was inside the house in a matter of seconds.

Eugene McGlinty heard the familiar noise. *That damn step* he thought, recognizing the source of the noise that had awakened him. He made a mental note to get the step repaired once-and-for-all before rolling over and pulling his blanket up over his shoulders. This left his back exposed to the bedroom door.

Unfortunately, his ignoring the step's warning coincided with Buddy Curran preparing to present himself as the ugly alter ego of the proverbial sandman.

Curran had almost completed his trip to the second floor when the loud creak brought him to a sudden halt. He removed the gun from his pocket, hugged the stairwell wall, held his breath, and perked his ears for any potential activity.

When silence reigned, it was time to take care of a little unfinished business.

39

Jill arrived back at Bobby's house. With a Boston Police car parked in front of the house, and a box truck double-parked and its driver making a delivery, she had to park farther down Hardy Street than usual. She was beginning to long for her regular lifestyle. Her cell phone was dead; her mailboxes—e-mail, voice mail, and U.S. Mail—were full; and she was exhausted.

She was also in love.

She entered and found Bobby on a different wavelength.

His thoughts were much more forlorn. "What do I do about Mickey's wake? I can't forgive him for what he did; but I feel like I should go out of respect for Jake and the rest of his family."

Jill, hoping for a more upbeat greeting, withheld any immediate response.

When Bobby turned his back and seemed prepared to drop the subject, she finally spoke up. "*You* have to make that decision. If you want me to go, I'll gladly go with you."

A bright light suddenly flooded Bobby's living room. He walked to the window and was shocked to see a local news station's mobile van setting up right across the street from his house.

"You've got to be kidding me."

"You want me to go out and deal with them?"

"Follow me." Bobby said, before heading for the other end of the house. "Remember the way you came in the other night? You know, when I had you pound on the backdoor with the umbrella? Go out that way, take a left, and then walk up the street from Marine Road, you know, on the beach end of the street.

"That won't be a problem. I'm actually parked down that way."

"Good. When you come back tonight, don't come here. Park where you dropped me off last night," Bobby pointed toward his backyard. "Call me when you get there and I'll slip out the backdoor and meet you."

Jill's noticed Trisha's diary as she passed through the kitchen. They had unfinished business they had yet to discuss. "Hey, I still need to talk to you about your mother's diary."

The bell rang before Bobby could respond. Assuming it was a reporter cold calling for information, he said, "Why don't you head out the back now. I'll call you."

Bobby opened the kitchen door that led to the back hall.

Jill focused on the diary. *Maybe I read it wrong.* She picked it up and said, "Do you mind if I take this with me? I promise I'll bring it back. I just want to read it one more time before we talk about it."

"Just don't lose it," Bobby said, quickly ushering her out the door.

∽

Dr. Eugene McGlinty rolled over to the cold barrel of a handgun pressed deep into his right temple.

Buddy Curran grabbed a handful of his mussed hair with a gloved hand. "You move and I'll splatter your fucking brains all over the pillow."

"What do you want?" McGlinty whimpered. Still half-asleep, he was staring into a pair of ominous steel-gray eyes made even more distinct by the black mask covering the remainder of the intruder's face.

"My boss thinks you're going to cooperate with the cops on this Barron case. He told me to 'kill you.' Is there any good reason why I shouldn't?"

Scared and mindful that he was the witness whom Mickey, Willie, and their ilk gained the least amount of comfort from, McGlinty begged for his life. "I won't say a word. Why would I?"

"Because the cops are going to come at you hard. They're sitting outside your house right now. My guy thinks you're going to cave in. So do I, for that matter."

McGlinty argued for his salvation. "I have nothing to gain by opening my mouth. You can always come back at me. I don't want to spend the rest of my life looking over my shoulder. Besides, I have no loyalty to *any* law enforcement group. They tried to strip away my license to practice—you know, my medical license—you've got my word."

Curran drew back the weapon, yanked on McGlinty's hair, and smashed the steel butt of the gun handle off the left side of his face, opening a nasty gash. Killing McGlinty was out of the question, at least for the time being. Nonetheless, Curran was intent on reinforcing his point.

Nauseated, and now wobbly, the doctor had no idea his life would be spared. Resultantly, he repeated his promise, whining, "I won't open my mouth. You have my word."

"I *better* have your word. You open your mouth about me even being here and you'll never see me coming the next time. You hear me? When they ask you about the people who were holding the woman captive, you know nothing. Right?"

Dazed and frightened, McGlinty shook his head from side to side. He managed to mumble, "Nothing." Shaking his head again, he recited the words he knew Curran wanted to hear, "I know nothing."

"Remember, the next time I won't even *wake* you … I'll just put two in the back of your fucking dome and a couple of more into your wife. You got me?"

"I've got you. I know nothing. I saw nothing."

Killing McGlinty was the most efficient way to prevent him from chirping to the police. Unfortunately, it would also send out a clear signal that this matter was light years from conclusion, and would place the Barrons, especially Bobby, under more intense police security.

Curran exited through the same door he entered. He was confident McGlinty understood his short-tem instructions. He remained on the endangered species list if things didn't work out with Bobby Barron; *or* if he reneged on his promise.

☙

"Can I help you?" Until this moment, Bobby Barron had never seen a news camera he didn't like.

"Vance Colchester," boomed the well-coiffed figure as he extended his right hand. "Channel Six News."

"How you doing?" Bobby said, ignoring his outstretched hand. He noticed his neighbor Larry Fitzgerald taking in the activity from across the street.

"You're Bobby Barron, correct?" Colchester asked. "We're here about the activity that occurred earlier. Several sources have disclosed that a woman, whom we believe to be your mother—"

Bobby cut Colchester off in mid-sentence. "I'm an *attorney*. It is my understanding that the Boston Police have an active investigation underway and—"

"Can you substantiate your mother's involvement?"

Bobby was upset at being cut off. He resorted to a more serious tone as he stared down the reporter. "Look. I'm trying to explain the situation to your satisfaction. If you interrupt me again, I'm going back inside. I am an officer of the court. In that capacity, nothing takes precedence over the protection of proper investigatory procedures. Given that, I will not compromise an ongoing police investigation."

"I understand, but—"

He was on a roll. It was time to turn the tables on the overbearing reporter. Bobby cut him off, and proceeded to treat him like a first-year law student in the process. "I don't think you're listening ... what did you say your name was? Vince?

"*Vance* ... Vance Colchester—"

"Right, right, *Vance*. Look, any comments I make regarding specifics of the case would serve no useful purpose at this time. They could, in fact, have an adverse effect on the police investigation." With a syrupy indignance, Bobby added, "I will not participate in conjecture or entertain half-truths or manufactured allegations."

"But, Mr. Barron—"

"I have nothing else to offer at his point. If the police uncover concrete evidence, and clear it for dissemination to the press, you folks will be the first to know. I have retained an individual to handle any additional media activity. You may know her. Her name is Jill Thurman."

Colchester pulled out a notepad. He did not recognize her name. His eyes narrowed in confusion and he repeated the name to ensure he had it correct. "You said Jill *Thurman*? T—H—"

Bobby cut him off again. "If you want to wait a moment, I'll go inside and get her contact information for you."

Bobby headed back into the house without waiting for the reporter's response.

Jill had already accessed her car and exited Hardy Street.

୧୨

"I already spoke with Jackie O'Brien over at the funeral home. I want two men stationed inside in plain black suits before the doors open at four. No Southie guys, but put a couple of guys in there who *look* like they're from Southie.

The police captain nodded, writing notes in a small black leather-bound notebook.

"Have them interact with the visitors at Carberry's wake, you know, like their employees of the funeral home. They can keep the Mass card plate clean and provide any services that may be required. Send them up there as soon as possible so they can get a crash course in what they should do, you know, how they should act. Have them see Jack's daughter, Tara. She's expecting them."

The police captain nodded, adding Tara's name in his notepad.

Lyons looked around his office. "Am I forgetting anything?"

The captain stepped forward and placed a manila folder on Lyons's desk. "Here are the people we're looking for commissioner. The first guy's name is

Willie Marcus. He's was in on it with Mickey Carberry. They've been running together for quite a while. The mother remembers him well. He's the one who originally picked her up out at Harbor Point. She identified him. So did her son.

"The other guy is a low-level accomplice, a wannabe. Young kid named Sammy Jackson."

Lyons shook open the folder. Eight-by-ten photos of Willie and Sammy slid out onto his desk.

The commissioner tossed the first picture aside. "I know Willie, but who's the kid?" He turned the photo toward the assembled group and held it up. "Christ, he's just a baby," he said, flashing the picture for the captain's staff.

"We've got paper on him. He's from Dorchester. Tough kid. In and out of trouble since his early teens."

A detective spoke up from the background. "We can pick him up anytime. We thought it best to wait and see where he leads us."

Lyons pondered that thought then said, "Neither of these guys are brain surgeons. I'll lay odds they both show up at the wake. Let's just wait until they leave and grab them outside so we don't disrupt the services anymore than necessary."

The detective nodded.

The commissioner explained his thought process. "Removing two more of these morons from the street will diminish the capacity of their acting in concert with anyone who's left. Plus, it'll give us a chance to question them. Maybe we can uncover additional participants."

Unfortunately, their most pivotal witness, Dr. Eugene McGlinty, was following the paramount law of self-preservation: *The less said the better.* To that end, he had already arranged to spend extended time at a friend's hunting cabin deep in the secluded woods of northern Maine.

His plan would be well received by Buddy Curran and Pick Piccorino, but even they didn't know he was leaving—which was just the way he wanted it.

As the staff filtered out, most of them failed to understand that Willie and Sammy were yesterday's news.

Buddy Curran should have been their paramount concern.

ひ

Jill rose from the couch. *Well, at least I know I'm not nuts.* She placed Trisha's diary on a coffee table after reading about May 10, 1970 a second time. She was walking toward the bathroom when her phone rang. "Hello."

"Hey, what's up?" Bobby asked. "Any chance we can swing by and see my mother before the wake? You know, just for a few minutes."

Jill stared at her watch. "I was just going to jump in the shower. I'll be over as soon as I can."

"Shower, huh? You need some company?"

"No, I think I can manage it on my own," she teased. Jill segued into a more serious tone. "Hey, I really need to speak to you about something. I think it's important, but I don't want to discuss it over the phone."

"What are you breaking up with me already?"

"Bobby, I'm serious."

"Breaking up's serious. By the way, I gave out your office phone number to those people who were peeking through my window. I explained that you were my new press secretary and they didn't seem too happy at your unavailability. If they only knew you were slipping out the backdoor while I kept them occupied."

"You should have given them my home phone or even my cell phone. I'm never in the office."

"Hey, what do I know?" Bobby laughed. "Don't forget to park over on M Street. I'll cut through my neighbor's yard to meet you. We'll shoot over and see my mother; go to Mickey's wake and see Jake; and then I'll treat you to dinner down Amrhein's. Then you can have your way with me after you ply me with a little alcohol. How's that sound?"

"You have a sick mind, Barron. I'm going to tell your mother."

"She'll never believe you."

No, it's you that's not going to believe what I have to say about your mother.

ひ

Larry Fitzgerald grabbed his kitchen phone. "Hello?"

"Larry, it's Bobby Barron."

"Bobby, what the hell's going on?"

"I need a favor..."

⌑

He sat in a parked car, easily blending in with the mini-media circus clustered on the corner of East Eighth Street and Hardy Street. That was fine with him. Their activity provided the necessary camouflage for his presence.

He planned to meet with Bobby Barron, but not in a group setting. His years of experience had taught him to blend in and wait for the right time to make his move. His internal antennas went up when a neighbor left his home and climbed up Barron's front stairs. When the guy was ushered in, he immediately smelled a rat.

He fired up his car and cruised up East Eighth Street for a quick trip around the block.

When he turned left on M Street, he was not surprised to see a flashy red Volvo double-parked on the left hand side of the street, halfway down the block.

He pulled over to the right.

⌑

Bobby slipped on a suit coat. "I need to get out of here, Larry. Like I told you on the phone, just hang in here for ten minutes while I slip out the back. I can't deal with the press right now. I've got to visit my mother in the hospital, and then go to a wake. I don't want these people following me."

"How is your mother by the way?"

"She's doing well. I'm going to walk into the living room with you. We'll walk over to the window and peek out so they see me. Then we'll start moving this stuff around like we're straightening up the place. I'll take a load to the other end of the house. I'll come back once and repeat that and then I'm out of here. Just wait about ten minutes, and then you can take off."

"Where are you going once you slip out the back?"

249

"I've got someone waiting for me over on M Street. Ted Lyons sent the cops down to tell these people they can't enter my property and ordered that cruiser that's sitting out there. There's no way they can see the cut-through into the Keller's yard from here. You with me?"

"Yeah, but what about locking up?"

"The door will lock as soon as you pull it shut. I just need a little diversion. What do you say?

Before Larry could answer, Bobby's cell phone rang. He looked at Larry and smiled. "Timing's everything. Wish me luck."

Bobby grabbed an armful of clothes, deposited them in the next room, and walked out the backdoor.

 барон

Barron appeared out of nowhere, just as he expected. He walked around the front of the car and slid into the passenger side seat of the red Volvo. He leaned over and kissed whoever was driving and then the car lurched forward.

He waited a few seconds then fell in behind them.

Jill headed past the Old Colony projects and turned onto Old Colony Avenue.

He maintained a safe distance between them. Success was predicated on surprise in his profession.

The drove over the Jimmy Kelly Bridge and exited at South Station. When they headed down Kneeland Street, he assumed they were heading to the hospital to visit his mother. This created a plethora of possibilities. *If they park on the street, it will be a lot tougher as there will be more witnesses and easy access into the building. Maybe they'll park in the garage on the far side of Washington Street. That would be perfect.*

Jill turned left on Washington Street but passed the entrance to the garage.

He was disappointed, but a lack of parking spots along the adjacent streets buoyed his sagging spirits. The farther they got from the hospital's front doors, the less foot traffic they would encounter. It would also eliminate the opportunity for them to access the building quickly.

Jill circled the block and they passed through Oak Street.

He was confident of a clean shot at Bobby if they parked this far from the hospital.

Jill pulled into an empty spot.

He slipped into another empty spot several car lengths behind Jill; knowing from experience that approaching them from behind was the most effective route to success.

ℰℱ

"What's up, Shadow?" Pick Piccorino whispered into his cell phone.

"Nothing yet," said Pick's erstwhile—*or so Shadow had thought*—attorney. "It's going to take some time."

"Despite having nothing but time, I don't *have* any time. If I can't get Dunlap's case tossed soon, he'll walk out of here owing me nothing. It's all *about* time."

"Buddy's on top of it. He's going right at Barron. He'll persuade him to do the right thing. It's just hot right now. Barron's house is lit up like the fucking White House at Christmas with all the news cameras. Buddy's got a plan, but, like I said, it's going to take time."

ℰℱ

It has to happen before he gets to Washington Street, he thought. He exited his vehicle and fell in behind Bobby and Jill as they headed up Oak Street.

Bobby put his hand to his ear. His pace slowed, and then stopped. He ducked against a concrete wall of the Wang YMCA. Bobby jammed his left forefinger into his ear in an effort to hear his phone over the gusting echoes of the chilly November wind.

Shit! He couldn't stop, and it would look too obvious if he turned back toward his car. He had to pass Bobby and Jill. *I'll turn the corner. When they start moving, I'll have to head back toward them.* As he passed them, he could briefly hear Bobby's end of the conversation. "...I'm right outside the hospital, I'm heading for her room..." before being unable to detect any additional conversation.

He turned left at the corner and positioned himself at a bus stop, just beyond their view. *As soon as they begin moving in my direction, I'll head back toward them and catch them off guard.*

℘

Marie Phillips was shocked to see all the coverage on the NECN mid-afternoon newscast. *No wonder Bobby had been so closemouthed.* Reaching for the phone, she called his cell.

Marie received several arcane responses. She finally asked, "What hospital is she in?"

"New England Medical Center."

"Is she okay, Bobby?"

"Hold on, I'm having a hard time hearing you." Bobby ducked closer to the building to shield the earpiece from the wind.

"What did you say?"

"I said, is she okay?"

Jill stepped closer to Bobby, allowing an approaching stranger enough room to pass.

"Yeah, I'm right outside the hospital, I'm heading for her room right now."

"Is there anything I can do?"

"Not at the moment."

"What about work?" Marie asked. "Are you coming in?"

"Not for a few days. "I'll call you after the funeral tomorrow and we'll come up with a game-plan as far as my return." Bobby signed off after twenty more seconds of give and take.

He and Jill regrouped and headed for the hospital.

At least that was their intention.

℘

252

Once they resumed walking, the stalker made his move. Reaching into his right-hand jacket pocket, the feel of the cold metal bought him an added level of comfort. *People never know how to react,* he thought.

As he closed in on the couple, the stalker whipped the unit out of his pocket and jammed it toward the center of Bobby's face.

Bobby lashed out instinctively with his left arm to deflect the attack.

The stalker's tape recorder flew out of his hand and crashed to the sidewalk. Its batteries and various components shattered and bounced in a half-dozen different directions.

c⁄ɔ

Buddy Curran was intent on one thing. He was going to maintain full control in any face-to-face meeting with this Barron character. He parked his car on the left hand side of West Fifth Street, next to the Highland 1 Hour Dry Cleaners on Dorchester Street. This gave him an unobstructed view of the activity in and around the front door of O'Brien's Funeral Home.

Presuming that Barron planned to pay his respects to his old friend, Curran looked forward to meeting his prey upon his exit.

Whatever secret details Barron knew about framing Tim Dunlap would soon be unveiled. The follow-up plan to free Pick Piccorino would then begin.

40

Bobby raised his fists instinctively, blurting, "Who are you want?" It was an amalgam of what was going on in his head. Properly stated, it would have sounded more like "*Who* are you?" or "*What* do you want?"

Bobby rephrased the question when the perpetrator didn't answer. "Who are you?"

"My name is Frank Hart. I'm a freelance news reporter. I was wondering if I could get a couple of minutes with you to discuss the activities surrounding your mother."

"Who did you say you worked for?"

"I'm an independent. I chase stories and sell them."

Bobby's face was as white as blackboard chalk. He shook his head, grasped Jill's arm, and said, "Let's go."

He turned back toward the reporter to see whether he was going to follow them, earning himself a full-on blast of a camera flash. As Bobby reoriented his eyes, the reporter continued peppering him with questions.

"Do you have any idea why your mother was kidnapped? Are you going to visit her now? Would you mind if I accompanied you?"

Bobby pulled away from Jill. Two days of fear, panic, and complete uncertainty managed to roil an inner-rage that finally erupted.

Bobby locked his hands on the collar of the reporter's nylon coat.

The reporter's camera crashed to the ground when he attempted to defend himself.

Bobby twisted his powerful hands in opposite directions to tighten his grip, rendering Hart unable to breathe. Swinging his right leg behind the legs of the reporter, Bobby pulled him forward so they were nose-to-nose before rolling his right shoulder into the reporter and violently hurling him in the opposite direction.

As the two men plunged toward the sidewalk, Bobby invoked an old football trick. He directed as much of his body weight as possible toward the center of the reporter's torso as they struck the sidewalk.

The reporter's lungs deflated. Two of his ribs cracked. The tactic proved far more effective on concrete than grass.

Jill stood helpless and frightened.

Bobby's behavior was uncontrollable. "Stay away from me. You hear me?" Bobby latched back onto the reporter's throat and grabbed a healthy handful of hair, pulling him into a sitting position.

The reporter's ravaged ribs resulted in an agonizing, animal-like scream of agony.

"You come near me again and I'll kill you," Bobby screamed, shoving his upper torso forward with a vigorous one-handed thrust to his throat.

Bobby grabbed a still shocked Jill's left hand. He pulled her across Washington Street toward the hospital. They stopped at the registration desk of the Emergency Room and Bobby summoned a security officer. "I noticed a guy across the street who might need some assistance. It looks like someone beat him up pretty bad. You may want to send someone over to look at him."

The security guard thanked Bobby, applauding him for 'his civic responsibility.'

"Most people would have walked right by the guy," he said before heading out the main door to evaluate the victim.

"Most people wouldn't have beat-up the guy in the first place," a still shaken Jill whispered as they walked toward the elevators. "I trust you're not *always* so civically responsible."

Bobby knew better than to respond. His brief romance with Jill was going to be short-lived if he didn't get a handle on his emotions.

୧୨

Bobby and Jill found Trisha in good spirits when they arrived at her room. Dr. Wissard had been in for a visit and an update, and she had improved significantly since the last time Bobby had seen her.

Bobby bent over and kissed his mother on the cheek. "How you doing, Ma?"

"I feel great, honey. The problem is they told me I would be going home and now they are saying I might have to stay another day or two. What about you? You look a little frazzled."

"Please, you don't want to know."

Jill rolled her eyes.

Bobby changed the subject. "So, what do you remember?"

"I was really sick. It was actually weird, you know, kind of like a dream. At times I thought I recognized people's voices."

"Oh yeah? Whose voices do you think you heard?"

"Oh, I don't know. It was all so surreal."

"Did you see any of them?" Jill asked.

"Oh, yeah. There was this guy, Willie. He claimed to be some type of government agent." Trisha looked at Bobby. "That's how it all started. He claimed *you* were being arrested for some type of illegal activity."

Bobby shook his head. *Great! This is just what Jill needs to hear right now,* he thought, before Mickey's involvement and utter betrayal suddenly re-entered his mind.

Trisha expounded on everything she remembered and her story ended with a bang. "What was really weird was when they finally agreed to release us the people that *had* been involved disappeared and Fairly Curran ended up driving me and the doctor back to our house. How *is* that doctor doing by the way?"

256

Bobby sat up in his chair. Sneaking a peek at Jill he said, "*Who* drove you back to the house?"

"Fairly Curran."

"Who's Fairly Curran?" *And why does that name ring a bell?*

"I went to school with him—years ago—well, not that many years ago," Trisha corrected herself, not wanting to reveal her age in front of Jill.

"Did he know you?" Bobby asked.

Trisha laughed. "I doubt it. We were *kids*. It was the old Nazareth School at O and Third Street. Saint Brigid's wasn't even built then, well they were building it at the time. That's how long ago it was."

"But you're sure it was him?"

"Oh, I'm sure."

"Did you tell the police?" Bobby asked.

Trisha paused, "I don't think so, but I don't remember. I was still pretty groggy when we spoke."

Fairly Curran. The name nagged at Bobby.

∽

Bobby apologized to Jill in the lobby of the hospital. He pledged that his earlier behavior was aberrational and Jill accepted the apology, reconciling that he had been through an inordinate amount of pressure.

The reporter's suspect actions resulted in his paying the tab for the nefarious acts of several truly evil individuals.

As they exited the hospital, a temporarily relieved Bobby transitioned back into his pending problems. "I've got bad vibes about this guy, Fairly."

"What parents would name their kid Fairly?"

Bobby ignored Jill's question and repeated his thought. "I'm telling you, when I say I got bad vibes, we're missing something here."

He reached for Jill's hand as they crossed Washington Street and she readily accepted his advance.

All was not lost!

℘

The waiting line at O'Brien's Funeral Home extended well down Dorchester Street. The Carberry family was large, well known, and highly respected in the South Boston community.

The long line lent credence to that fact.

Jill and Bobby waited thirty minutes to get inside and another ten to reach Mickey's body.

The kneeler was removed to facilitate the movement of the long line. Mrs. Carberry was first in line, sitting in an upholstered chair.

Bobby took her hands in his. "I'm so sorry to see you under these circumstances, Mrs. Carberry," all the while wondering *Does she know what Mickey did to my mother?*

Jake was next in line and while Bobby conversed with Mrs. Carberry about his days of yore with Mickey, Jake took the time to slip around him and give Jill a healthy hug. "How's he doing?" nodding towards Bobby.

"Oh my God, Jake, you wouldn't believe it. We went over the hospital to visit his mother before coming here and some reporter followed us. They ended up in a fight. It was awful."

"What happened?" Jake asked, before feeling a tap on his shoulder. He turned to encounter Bobby.

"Hey, Jake, how you doing?" Bobby asked.

Their firm handshake evolved into a bear hug.

Bobby released Jake and said, "I need to speak with you privately. Any chance? I just need a minute."

"Sure, I need a break anyway. It's been non-stop since the doors opened."

Pictures of Mickey were on display throughout the funeral parlor. Their path to the small parking lot outside the backdoor of O'Brien's stalled on numerous occasions, as both Jake and Bobby bumped into friends and acquaintances who wanted to catch up.

258

Jill meandered a short distance behind them.

Once they stepped outside, Bobby got right to the point. "Who's Fairly Curran?"

Jake took a deep breath and laughed. The cool November air felt good. "Don't let Fairly hear you call him that. Fairly Curran is better known as "Buddy," and Buddy Curran is a nasty guy. He was a friend of Mickey's. As a matter of fact, I'm surprised he's not here tonight, probably will be before the night's over." Shaking his head, he said, "Plenty of other lowlifes have shown up. Anyway, what's your interest in Buddy Curran?"

"I just came from visiting with my mother—"

Jake cut Bobby off. With a poker face he asked, "Hey, did some reporter follow you?"

Bobby stared at Jake. "Christ, is there *anything* you don't know?" When he looked at Jill, it quickly sunk in. "What are you guys doing, talking behind my back? I thought we were partners?"

"We're not going to be partners when that lawsuit comes in for piledriving that reporter, mister. You should've seen him, Jake."

"Guy scared the heart out of me," Bobby said, before revisiting the previous subject. "So, how well do you know this guy?"

"Not well at all. I mean, I know him enough to say hi to, but that's about it. I do know plenty of people who know him. Why?"

"I'm not going to sit around and wait for him to come after me. Can you set up a meeting with him through your friends?"

"Bobby, you've got to understand, these guys don't set up business meetings. With them, it's all about intimidation."

"I understand. Don't forget, I represented a lot of those people. The problem is I can't just sit around and wait for something to happen."

Jake's disposition suddenly changed. "Wait here," he said, a sudden sense of urgency obvious in his voice. "There was a guy here earlier who might be able to help. I'm not sure if he's still here. Let me take a look."

જી

Buddy Curran stared at the Massachusetts Bar Association photo of Bobby Barron, then at the guy with the smoking-hot red head standing in the waiting line outside O'Brien's, and thought *That's got to be him.*

Curran reached into the glove compartment of his Oldsmobile and pulled out a piece of paper Shadow had given him. It was loaded with information on Bobby Barron, but he could not find any significant other listed. This cast Jill as the proverbial fly in the ointment. It was important that he discuss the situation one-on-one with Barron.

Fifteen minutes later, Bobby Barron marched down the driveway of the funeral home.

He'd jettisoned the redhead and seemed to be walking directly toward Curran's Oldsmobile.

☙

With the backside of O'Brien's parking lot out of his view, Buddy Curran couldn't possibly have known what had transpired in the minutes leading up to Bobby Barron's approach.

Notwithstanding, a mitigating factor had emboldened Bobby to follow this course of action.

Five minutes earlier, Jake had come back outside, accompanied by another gentleman.

Jill was gone, having excused herself to use the ladies' room.

The timing couldn't have been more perfect.

"Bobby, say hello to a friend of mine. Jack, this is Bobby Barron."

Jake pointed at Bobby and said, "This is the guy I was telling you about. Tell him what you just told me."

Jack leaned toward Jake and whispered, "Hey, the last thing I need is a beef with Buddy. Please Jake, I've got enough problems."

"Relax, Jack. What did I tell you?"

"I just don't want my name brought into it. When you asked me about Buddy, I didn't know it was going any further than you and me. It was just funny that I saw him on the way in, and then you asked me if I'd seen him lately. I need you to keep me out of this, Jake."

Jake threw his arm around him. "Jack, how well do you know me?" Asked rhetorically, Jake continued, "Your name will never be brought up, you've got my word. I just wanted Bobby here to be able to thank you for the tip. As far as we're concerned, we never met. Right, Bobby?"

Bobby nodded. *He had no idea what they were talking about.*

Jake's assurance was good enough for Jack Bradshaw. He was only in attendance to provide additional cover against any possible evidence that could lead back in his direction. He was also officially convinced that Jake's brother Mickey was now truly sorry for savagely beating his son and his son's loudmouth friend.

When Jack Bradshaw walked away, Jake said, "Jack hangs in the same bar as Buddy Curran. I asked him if he'd seen him lately. He told me he was sitting in a car right across the street. I popped outside to get some air and there he was. If you walk out to the end of the driveway, he's right across the street, parked next to the cleaners. How do you want to handle it?"

Bobby analyzed the situation. "My thought is he's just going to continue to do more of the same, you know, threaten me. I mean, he's not going to kill me. Right?"

"It's your call. If your question is, *will* he kill you right now? My answer would be no. If your question is, *would* he kill you? My answer would be in a New York minute!"

Bobby was tired of looking over his shoulder and frightened about the well-being of his mother. The time had come to confront his demons. Bobby walked down the driveway and straight for Curran's car.

Jake had taken one more undisclosed precaution while he was outside looking for Curran's car. He had removed Mickey's gun from the trunk of his car and jammed it down the front of his pants. For once in his life, he was glad to be wearing a suit coat.

Jake gave Bobby a few seconds, and then walked through the funeral parlor, his eyes focused in a distant manner to avoid making contact with anyone out of fear of having to stop and talk. He exited the front door as casually as possible, walked down the granite steps, and headed across Dorchester Street.

Much to Jake's surprise, Bobby was engaged in what appeared to be a deep conversation with Buddy Curran.

ↁ

Bobby traversed Dorchester Street as if he owned it.

He wasn't putting up with this nonsense for one second longer. As he approached the driver's side window of Curran's car, his adversary's thin frame and overall lack of size struck him. From six-feet away and closing fast, it was obvious that he was no threat to Bobby—unless, of course, he shot him.

Feeling more than a little Clint Eastwoodesque, they locked eyes as Bobby approached.

Curran lowered the window.

Bobby even sounded a bit like Eastwoood when he uttered, "Are you *looking* for me?"

Curran's threatening glare belied any physical shortcomings. His silence was frightening.

Bobby quickly second-guessed his rash decision. "I'm not looking for any trouble," Bobby explained. "You want to talk? I'll tell you anything you want to know. I just don't think I know what you people *think* I know."

"Get in the car," Curran said, thrusting his right thumb toward the passenger seat.

"I'm not getting in any car. You want to talk, we can talk right here."

"Well, back the fuck up and let me out."

Bobby backed up. He noticed Jake walking on the opposite side of West Fifth Street.

Curran stepped from the vehicle. He couldn't have been more than five-foot-ten.

Bobby stared down at him and thought *He looks so much older than my mother.* Fortunately, Bobby knew nothing of his past transgressions. There was no quantifiable correlation between size and effectiveness in Buddy Curran's malevolent world.

What was also fortunate for Bobby was they needed him and, therefore, couldn't do him any *permanent* harm.

This didn't stop an enraged Buddy Curran from putting on a show. "Who the *fuck* do you think you are?" he hissed. He shoved his right hand inside his leather coat and said, "I'll blow your fucking head off!"

Bobby stepped back. He was now unequivocally convinced he had made a tactical error. Thoughts of running entered his mind.

"Buddy? Jake Carberry. How you doing?" said a voice off to the left.

Curran's right eye twitched and his head turned. He withdrew an empty hand from his coat and found himself staring at Jake Carberry. "Jake. Yeah, right,...Hey, I'm sorry about Mickey. He was a good kid." He shook Jake's hand.

"Yeah, thanks. I was just out getting a little air." Jake turned to Bobby. "Bobby Barron, right?"

"Yeah," said a still shaken Bobby. "Hey, I'm sorry about Mickey, too. I must have missed you. I was already inside the wake," Bobby said, pointing at O'Brien's before accepting Jake's extended hand.

Turning back to Curran, Jake said, "Well, you look like you're talking business. I'll leave you guys alone."

Jake successfully neutralizing the potentially volatile situation allowed Bobby to seize on the opportunity. "Listen, Mickey Carberry was a friend of mine. He screwed me and I'm still haunted by that. However, you guys are making accusations that simply aren't true. Can you set up a meeting with Dunlap?"

"All I know is what I was told. How you straighten it out is your business. Bottom line, my guy's convinced *you* set Dunlap up, and from what I hear, everything is pointing in your direction. My people want you to make it good."

Bobby didn't dare interrupt him.

Lowering his voice, Curran said, "Look, kid, you've got a lot of balls, you know, approaching me like this. But that ain't going to get you anywhere, you hear me? *Here's* the message. Make it good." Pointing at O'Brien's, he added,

"You don't want to be Jackie's next customer, but if you don't do the right thing, that's exactly where you're going to end up."

Bobby understood that no matter what he said, he wasn't going to sway Curran. "Look, I don't want to be a wise guy. I'm telling you, the only way we're going to solve this is by setting up a meeting with Dunlap."

"He's in fucking prison," Curran reminded Bobby.

"That's the best I can do." Bobby said with a shrug, before reversing direction and walking back across Dorchester Street.

As he approached the front door of the funeral home, he watched two men in black suits escorting a third man down the same driveway he'd used minutes earlier.

While the escorted party was wearing respectable clothing, Bobby would never forget those bushy eyebrows. They reached the bottom of the driveway just as a police car—white and blue lights flashing, but no siren, per Ted Lyon's orders—whipped into the opening to transport Willie Marcus to the police station for questioning.

Young Sammy Jackson's total lack of respect for his dead comrade had saved him from a similar fate.

At least for the time being.

❧

"We're in the same spot we were in when this all started," Bobby said, taking a swig out of a bottle of *Corona*.

Jill swirled her icy green Margarita with a straw. Amrhein's restaurant was a recently renovated and significantly up-scaled version of a South Boston institution that dated back to the 1890s. "Anyway, I read your mother's diary."

Bobby slumped noticeably. The mere mention of his mother caused him to ask, "You don't think they'll go after her again, do you?"

Jill leaned her head closer to Bobby. "You're not *listening* to me. Portions of your mother's diary are very explicit."

"What do you mean *'explicit?'*"

Jill took a deep breath. She carefully couched the attribution. "According to the *diary*, your birth was the result of a rape in 1970."

"What are you talking about?"

"It's in the diary." Jill dug it out from her oversized pocketbook. "Your birth resulted from a rape."

Bobby stared blankly at her before focusing his eyes on the diary. He repeated his question, "What are you *talking* about?"

Jill opened it and began reading to Bobby. "Everyone was celebrating the Bruins winning the Stanley Cup and I was stuck at work. It was all worthwhile when this gorgeous guy named Tad came into the store around nine to buy something. How was I to know that such a gorgeous guy could also be a rapist?"

A disbelieving Bobby took the diary from Jill's hands.

Jill coaxed Bobby to slide over and joined him on the opposite side of the booth. She said, "There's a number of other things you should see."

Bobby reread the passage. "What else is in there?"

Jill gently reclaimed the diary and rifled through the pages.

A perky young waitress appeared out of nowhere. "You folks decide on anything yet?"

"You know what? We're actually going over an important matter and we're going to need a little more time," Jill said. "Would you mind getting me another margarita?" Looking at Bobby, Jill asked, "You want another beer?"

Without removing his eyes from the diary, Bobby said, "Bring me a dozen."

౭౨

"Are you serious, Buddy?" Shadow barked into his cell phone.

"That's what the kid said."

"There's no fucking way we can do that."

"Why not? Pick's got the juice."

"He's not at the fucking Ritz, Buddy. He's in *prison*."

"First of all, don't raise your voice to me. I know where the fuck he is. You want me to whack this kid? What good will that do? The kid's gone, but the problem remains." Mulling over his thoughts, Curran said, "Actually, things get *worse*. The kid is the key. Feel Pick out, see what he thinks."

A noticeably subdued Shadow said, "Okay, let me get this straight. This kid's simply going to march into prison and meet with Pick?"

"That's *not* what I said. Barron said he would be willing to 'Meet with *Dunlap.*' I don't think he has a clue about Pick from what he said to me." Curran drew a deep breath before beginning his explanation. "Barron goes into Rice—"

"Ostensibly, he goes in to meet Dunlap, and Pick intervenes."

"I don't know what the fuck you just said," Curran responded with a chuckle, "but I *think* you've got it."

❡

Bobby took a long swig of his third Corona—the fourth already ordered—and admitted, "It's all plausible." He'd seen the handwritten evidence with his own eyes. Moreover, despite lifelong stories to the contrary, he had known for quite some time that his father did not die in Vietnam. "Where do we go from here?"

Jill had returned to the opposite side of the booth. She looked into Bobby's eyes and said, "Thirty-eight years is a long time. What *can* you do? Just be thankful you've got your mother back."

"I already told Curran I would meet with Tim Dunlap," he reminded her. "Plus, what's to say they won't do something to my mother down the line?"

A confused Jill said, "I'm not following you."

"*I'm* not following me at this point."

"Bobby, you're mixing two totally separate issues." Jill attempted to provide a coherent analysis to Bobby's predicaments. "*This* situation with your mother is between *you* and *her*. All this *other* craziness seems to be something you need to address immediately, but it has *nothing* to do with what's in your mother's diary. Right?"

"Yeah, I suppose you're right."

41

Jake Carberry stood at the foot of his bed, rifling through the drawer of the armoire that housed most of his wardrobe. *I've got to get kick-started. Why is it that whenever you needed black socks you always find every blue pair you've ever owned, and vice-versa? And why was it that artificial light—be it a lamp or an overhead—never shone bright enough to assist in separating the two colors?*

His day wouldn't be improving much.

Burying his brother Mickey was the next item on his agenda.

❧

Johann Sebastian Bach ultimately proved to be the most renowned member of an already legendary musical clan whose Hungarian roots traced back over well over two-hundred years.

Born in 1685 and orphaned in 1695 Bach earned a scholarship to the world-renowned Saint Michael School in Luneburg, Germany in 1699.

His life's work embodied the necessity for recording history, with one possible exception. Despite his brilliance, even Bach would have had a difficult time accepting his "Fugue in D minor" being relegated to a ring tone for a cell phone, circa 2008. After all, even brilliance of his dimensions required parameters.

Bobby Barron now found himself victimized by this fact. Having finished off nine *Corona's* at Amrhein's; been apprised that he was the progeny of a rapist; and been threatened by still another local gangster over something he had nothing to do with; a loud version of Bach's "Fugue in D minor" merged seamlessly into his dreams as the chosen default tone for his BlackBerry's alarm clock.

In the throes of a considerable hangover, Bobby deduced that Jill had already exited his bed—or perhaps she had never slept there—as that side of the bed seemed undisturbed upon further inspection. Bobby hoped he hadn't embarrassed himself too much. He looked over to a small night table where the offending BlackBerry was charging. *Did I charge it or did Jill do it for me?*

He stumbled over to the night table and performed several quick manipulations to dismiss the annoying alarm. He then produced Jill's cell number and hit SEND.

"Hey, what are you nuts, leaving me alone?" Bobby asked, when she cheerfully—no, far *too* cheerfully—answered her phone.

"Hey, I took good care of you, buster. I quit after two margaritas."

Bobby laughed. It made his hair hurt. "I should have followed your example. Hey, I'm going to Mickey's Mass, but I'm not going to the grave."

"Yeah, yeah, you gave me your whole itinerary last night," Jill reminded him, "but I'm going to get fired if I don't get in to work and explain myself. They must think I'm out of my mind. I simply went dark on them. You also said you were going to visit your mother after the Mass."

"I remember that," Bobby lied. Snippets of their conversation from the previous evening bled back into his memory. He could hear Jill's voice reciting various passages from his mother's diary, most notably, "Your birth was the result of a rape."

"You still there?" Jill asked.

⌘

The presiding priest at the newly refurbished Gate of Heaven Church called on Jake to eulogize Mickey.

Bobby sat there thinking *What positive things can you possibly say about a guy who steadfastly refused to conform to generally accepted societal standards?*

Jake not only did the job, he did it remarkably well. For fourteen minutes, he enthralled the assembled audience with an anecdotal history of Mickey's life.

Friends and family wept.

Even Bobby found himself conflicted by competing sensations of sadness, overlaid against the fact that this guy—*his lifelong friend*—had participated in the kidnapping of his mother.

Mickey's brothers escorted his body out of the church at the conclusion of the Mass.

Bobby slipped out a side door onto I Street. He headed down the hill toward his car, all the while dreading his next task.

During the Mass, he wondered whether to drop the matter entirely, questioning what good could possibly result from it. In the end, however, he knew he had to get it off his chest. The Buddy Currans of the world weren't going to vacate his life until they got their way, and that reality was already occupying far too much space in his head and time in his life.

Maybe confronting my mother won't be the worst thing I've ever had to do. I still have to go to Riverfork and see why Tim Dunlap is creating all this aggravation a full year-and-a-half after he went to jail.

ᥱ᠕

Pick Piccorino—who had arrived at Tim Dunlap's cell ten minutes earlier and seemingly out of thin air—finished his explanation. After a brief pause, he said, "So, what do you think?"

Dunlap chose his words carefully. "I know how important this is to you. However, the problem remains the same. I don't think Bobby Barron had anything to do with my being in here."

"Are you shitting me?" Pick grumbled. He raised his voice several octaves. "*Madone!* What am I going to do with you? I'm going to ask you one last time. Did *you* rape that girl?"

It was the equivalent of the unanswerable question, "Have you stopped beating your wife?" Whether Dunlap answered yes or no, he was not going to satisfy Pick's one-track mind. Answering "Yes" could ostracize him from the invaluable protection Pick's crew provided, not to mention possible retribution. A "No" would advance Pick's argument that he needed to stick up for himself. That entailed his working in concert with Pick against Bobby Barron.

In the end, the choice was easy.

"Maybe you're right. When can we meet him?"

Pick's dour demeanor instantly disappeared; replaced by a wide, toothy smile. Clapping Dunlap on the shoulder, he squeezed his cheek and said, "That's my boy! I'm going to set up a special face-to-face."

He winked, adding, "You know what I mean?"

 ∾

Bobby headed down the hall of the New England Medical Center. He couldn't shake the butterflies. He arrived at Trisha's room and her improved physical appearance shocked him. *This was going to make things that much more difficult.*

"Hey, what's up?" Trisha asked. She rose out of a chair for a hug and kiss.

"You look great," Bobby responded, thinking *But not for long.*

"They're releasing me tomorrow morning. Think you can pick me up?"

Bobby nodded. "Sure. But, first I have to talk to you about something."

 ∾

"The diary is true," admitted an ashen Trisha.

"What about Nan and Pa? Do they know?"

"To an extent," Trisha answered. "It's a long story…."

And out it poured. It was a tropical rainstorm—in the form of tangible information for Bobby—followed by bright sunlight representing the decades of Trisha withholding the truth.

Trisha delved deeper and deeper into the recesses of her suppressed memory to explain everything to Bobby. The more she spoke, the better she felt. It was amazingly therapeutic. At times, she would miss key points and she would backtrack.

At one point, Bobby shook his head and slowly mumbled, "All this time?"

"Bobby, we're talking about a *different* time. Pregnancy was the Scarlet Letter of my generation. It ruined entire families. It's not like today, kids having kids and society turning a blind eye to it. I entered a home for unwed mothers in Dorchester. It was *awful*. Then you were born and my whole life changed. My parents wanted me to put you up for adoption. For nine months I fought them…" A torrent of tears flowed as the memories resurfaced.

"I'm so sorry, Mom." Bobby said, hugging her fiercely.

Through muffled sobs, Trisha said in a low voice, "I feel like I've gotten the weight of the world off my shoulders."

Bobby released her. "Did they ever catch this Tad guy?"

An irreverent smile suddenly replaced the tears. "I made sure they didn't, but *I know* who he is. I have since you were a few weeks old."

The sequel was every bit as disturbing and enlightening as the original tale.

Suddenly, everything began to make sense.

42

"You've got to be kidding me?" Jill gasped. Her hands involuntarily covered her mouth and her luminous green eyes nearly popped from their widened sockets. She sat on Bobby's living room couch as he relayed what he had learned from his mother.

He conveniently left out one key point.

"I thought she was kidding; but that's not even the *craziest* part of the story."

"What can *possibly* be crazier than that?"

Bobby sat opposite her in an upholstered chair. He took a deep breath. Exhaling, he rubbed his face with both hands and said slowly, "All these years she *knew* who raped her."

"*What!* Why would she *ever* cover up for someone who raped her?"

"It gets even crazier!"

"Come on. How can it possibly get any crazier?"

Bobby spoke slowly to gauge the effect on Jill. "Tim Dunlap is my *father*."

Jill's slacked jaw, wrinkled forehead, and disbelieving eyes said it all. As she digested the ramifications of that bit of news, Bobby continued.

"They think *I* set Dunlap up. The crazy part is they kidnapped my *mother* to put leverage on *me* to come clean."

"Wait, wait. I'm confused," Jill said, shaking her head, then her hands, in an effort to slow him down.

Bobby repeated the chain of events. "They kidnapped my *mother* to get at *me*. But it was my *mother* who set this whole thing up."

"What are you talking about?"

"Tim Dunlap is Tad. Timothy A. Dunlap. T - A - D. It's his initials."

Jill paused to process the information. "Wait a minute. Tim Dunlap is in jail for raping a young girl in Brighton. They tried to blame the—"

"Other guy," Bobby said, completing her thought. "Except Dunlap didn't rape that young girl."

Jill's total confusion was obvious.

Bobby attempted to simplify things. "It was a DNA case. The crux of the case hinged on Dunlap's sperm being all over his monogrammed handkerchief. The TAD never registered until my mother told me what she had done. The handkerchief had a huge D in the middle. When you look at it, it was a smaller T, a D, and a smaller A. It was T - D - A, *not* T - A - D."

"Unbelievable," Jill said, masking the fact that it was still too much to comprehend.

"What's more unbelievable is that the guy who was originally accused of that rape—and who probably did it—had the *same* initials. His name was Thomas Davenport. Amazingly, even his middle initial matched. What were the chances of that? When they inventoried the rape evidence for that young girl's case there was a white handkerchief among the items that had been confiscated from the alleged rapist."

Jill nodded, and then shrugged. She was unsure where Bobby was heading.

"At the time, my mother showed an inordinate amount of interest in that particular case. She even took time off work to accompany me to police headquarters to review the evidence. While we were there, she spilled some coffee. Of course, we thought it was an accident. While the technician and I were running around to clean up the mess she replaced the existing handkerchief with a handkerchief she had held onto since 1970."

"Oh, my God," Jill said, placing her hands over her mouth.

Jill's complete captivation encouraged Bobby to continue. "She then began an anonymous behind-the-scenes phone calling campaign claiming to police that Dunlap was the actual rapist. At the time, there was a lot of speculation as to why a big shot attorney was defending such a low-life. Dunlap told me that he was forced to do it by the mob because the guy was a degenerate gambler and they didn't want to lose his business. But when the DNA test on the handkerchief proved to be Dunlap's, conventional wisdom was that he got involved to cover up for his own act. The mob guy didn't care, because he still had his gambler on the street and could continue to extract his weekly payments. The fact that he was a rapist mattered little to him, as long as he kept betting, losing, and paying."

"But couldn't they tell the handkerchief was over thirty-years old?"

"I asked my mother that same question. The answer is no." Shrugging his shoulders, he said, "Dunlap's in prison, right? Remember, she knew Dunlap was my father since *1971*. Her renewed interest evolved out of her rage that Dunlap was representing someone who did the same thing *he* had done to her years earlier. You see, normally he wouldn't have been involved in this type of case. He was big-time. In the end, one isolated quote in a newspaper triggered this entire event. Absent him being quoted—or my mother *reading* it for that matter—none of this would have happened.

"Wow, but you can see why she would think that way, you know, have that type of reaction."

"Oh yeah, absolutely. She was infuriated that he was defending this guy. Anyway, getting back to my mother's story, after Dunlap raped her she was able to escape by kicking him in the face. Dunlap had cleaned himself off with his handkerchief and she inadvertently grabbed it when she was pulling her pants up. She tossed it on the ground once she realized what she'd done, but when it landed, she noticed the monogram and decided to keep it as proof. Remember, this was pre-DNA days. She only kept it because of the monogram."

"It's like a movie," Jill said.

Bobby nodded in agreement. "Three things worked in her favor. The first two were the absolute lack of any light in her hiding spot; coupled with the fact that the paper bag she had placed it in was the perfect receptacle for this type of evidence. In fact, that's how evidence is stored in today's sophisticated laboratories; plain old heavy brown paper bags. The third key was the high quality of the linen handkerchief. The monogram was simply the icing on the cake, especially with the advent of DNA testing."

"Unbelievable," Jill whispered. The entirety of the story was slowly sinking in.

Ever the attorney, Bobby felt obligated to give a brief closing: "She was sixteen years old. She found a discarded paper bag and threw everything in it, took it home and hid it behind the back of a drawer on a side of the house that bordered an alley where no sunlight ever hit. She unwittingly replicated perfect laboratory conditions for DNA storage. Then, thirty-something years later—after reading an innocuous story in a newspaper—she gets even with the guy who raped her."

Bobby grew quiet, awaiting Jill's reaction. *He knew Dunlap was his father, but Dunlap had no idea. There had to be a way to use this knowledge to his advantage.*

∽

"Make sure he understands," Pick said to Shadow. "I don't want him going in there half-cocked like it's a regular visit. I used up a lot of favors to make this happen."

"I'll call Buddy now."

"Make sure you tell Buddy not to lean on him too hard. I don't want to scare him off."

"You're sure you can get him in?"

"Just do *your* job; I'll take care of the rest."

∽

The early morning phone call from Buddy Curran had been disconcerting enough for a dog-tired Bobby. He and Jill had spent a particularly enjoyable evening advancing their personal relationship.

Their extracurricular activities had left him resultantly sluggish.

What was more disturbing—and gave him great pause—was Buddy Curran's request that he accompany him and some lawyer to Riverfork.

Fortunately, his top advisor and media consultant was only an arm's length away, wrapped in a comforter.

"Who was that?" Jill asked.

"That frigging nut job, Buddy Curran. He wants to go with me when I visit Dunlap. He wants to bring some attorney, too."

"Are you still going to go through with this now that you know about Dunlap? It seemed like you were leaning the other way last night."

"I really don't have a choice." Bobby flopped back onto the bed and snuggled up to Jill.

"You've had enough, buster," Jill giggled, trying unsuccessfully to wriggle out of his grasp.

"You're the only good thing I have to look forward to," Bobby said with mock desperation.

Just as Jill's urge began to shift, Bobby released her and rolled off the bed.

"I've got to take a shower. They're picking me up in an hour."

∽

"Billy, we all set?" Pick asked.

Prison guard Billy Turpin looked nervous. "I'm going to lose my job if we keep doing shit like this. I'm not going to be very useful if I end up sitting next to you in here, you know what I mean?"

"Relax, kid, this is a one-time deal. Tell Steiner I'll take care of him. Just make sure I have that room to myself and make sure they take Dunlap up there. Eleven o'clock."

∽

Buddy Curran appeared on Hardy Street at the appointed time. He honked the horn before his Oldsmobile came to a complete stop.

Bobby climbed into the back seat. He assumed the creepy-looking guy sitting next to Curran was the attorney. With all that had gone on, he had yet to make the connection between the previous phone conversations with attorney Carl Bionda—when his mother was still being held captive—and the creepy looking guy that Curran alluded to as 'an attorney.'

Suddenly, Larry Fitzgerald's previous description of the alleged tile guy with the gloved hand: *'Kind of creepy looking ... weird eyes, you know, almost like a glass eye or something. He was tall...'* flooded back into his head.

Another piece of the jigsaw puzzle fell neatly into place.

The trio set out for the pastoral central Massachusetts town of Farrell, and the Riverfork Institute of Correction.

Bobby's father was waiting for them.

43

The Riverfork Institute of Correction was a massive rust-colored brick fortress. The white sign on one of the building's side doors clearly read AUTHORIZED PERSONNEL ONLY. Below that lettering was sub-text naming the manufacturer and describing the door's elaborate alarm system.

It also explained—quite clearly—that "Any unauthorized individual found in this area would be subject to immediate arrest."

Even to an untrained eye, it was obvious that it was not the visitors' entrance. The door magically opened when Buddy Curran, the creepy guy lawyer who Buddy kept calling "Shadow" during their ride, and Bobby Barron hit the top step.

Pick's favorite prison guard, Billy Turpin, ushered them into the building, slamming the door shut behind them.

The guard punched in a series of numbers on a security keypad until a green light blinked. His then replaced the five-foot long, four-inch by four-inch piece of hardwood timber that fit neatly into two large steel brackets, toggling the door shut in the event all other measures failed.

Shouldn't the piece of wood be on the outside to keep prisoners from getting out? thought Bobby. He then reconsidered his thinking. In essence, they were breaking *into* prison.

"Which one of you is Dunlap's attorney?" Turpin asked. He produced a piece of paper from his left breast pocket and awaited an answer.

Bobby knew enough about Buddy Curran to know he was not an attorney. The other guy, who had been identified as an attorney by Curran during their early morning phone call, and whom he believed to be Carl Bionda, had to be the guy. *It has to be him,* Bobby thought—prompting him to point at Bionda—who was already pointing back at Bobby.

"I'm not Dunlap's attorney." Bobby said. *I'm his son.*

"Wrong," Buddy Curran replied. "For this little exercise, you're Dunlap's attorney."

"You've got to sign this," Billy Turpin said, handing him a Riverfork Institute document entitled: *Lawyer/client confidentiality* with a sub-title *Visitors' Rules and Regulations.*

Timothy Aloysius Dunlap was clearly spelled out under CLIENT.

Tad, thought Bobby, who was tempted to change the T to a D.

The ATTORNEY portion was blank.

"I'm *not* signing this," Bobby protested.

"Look, my orders are clear," Turpin said. "No signature, no visit."

Bobby shrugged his shoulders. His indifference was palpable. "Cancel the visit."

Buddy Curran squeezed Bobby's left elbow. The diminutive, albeit domineering, Curran led Bobby to a corner of the hallway. "Listen, you cocksucker, sign the fucking paper. If you don't sign that fucking paper I'll hunt your mother down as soon as I set foot back in Southie and put two bullets in her fucking forehead. You hear me?"

It was classic mob mediation. It was also additional proof that size did not necessarily parallel strength.

Bobby turned to Turpin. "Have you got a pen?"

Bobby scribbled something that he hoped wouldn't remotely resemble his official signature under any type of in-depth scrutiny. He handed it back to the guard.

Scrutinizing it, Turpin said, "You've got to *print* your name, too," handing the document back to Bobby.

•

Bobby's hand shook as he printed his name on the document. Turpin examined it again. He looked at Bobby, then back at the sheet, and said, "Hey, I knew you looked familiar. Robert Barron. I've seen you on TV."

Bobby nodded. *So much for his anonymity.*

The guard led the group down the hallway. Turpin produced a large key ring and unlocked a green metal door. He pushed it open and waved his hand, signaling for them to enter. The guard stuck his head inside the room while holding the door open with his body. "You know the drill, Pick. Just bang on the door when you're done."

Pick? What the hell's going on here? That's got to be Pick Piccorino, Bobby thought.

A table with a half-dozen chairs was set up in the middle of the room. Tim Dunlap sat on the far side of the table, a stoic look covering his face.

Jesus Christ, he looks good. A little pasty, but he looks fit. He has no idea that he's my father. Not knowing how to react, Bobby gave him a slight nod of recognition, opening the door of acceptance.

Dunlap stood up and approached him. "How have you been, Bobby?"

"What's up?" Bobby responded in a shaky voice as he surveyed the room.

A dictatorial Pick Piccorino took over. He stepped forward and said, "Bobby, Pick Piccorino." He offered his hand and gave Bobby a death grip handshake designed to show he was serious. Never taking his eyes off Bobby, he said, "Have a seat." It was more of an order than an invitation as he pointed at several empty gunship-gray folding metal chairs.

"I'm fine," Bobby said, refusing his invitation to sit.

Bobby was intent on getting down to business. He pointed at Curran and Bionda and said, "I was asked by these two gentlemen to come up here and see Tim. Now, I agreed, and I even signed some lawyer/client confidentiality agreement to get in here. If it's okay with you, I'd like to speak with Tim in private."

"Is that how you want it?" Pick asked in a reasonable tone.

"Yeah, it's the only way—"

"The only way *what!*" Pick bellowed in a venom-laced voice. "The only way *anything* gets done in here is *my* way. You got that, *lawyer-boy?* Now sit the fuck down and shut the fuck up." He got right up in Bobby's face. Spittle rained from his mouth, its residual effect dotting Bobby's face and upper body and the accompanying stench disgusting him.

Bobby backed up.

Piccorino closed the gap again, producing the same results. He was maniacal, screaming, "God blessed you with *two* ears and *one* mouth for a reason—to *listen* twice as much as you talk! In *here*, you might as well have *eight* fucking ears the size of an elephant's, because I'll be doing all the talking."

Bobby backed up again and looked over at Dunlap.

His head was hanging and his eyes were riveted on the gray tile floor.

Pick relinquished some space, but his diatribe continued, albeit several octaves lower. Pointing at Dunlap, he said, "You see my boy Tim here? He wants to help me tip my RICO case, but he can't do it sitting on his ass in here. Now, *you* know and *I* know that he didn't rape that fucking broad. I'm done playing games here. You've been given plenty of chances, plenty of warnings, and plenty of time. I'm here to tell you your fucking *time's* up, they'll be no more *chances*, and they'll *definitely* be no more *warnings!*"

Bobby stared at Pick. Another piece of the puzzle nestled into place.

Bobby acted confused and whispered to avoid another outbreak of rage. "So that's what this whole thing is about? Legal help for you? All this craziness for legal help?"

A defiant Pick stared at him but maintained his silence.

Bobby raised his voice several octaves and summarized the situation. "You want help from a guy who's *lost* his license to practice? Did you ever think to come to *me* for the help?" He then pointed at Bionda. "Plus, isn't he an attorney?"

Pick rose from his chair and immediately morphed back into his psychopathic behavior. "Yeah, he's a fucking attorney!" he screamed. "But he's not a RICO specialist and he wasn't around when I came up with this idea. I don't *want* him, and I don't *need* you." He pointed at Dunlap and said,

"That's the fucking guy I want. You know fucking-right-well he didn't rape that broad—"

Bobby cut Pick off. His emotions overflowed, but he chose a low-key approach. "Maybe he didn't rape that young girl, I don't know—" Then the eruption began.

It was hot lava careening down the side of a mountain, oblivious to anything and anyone in its path. It transpired with no consideration of the consequences; and complete abandonment of the tenets, doctrines, and mantras instilled in him during law school and subsequent real-life experiences. Anger had finally begotten anger, and Bobby wasn't backing up—not one inch. The volume of his voice increased with each word. "As a matter of fact, if I had to bet on it, my money would say he *didn't* do it."

Bobby's capitulation to their claim set off collective confusion. It was obvious on their respective faces, but Bobby maintained the floor.

He turned to Dunlap, "Yeah, that's right, maybe you didn't rape that girl in Brighton, but you did rape my *mother* back in 1970." He stepped toward Dunlap. His rant continued. "Nice to meet you, *Dad!* Say hello to your son, you fucking piece of shit." It was classic Jack Nicholson with a noticeable inflection of Bobby's unavoidable South Boston dialect.

Bobby turned back to Pick. "I've got no beef with you. You want help? *I'll* help. But you might as well kill me—right *here* and right *now*—if you think I'll ever do *anything* for this piece of shit."

Pick stood his ground, but abandoned any thought of advancing.

Once Bobby had leveled the playing field, his voice returned to a normal and self-effacing tone. His years of training and experience finally reappeared.

He pointed at Dunlap and said, "You raped my mother back in 1970. Where do you think the handkerchief came from? You know, the monogrammed handkerchief with your come all over it? Maybe you didn't rape that young girl in Brighton, but let's face it, you got what you deserved."

"So you *did* set me up," Dunlap said.

"I didn't say that. I had *nothing* to do with setting you up."

Bobby turned back to Pick and reiterated his position. "I'll help you. We can draw something up right now. I'll start tomorrow, but there's one condition. You do *nothing* to help him," pointing at Dunlap. "He *raped* my mother."

"How can you possibly know that?" Pick asked.

"She told me."

Tim Dunlap had heard enough. He shook his head in disbelief. "I have *no* idea what you're talking about. More importantly, *you* have no idea what you're talking about."

Bobby looked at Pick. "The way I understand this is you've forged an alliance with Tim. You get him out by getting me to admit that I tampered with evidence. Only there are a couple of problems? *One:* I never tampered with any evidence. *Two:* Because I never tampered with any evidence, I cannot provide you with any information to free him. But, understanding he's nothing more than a means to an end, I can provide you with the same services you're seeking from him without your having to wait for his release—and then his reinstatement—both or either of which could take a very long time."

"If I had the dough, I'd already have someone working on this," Pick countered.

"I told you, I'll do it for *free*. The only pledge I need from you is that from this point forward you leave me and my family alone, and you do nothing for him," pointing one last time at Dunlap. "Do we have a deal?"

An unflappable Dunlap remained composed. "Pick, if you want Bobby to take this case, that's fine. Not only is it fine, it makes sense. He's right-on in just about everything he said, the one exception being the part about my raping his mother." He turned his attention to Bobby and asked, "How long have I known you, Bobby? Long time, right?"

Bobby shrugged, his body language suggesting *what difference did that make?*

Dunlap continued, "Look, all I'm asking for is an explanation. Honestly, I have no idea what you are talking about."

Pick jumped in. "I've got to tell you, kid. This fucking guy has defended you since the day I met him. I've ridiculed him. I've broke his balls. I've mocked him. Yet, not *once* did he ever agree with my assessment that you set him up. The guy deserves to hear the whole story about whatever it is you're claiming."

Bobby said. "Fine. I explain the story. Then I'll take your case, *pro bono*. In return, me, my family, and my friends are off-limits from today on; and this guy gets no help or assistance from you."

Bobby paused to let the offer sink in.

When Piccorino stared him dead in the eye, Bobby said, "Deal?"

"Let's hear it," Pick said.

☙

Tim Dunlap wracked his brain for a response as Bobby walked them through his story.

Early on, he'd repeatedly interrupted Bobby.

Pick finally invoked his version of courtroom justice in the form of "Tim, shut the fuck up and listen."

Given that, even Pick couldn't refrain from questioning Bobby's tale from time-to-time.

Bobby had an adequate response for each of his questions.

Seventeen minutes after Bobby's opening statement had commenced, he yielded the floor to his adversary, and at this point—at least according to Bobby's story—his father.

"Where do I start?" Dunlap asked. The wild allegations confused him, but his mind was working overtime to conjure up a response. "I *think* I have an answer, and I'm reasonably confident that I can prove to you that I had nothing to do with any of this. Of course, I'm going to need some time to do a little research and to speak with some people who need to hear this story. In the meantime—"

The steel door to the room burst open.

The group went silent.

Billy Turpin looked nervous. "Pick, what's going on? You said 'about fifteen minutes.' Steiner's not too happy. We've got to break this up. We've

284

got a shift change coming up. Kineavy's going to be here shortly, and we've got to be out of here before he shows up."

"I'm going to need some time to respond," Dunlap argued.

"Give us two minutes, Billy."

The guard pulled the door shut behind him.

"Two minutes isn't going to give me near enough time to answer these charges," Dunlap protested.

"Relax," said Pick. He looked at Bobby and said, "Alright, here's the deal. Nobody will bother you or your family. You work in good faith and all this shit ends." He turned to Buddy Curran and said, "Are we clear on that?"

"Whatever you say, Pick."

"That's what I say, and I want you to spread the word as soon as you get back. Anything changes, I'll contact you."

Pick turned back to Bobby. "Now, are you going to take the case? Otherwise, we're back at square one."

Bobby sat stone-faced.

Pick raised his voice for emphasis. "Look, you made a lot of crazy accusations here. Some of it makes sense in my mind, because I've got to tell you, I always wondered why he didn't come back at you. But that's *his* business. Let's leave it like this. If you're going to take my case, that allows us to meet one-on-one. If I think Tim's got a legitimate beef, I'll set up a face-to-face meeting. In the meantime, you and your family have got nothing to worry about. What do you say? Deal?"

A drained and weary Bobby stood up and shook Pick's hand. "Deal."

EPILOGUE

Irony: Pronunciation: 'I-r&-nE also 'I(-&)r-nE

Function: noun

Inflected Form(s): plural -nies

Etymology: Latin ironia, from Greek eirOnia, from eirOn dissembler

Irony: The incongruity between the _actual_ result of a sequence of events and the _normal_ or _expected_ result...

Bobby Barron
From: Bobby Barron [rgbarron@barronandassociates.net]
Sent: Sunday, December 6, 2008—5:10 PM
To: Jthurman@ABOUTFACE.com
Subject: Here's the poem I was telling you about—check it out. It's called "Irony!!"
IRONY

An arid daylight shines along the beach
Dried to a grey monotony of tone,
And stranded jelly-fish melt soft upon
The sun-baked pebbles, far beyond their reach
Sparkles a wet, reviving sea. Here bleach
The skeletons of fishes, every bone
Polished and stark, like traceries of stone,
The joints and knuckles hardened each to each.
And they are dead while waiting for the sea,
The moon-pursuing sea, to come again.
Their hearts are blown away on the hot breeze.
Only the shells and stones can wait to be
Washed bright. **For living things, who suffer pain,**
May not endure till time can bring them ease.

Amy Lowell

Jill: Like I was telling you, when we were cleaning up the mess, I noticed this small frame on my mother's bedroom dresser with this poem in it. Been there for years (who goes in their mother's bedroom?). My mother told me it was her favorite poem. Look at the last two lines, starting with, "For living things...." Think about it! She was out walking the beach, minding her own business... Bobby

This message has been scanned for incoming viruses by PJKB - Version 83.11.979

Jill Thurman
From: Jill Thurman [Jthurman@ABOUTFACE.com]
Sent: Sunday, December 6, 2008—5:14 PM
To: 'Bobby Barron'
Subject: Here's the poem I was telling you about—check it out. It's called "Irony!!"

WOW!!! you gotta be kidding...that's so weird! and here I am thinking the IRONY of this whole ordeal was our getting together. call me – J

A REVELATION

"Bobby, you *can't* do that to me," Jill yelled from the bedroom of her Marina Bay condominium.

"I promised Pick. He says he has important information he has to get to me right away." Laughing, he said, "I mean, it's not like I can have him deliver it here, or we can meet halfway for lunch."

Jill emerged into his sightline; a turquoise wrap wound tightly around her just-washed hair and a matching terry cloth towel barely covering the remainder of her body.

She lit into Bobby again. "I have a *deadline*. They have to get those photos, Bobby."

Bobby hugged her and playfully nibbled on the left side of her neck as he subtly attempted to separate her from the towel. "Forget Pick *and* the photos," he said, dragging her toward her bedroom.

Spinning out of his grasp, Jill said, "No way. Not unless you agree to do the photos."

"That's *blackmail*," Bobby said. "How about this? You take the ride with me to see Pick and we reschedule the pictures for later today? This is going to be the biggest selling story *About Face* ever had. Those were your *exact* words?"

"Let me make a call, you spoiled brat."

Twenty minutes later, they were in Bobby's Durango and on their way to Riverfork.

"What do you have to go out there for?" Jill asked.

"I'm not quite sure. Pick is a bit of a micro-manager. He's a control freak and he says he says he has some sensitive information that he doesn't want to discuss on his cell phone."

"I didn't think you could have a cell phone in prison."

"Cell phones are actually right next to hacksaws on the list of prohibited items," Bobby said with a laugh. "But Pick's not your average prisoner."

"Will you have the same setup today, you know, will you be breaking *into* prison?"

"Pick didn't mention that. I think I'm just going in as the attorney for a prisoner. We get a little more latitude due to the confidentiality rules, but you never know what Pick has in store."

Traffic was minimal. The quality back-and-forth banter—representative of the early stages of any truly great relationship—shortened the trip considerably.

Jill got a sudden urge to patronize the town's businesses as they passed the town of Farrell's picturesque common and downtown shopping area—all two blocks of it. She had originally planned to catch up on some reading while Bobby was inside; but with Christmas season looming she suddenly changed her mind. "Would you mind if I jumped out here? It's so beautiful, and it beats sitting in the car."

"No, that's actually a good idea. Do you have your cell phone in case I need to get ahold of you later?"

Jill brandished her cell phone. "Just call me when you're on your way back. I'll meet you right in front of that big clock," pointing at a giant forest green clock towering over the north side of the town common.

It represented the fact that Farrell had once been "The Watch Making Capital of New England."

Jill was off after a quick peck on the lips.

Bobby took the time to admire her statuesque figure in his rear view mirror as he swerved away from the curb. Following the signs, Bobby arrived at Riverfork, settled into a spot in the visitors' lot, and headed for the visitors' door.

He followed the rudimentary set of obligations expected of every visitor; at least until he recited his name and that of his client.

He was quickly bestowed VIP status.

"Right this way, Mr. Barron," said a uniformed guard, unlocking and relocking several doors as they moved deeper into the prison.

The guard unlocked one final door and held it open for Bobby to enter.

It wasn't the same room where they'd previously met, but it was eerily similar, right down to the fact that Tim Dunlap was still seated at a table.

Pick Piccorino stepped forward and broke the ice. "Hey, Bobby, thanks for coming out."

Bobby nodded toward Dunlap, "I thought we had an agreement?"

"Relax. I just need you to hear Tim out—"

Reinforcing his protest, Bobby reminded Pick, "We had a deal. *Him* or *me.*"

"We've got a deal, kid. Relax. Give him five minutes, that's all I'm asking."

"I can't do it," Bobby protested.

Tim Dunlap interrupted their disagreement. "I've known you a long time Bobby. I was always good to you, and you're one of the fairest guys I've ever met. Is five minutes of your time too much to ask?"

Bobby bit. "What can you possibly say in five minutes that'll make a difference? You're my *father*. How sick is that?" Turning to Pick, he said, "I'm out of here," walking toward a door that was undoubtedly locked.

Dunlap avoided another inevitable explosion by Pick when he said, "I'm *not* your father, Bobby. If you give me five minutes we'll put this whole thing behind us."

Bobby turned around.

Pick gave Bobby a wry smile. "Hear him out, kid."

Bobby stared at Dunlap, before asking once again, "What can you *possibly* say in five minutes that would change anything?"

Dunlap ignored the question and unsnapped the leather straps of a well-worn leather briefcase.

Bobby's stomach churned when he noticed the embossed initials along its top panel—*TAD*.

Dunlap reached in and pulled out a manila folder. Placing it in front of him, but leaving it closed, he looked across the table. "You had me going, Bobby. It was surreal. You were so sure that I had violated your mother that I was ready to plead guilty. Once I got my bearings and had time to piece it together, it all came clear in my head."

"What are you talking about?"

"Simply put, I'm *not* your father."

Bobby looked at Pick, then back at Dunlap, who continued. "But, I am your *uncle*. Your *father* is my brother Tommy...."

∽

Bobby called Jill as soon as he exited Riverfork. He didn't want to reveal his newfound secret or personal shock over the phone. He felt as if he would burst before reaching the center of town, and their mutually agreed upon mustering point under the giant green clock.

There she is, he thought, sliding into an empty parking spot.

Jill jumped into the car, and Bobby immediately dropped the bombshell.

"What?" an unconvinced Jill said. "How can you be sure? I mean, doesn't that seem a little far-fetched?

"My first instinct exactly."

"And what did he say?" Tugging his arm, she said, "Tell me *exactly* what happened."

Once Dunlap had explained away his alleged innocence, Bobby had performed the cross examination of his life. He was on his game, but—true to his old form—Dunlap was adequately prepared, parrying each aggressive advance by Bobby with a logical answer...

∽

"What are you talking about? My *uncle?*" Bobby asked.

"It was *me* that had to make a leap of faith here" Dunlap explained. "When you made all those crazy accusations, I thought you were nuts. What was already disturbing to me is that I didn't rape the young girl in Brighton. Nevertheless, in retrospect, especially after listening to you and understanding your involvement in prosecuting me, I couldn't help but come away thinking that you had framed me for this alleged injustice on your mother. Am I right about that?"

"I had *nothing* to do with framing you for anything. Before we discuss anything else, you've got to understand that. I had nothing to do—"

Dunlap cut him off. "I believe you. I never thought you did, at least until you explained the situation regarding my handkerchief. I think Pick has already made it clear to you on several occasions that I never held you responsible."

This was Pick's cue. "Bobby, I told you, this guy's been your biggest supporter. Like I've been saying, I thought he was fucking nuts, but he *never* agreed with me when I said you set him up."

"Yeah, but what's this shit about your being my 'uncle?'"

"Since you left, I've been burning up the phone lines," Dunlap said. "Pick's got a cell phone. He let me use it to gather the necessary material, and he then helped me get it in here."

"Hey, whoa, what the fuck ... I got another rat here?" Pick bellowed jokingly in an attempt to keep the mood light. "You two fucking guys won't be happy until the three of us are locked up in here together."

Dunlap smiled and continued. "I called people I hadn't spoken to in decades. I had my daughter ... she's the only one of my three kids who even speaks to me," he said, the sadness evident in his voice. "Anyway, I had my daughter dig through a pile of old files and personal information to come up with the necessary evidence. Fortunately, all I have is time."

Dunlap opened the manila folder. He removed several yellowed newspaper stories, and then placed his hands over them to shield them from Bobby's view. "I wanted to believe you were all wrong about this rape—"

Bobby cut in. "To say I'm 'wrong about this rape' is calling my mother a liar. I already explained the story, Tim. I didn't have to." Raising his voice for effect, he said, "She saw *your* picture in the newspaper, yet never said a word to *anyone*. We're talking thirty-something years! She could've fingered you at *any* time, yet she chose not to. It was the fury of seeing you involved in a similar situation—defending someone else who, in *her* eyes, had caused the same pain she had been forced to endure because of your actions—which put her over the top. Do you blame her?"

"Not if I did it, Bobby, but I didn't do it, my twin brother Tommy did."

"Twin-brother? Do you have a twin brother?"

"No."

Bobby smelled the makings of a scam. He looked cynically at Pick, then back at Dunlap. "What are you talking about?"

"I *had* a twin brother. He died on April 15, 1976. Car wreck in Newport, Rhode Island. Twenty-seven years-old, the last seven or eight of those years fueled by alcohol, drugs, and constant rage."

Dunlap lifted up his hands and slid one of the old yellowed newspaper stories toward Bobby.

The *Boston Globe* headline read "Man Dies In Early Morning Crash." The story included the following passage: "…The dead man was identified as Thomas Dunlap, 27, of Allston, Massachusetts.…"

Bobby looked at Dunlap. "You've put a lot on my plate."

"I understand."

"Let me get this straight. Your *brother* raped my mother? He died in a car wreck five or six years later, and you had nothing to do with it? *Nothing at all?* Is that your story?"

"Exactly," said Dunlap, with a solemn shake of his head.

"Kind of *convenient*, wouldn't you say?"

"Very convenient," Dunlap agreed. "I'll even stipulate that on its own merit it wouldn't be enough to sway you. But there's more."

Sliding a second newspaper story across the table—another old *Boston Globe* production—took the story to a different point in history.

The date on the newspaper was May 11, 1970.

Bobby immediately recognized the significance of the date. *The day after my mother was raped.*

He read the story: "Last evening, officers from District 11 picked up an incoherent man adjacent to the Columbia Point Housing Project. Police report that Thomas A. Dunlap, a student at Boston College, was discovered walking naked along Mt. Vernon Road around 11:15 p.m. Dunlap was placed into protective custody. Police say that Dunlap had been drinking and had inadvertently wandered into the projects, where he was beaten, robbed, and had his car stolen. After interviewing the victim, investigators theorized that his attackers stole his clothes to prevent him from pursuing them and from reporting the incident to police."

Bobby looked at Dunlap. "You really had a twin brother?"

"It'd be pretty hard to set this up," Dunlap said, "especially when you consider that his nickname was Tad. My brother loved to party. The sad part was he was a better athlete than I was, but he pissed everything away. He was the king of intramural sports at BC; won a bunch of championships, all different sports, you know. It was right up his alley; play your ass off, then drink your ass off to celebrate. There was no shortage of people to enable his behavior back then. They wore out a path to their favorite bar, at least until they banned him for life." Shaking his head at the memory, he added, "That's how messed up he was. You had to be pretty screwed up to get barred from that dump."

"What about the DNA?" Bobby asked. "Do all twins share DNA?"

"Good question. My daughter researched that for me. *Identical* twins are the byproduct of a fertilized egg that's been divided in two, so they share identical genetics.

"So not *all* twins share the same DNA. Right?"

"That's true; not all twins are identical. Tommy and I were. I had a twin brother. You have that proof. My brother was nothing but trouble, and the combination of his drinking and his temper lead me to believe he was capable of doing what you accused *me* of doing. With limited resources and little time, I was able to place him close to the *scene* of the crime, on the *night* of the crime. All I can say on his behalf is, I'm sorry, and I apologize."

Bobby sat in silence for a full minute. He then lifted himself out of the chair. "*You're* sorry. What about *us*? Where do we go from here? I'm still a little stunned, but we've got to straighten this mess out."

Only then did the irony of those words settle in on him.

This entire ordeal had started with a similarly worded phone call. '... "*You framed Tim Dunlap, and unless you figure out a way to straighten it, out we're going to kill your mother first, then kill you when we get our fucking hands on you ... For now, consider your mother to be a little insurance, but you better start thinking about how you're going to make this good....*'

Paradoxically, it was time to take their advice, and 'make this good,' as his *only* uncle's future was at stake. He extended his hand.

When Tim accepted it, Bobby pulled him forward. "I accept your apology," he said, his voice husky with emotion. "I can only hope that you can accept ours."

A relieved and emboldened Tim Dunlap turned to Pick. "Get in line. It's going to be a lot easier to get me out of here than you. But once I'm out you could become the first client of *Dunlap & Barron, LLP.* What do you think?"

Bobby knew that the secret would be getting "Uncle Tim"—*this was going to take some getting used to*—out without having to offer Trisha up as a sacrificial lamb. *Where do we start?*

Bobby needed to huddle up with Jill before all the difficult work kicked in. *She's never going to believe this.*

She would be waiting for him under the giant green clock in Farrell.

Bobby took a deep breath. *I've got ten minutes to get there, but a lifetime to convince her.*